PORTRAIT

OF AN

AVIATOR

BRYAN W. CANTRELL

PORTRAIT
OF AN
AVIATOR

BRYAN W CANTRELL

Portrait of an Aviator

PUBLISHER'S NOTE

This work depicts actual events in the life of the author as truthfully as recollection permits and/or can be verified by research. Occasionally, dialogue consistent with the character or nature of the person speaking has been supplemented. All persons within are actual individuals; there are no composite characters. The names of some individuals and locations have been changed to respect privacy.

Printed in the United States of America

Special thanks goes out to all that gave so much love and support in my life. Thank you God for creating life in my destroyed body. Sorry Michelle for only talking airplanes and helicopters for twenty years. I would like to thank Alyssa and Nick for being the greatest kids. Never forget your passions or dreams.

PORTRAIT
OF AN
AVIATOR

It hurts to know my passion in life, my love for life, lead me to death's door leaving me nothing but a life of pain.

-Nick, the aviator-

CHAPTER ONE
Find Me

The confident man walked in, Aviator shades covering his eyes and olive drab flight jacket on his back. He was looking to drown any thoughts of imperfection. He tossed his flight jacket on the bar stool next to him and ordered a cold one. The first sip of the cold refreshing drink took his mind into a grand surreal place of mystery and reflection on himself. He loved his memories because they created the man sitting on the bar stool now. Halfway through that beer, he closed his eyes and pondered his existence.

Walking with a limp is one attribute that can be used to define me, or my rocky existence on this earth. But how did I get to this point. I never had a desire to hurt myself, yet here I am broken. The complete loss of my smell, and my taste, aids in my defining process. My vision from this ragged body lacks left peripheral in both eyes bringing a newfound hatred of the fast lane on the freeway. No dwelling on it, for life continues beyond my permanent injuries. Change would not happen, hence acceptance of the new Nick was needed for synergy in this perilous life. Never any regrets for following my passion into the air. My love of flying will remain in my soul until these eyes go dark and my heart grows still. Seems a blink in time is all it took to move me from the top of the world, to slightly below it. I still can't believe it. Yet so long ago, that convoluted day remains crystal clear in the grey matter of my befuddled mind.

I remember parking my dirty truck in a small patch of thin, growing wheat on the edge of the smelly loading area. The giant yellow plane sat in stark contrast to the brilliant green winter wheat growing on three sides of it. I wish Bruce could have contacted me before I got all the way back to Waterloo. Such is life. Jumping back into the beautiful plane was a motivational moment each day. I could fly her all day long, loving every minute of it. I figured the wind would probably stop the application as soon as the money handle dropped, but helping farmers will always be my priority in this life. The Visibility had drastically improved compared to earlier that morning while waiting anxiously for that mysterious morning haze to clear out. In this wild occupation, weather is a hurdle that must be jumped always. Running the 330 hurdles in high school truly puts it into perspective. If I did not clear a hurdle pain would soon follow. I had always seen Mother Nature as a mean bitch that one should never fight with. She will get even every time, much like the last hurdle of a 330 could do.

The starting process for the yellow beauty mentally began in my truck well before I got into the cockpit. Knowing I would soon be flying the yellow bird created excitement in the cab of the truck. Once in, the mental process converted to physical action. My eyes slid up and down the control panel visually inspecting every inch of her. My hand then slid down onto the cold metal of the throttle shaft pushing forward and back multiple times to feed the hungry carburetor inside of her big engine. She loved her fuel and seemed to need large amounts of it to maintain the fire inside her carburetor. When I compressed the small silver button, the circular motion of the fat metal prop shook the entire plane oscillating me side to side in rhythm with the prop swings. Much like the rhythm while slow dancing with a beautiful lady. Reliability of power was felt as much as heard. The thumping rhythm of the prop and engine flowing through my body was a comforting thrill and a peaceful place to be. The smell of the engine was invigorating. The prop wash blowing against my face started the natural flow of adrenaline needed to be successful in this occupation.

Soon I was five hundred feet above Cedar Falls, in my yellow lady headed north to Mason City, Iowa. The yellow metal wings on either side seemed to reach for miles looking for clean smooth air. We always seemed to find it. Each time I felt the wheels pop off the ground and take flight my mind enter a focused state of clarity. I was where I needed to be in life, flying the big yellow plane. Before long, I was flying over Johnson's green rectangle field of soybeans. The plane entered into a long 360-degree circle around the green field as I looked for obstacles to avoid. All looked clear so I put the yellow bird into a dive and started pass one. At the end of pass one, we entered a hard tight right turn, followed by another. The Soybean field that day

10

was so brightly striped between plant and dirt. It stood in great difference running under the sleek yellow wet looking wings of my plane. It reminded me of life in a desert. The green seemed to be thriving while the brown dirt seemed destitute and dead. As I made my last turn to dive back in, I noticed we would not be lined up on pass number two. I pulled back harder on the stick to tighten the turn when all of a sudden, she snapped hard left. I had never felt a turn so strong before. Oh man, here comes the ground and it was not going to move. I was helplessly out of control pointing straight down and scared beyond anything instantly. Damn it, right arm straight out, must protect myself. Firm impact followed with complete design transformation. What's that smell? Is it fire? What is that pain and why does it consume my entire body. My vision closed into a dark tiny pinhole beam then all black. Silence consumed all.

CHAPTER TWO
Passion Found

D o you remember where you were in life when something astronomically great happened to you? Those thoughts are normally encapsulated into the memory trenches in your head, never to leave. It seems like only yesterday when my pops walked into my room and said, "Nick, let's go fly." At four years of age, no questions where needed when I heard the word "fly." I dropped my toy planes and ran after him out the door. We jumped into his little brown truck and headed out to the Great Bend airport. Once there, we drove to our grey metal hanger, opened the door to reveal our pretty little Super Cub. Cub was short for, Piper PA-18 Super Cub. She was super to me. It was a great airplane, white with red and blue stripes from her spinner to her tail. She was a patriotic little beauty that always brought thoughts of July 4th.

Form the first moment I saw that plane, her registration number, N-number, N0404, has been reserved in a highly guarded area within my brain. The smell inside that cockpit of the little bird was a combination of airplane fuel and fabric glue, otherwise called dope. That became humorous with age. The Cub was so interesting to me. It was an airplane covered entirely of fabric. Meaning, all of the metal structures inside the Cub were covered with a fabric material. Pictures of old jeans and recycled T-shirts ran through my head when my pops told me that. Made of fabric or not, flying in it was a monumental part of my life growing up. After Pops pulled the little beauty out of the hanger we jumped in it, pops in the front and me in the back. In a manly voice he yelled, "CLEAR," and hit the starter. As the propeller started rotating, the Cub hiccupped and popped until the engine found a rhythmic hum. Then we taxied the plane down to the end of the runway. Pops stopped the Cub to visually clear the area before putting us on the runway. At four years of age I was already learning valuable airport techniques that would serve me for years to come.

We taxied her onto the runway for departure. As the power increased in the Cub her normal hum became louder as the motor and propeller gave all they had to get us in the air. The rush of cool air was refreshing as the sudden increase in speed pushed me firmly into my seat. Looking out, I could see we were rapidly accelerating. Before I knew it, the tires popped off the ground and we were flying. Watching the ground disappear below us was the best part of the takeoff. A few minutes later my pops leaned back in the little plane and yelled, "Nick, put your hand on the stick. Now move it a little in all directions, forward, back, left, and right while holding his right hand up demonstrating "a little" with his finger and thumb.

Nick, my hands are off the controls, you are flying this airplane now." I knew, without a shadow of a doubt, I was the luckiest boy on the planet. I was flying the Cub right then and there and I loved it. I was my own real life super hero that day. Pushing forward on the stick would cause the nose of the Cub to dive. When pulling back on the stick, we would enter into a climb. This was the beginning of a long wonderful journey in my life. Flying became my addiction from that moment on. In that plane with my father, I felt completely invincible and proud. Death might have been watching me that day, but it was unnoticed. There was no feeling of it in that patriotic little Cub flying.

A few years down the road, what felt like minutes in my young busy life, my pops took me back to the Great Bend airport to fly in one of the biggest airplanes on the planet, so I thought. My pops walked over to the bright yellow plane and jumped up on the wing. I had seen the plane before but figured it never flew due to its size and shape. The engine on the front was a crude and heavy looking structure. While standing on the wing Pops opened a big window on the side and slide into the giant cockpit area. I jumped up on the wings myself in awe of the size of it. Standing on the large wing of that giant plane, I felt even smaller than the young boy I was. It was so big and I was so small in comparison. Looking for my seat inside the cockpit of the yellow plane my pops, with a smile on his face, said, "Just jump on my knee Nick. Only one seat in this beast." I jumped in the cockpit and up on my pop's knee. He adjusted the seatbelt and flicked some switches, yelled "CLEAR" once again in a throaty voice, and pushed another little silver button.

The word "clear" is universally understood in the aviation world as a pre-start warning to all that might be near the plane. In this plane, it meant clear the prop area or else you will be chopped up and ran over. With the push of that small silver button the giant prop started to twitch, then began to spin in a jerky motion, shaking the entire plane.

I found it captivating that such a tiny little button was in charge of the giant propeller and powerful engine. The chills traveled down my back watching that prop chase the cylinders and feeling the cool air fill the cockpit area. With loud pops and groans, the engine started to breathe loudly. It came to full life with a deep moan as all the cylinders fired rhythmically. It was at that moment there was an understanding that engines needed to be felt as much as they needed to be heard. With the side window open, the smell of fuel burning was present. We could feel the heat from the engine blowing back. The rumble of the big motor caused several people to stop what they were doing at the airport and watch the plane. The feeling of importance consumed me. That plane dwarfed our little plane. The only advantage of the Super Cub, I had my own seat in the back of the Cub.

As it warmed up the engine began to run smoothly. It was then I could personify the harsh behavior of the beastly plane. The airplane began to exhibit human characteristics. I could hear it suck air deep into its cavernous lungs, followed with an exhaling roar. It coughed at first but then found its smooth rhythm much like the Super Cub, only with a deeper moan and stronger thump. The plane shivered and shook me as I sat in the cockpit on my pop's knee.

15

This was the greatest airplane ever made. The engine was the most powerful engine in the world. I just knew it. Looking back at my pops, I could see a big smile on his face. It was obvious my pops was amazed by this plane as well. Watching the wingtips jiggle in unison with the rotation of the giant propeller built a strong feeling of power. The enormous yellow plane roared louder as pops introduced some power and we started to roll forward.

We rolled about thirty feet into a dirty wet-looking area. A scary man walked towards us wearing a bizarre mask on his face. He connected a large green hose to a metal tube on the side of the plane. Under the windshield I noticed a small glass window peering into a large compartment located between the cockpit and engine. Through the little window I could see a green liquid rising in the compartment. In a few minutes the plane started groaning louder, as the power was increased. I watched as the big yellow wing came within inches of a silver tank as the plane turned out of the dirty area. We headed down the taxiway to the far end of the airport. This was not my first take off at this airport, but it was with this big yellow bull. This was where we had flown the Cub. The Great Bend Municipal Airport in Great Bend, Kansas, was my second home. At the end of the runway my pops lined the beast up on center. As high as I was sitting on my pop's knee in that big airplane, the massive white lines painted down the center of the runway stood in great distinction to the black asphalt runway. I had never noticed how big the painted strips were from the back seat of the little patriotic Cub. As he increased power to takeoff limits the motor screamed louder than anything I had ever heard through my ears. Not only was the noise heard, it was felt. The power of the enormous engine caused the green liquid in the little window to dance around. Even with earplugs in my ears and a headset wrapped around my head, it was deafening. Not only was the sound intense in my ears but also in my chest. It seemed that each rotation of the prop caused a thump of power in my chest. The intense sound reminded me of my hatred for firecrackers because they always hurt my ears. Strangely, the loud sound coming from that plane provided a security based on power and size and therefore, it was needed.

After that flight, I was going to suggest getting a giant engine for the Cub. At that moment I was in a state of elation and disbelief while feeling the power from the round engine beating inside me. Excitement filled the cockpit as if I was on Pappy Boynton's knee in a dark blue F4U Corsair. To me, the engine on the big yellow plane sounded the same as the fighter planes on TV my favorite television show ever. Each time the power increased I felt throughout my body. The green liquid, in the little glass square, looked as if it was dripping straight up, not down, from the loud vibrating power. We rapidly gained speed and soon lifted off the ground. I peered out the side window to watch the ground disappear below the giant yellow wing. Even in the air, the noise from the big motor was intensely loud, but the assumed power from it, assured me, we were safe. It was strange that my sensitive ears, thus hatred for loud noises, caused a feeling of security in that giant yellow screaming beast. Furthermore, my pops was with me to protect me. The yellow plane had to be a thousand times bigger than our little Cub. When you are six, things are big, and big things are enormous. That airplane was gigantic. We had been flying for a while when my pops yelled to me, "Are you ready Nick?" I nodded my head up and down. A few seconds later, the nose of the airplane was pointed down sharply. We were diving straight into a field of green. The butterflies inside my stomach were growing as the plane accelerated towards the earth. Apprehension filled my brain as we approached the ground. The thought of smashing into the ground repeated in my head.

The fear left as we leveled off at what must have been inches off the crop. The plane was so low I thought we were going to land in that green field, but we never touched the ground. Looking at the green vegetation passing under the big yellow wings, in such a rapid manor, created a newfound understanding of speed. *We must be flying close to a million miles per hour,* I thought. As we got to the opposite end of the field, the plane abruptly entered into a steep climb with a sharp turn. When we entered the tight right turn, I turned my head to look out the side window. It was shocking to realize that when doing so, I was actually looking straight down at the earth due to the tight angle of the turn. Everything looked so small out the giant window. Curiosity about that style of flying flooded my head as my stomach danced inside my body. I immediately wanted to experience more flying of that nature. *This is the best thing ever,* I thought over and over.

The cycle of diving and climbing with tight turns repeated about fifteen more times over that ominous green field. My pops yelled, "All done, let's go home son," and he pointed the big yellow plane back to Great Bend. Although excited to be flying with my pops, a comforting feeling draped over me when seeing the runway and hearing the tires chirp as they kissed the earth. Even though it was a thrilling flight a slight fear of death presented itself in my head. Having a new experience involving high power, and speed, had unsettled my nerves a bit. When the motor entered silence pops explained the flying we had just experienced was called "crop dusting." He further explained it was his job. It was how he made money for our family. He continued to explain it was an extremely dangerous job surrounded by death, but he loved it. I was excited to think about a job that involved diving into fields while flying great airplanes. My eyes could not stop starring at the big plane as my feet hit the ground that cool morning. *I am going to be a crop duster.* He told me it was an R-Model Thrush Commander with an R1300 Wright motor. He continued to explain it was the best crop-duster airplane in the world and had an 800-horsepower motor. We walked to the tail of the Thrush only to find the rudder and elevator on the big plane were both made of fabric, like the entire Super Cub. I thought the Thrush was too big to have fabric parts. Even at that age, I knew that I wanted do this when I grew up. I knew that I would follow in my father's footsteps and become a great crop-duster as he was. At six, one does not think about the small gap that exists between life and death. Death is not important to a six-year-old boy who lives on top of the world. There were dangers, but no fear of bleeding to death in a demolished airplane ever presented came to thought. This was the path that I would follow for the rest of my life with a giant smile on my face.

CHAPTER THREE
Just Boys

.

A short way down the road after the ultimate flight in the massive Thrush, Trevor, my older brother, and I were living strong in our imaginations. Daily, we would spend hours upon hours in the cockpits of our two Cessna 188 Ag Husky crop duster planes at the family business, Ag Air, in McPherson, Kansas. If not out spraying, the two planes were parked in a dirt area surrounded by tall green grass close to the office. The office represented our headquarters. A proud feeling came over me when in that plane and I was all so happy my family owned that company. Every now and then a whirlwind of dust would roll into the cockpit, making the scene in my mind develop greater. Even at eight and nine Trevor and I knew the name of every plane on the airport. The most important planes on the airport were the crop dusting planes. They had one seat, like fighter planes. The Ag Huskies were identical minus their stripes. One with green and orange strips the other with red stripes.

21

Trevor preferred the red stripes and I was more partial to the green and orange. The planes had identical smells. Year of crop dusting had permanently scented their cockpits with a fine smell of harsh chemical. Sitting in the cockpit on a warm day the smell was a mixture of Aviation fuel mixed with the musky odor of chemicals that had been in them. Minus our names painted on the sides, we each had claimed our own stinky plane as a fighter.

I remember McPherson clearly to this day. It was a slow flat country town but perfect to young boys to grow up in. The airport was there to supply our minds with a copious amount of entertainment. As we walked out to the tired spray planes, they morphed into two new dark blue F4U Corsair fighter planes. I could feel the chills run down my back, as I got closer to my plane. I was always ready to fly an important mission with my brother. We would fly in perfect formation with Pappy Boyington while shooting down enemy Zeros. We watched "Baa, Baa Black Sheep" religiously. We were the best fighter pilots in the world. When I pulled in behind a Zero, I could literally feel my heart beat increase. *"Sorry Jap but Capitan Nick is here to protect."* As I squeezed the trigger in my plane I knew I had saved the day. If anyone asked us, we were willing to tell whomever how great we were. We even told each other how good we were. "Trevor, did you see me shoot down all six of them Japs?" Both of us knew we were better pilots than the other. Anyone walking around the airport would hear airplane and machine gun noises emanating from the cockpits of two resting Ag Husky spray planes. Neither one of us could see over the panel of the planes at that age, therefore, at a glance, the machine gun noises seemed to be coming from two empty planes. It was just two young boys and their wild imaginations, flying for hours in our historical Corsairs for our country. I could, even now, travel back to my old Ag Husky and pretend to fly it some more. "Nick there is a bandit on your tail at six o'clock. I got it." "Thanks Trevor."

Fun memories brighten future day and bring smiles when thought about. Remembering great times of the past is great therapy for me soul. I think that is why I hold on to them so tightly. The smell of blowing dust still invites imagination. Trevor and I flew hours in our "Corsairs," while watching real crop dusters from the family business taking off each morning for daily jobs. Our imaginations swiftly changed from the best fighter pilots to manly crop-duster pilots. We soon became the best crop dusting pilots in Kansas, and in our minds. Of course our Ag Huskies were also aerobatic, in our rich fantasies. Those planes could do flips and rolls while spraying fields. My Husky still had its Corsair machine guns so I could kill bigger pests like ground hogs while crop dusting. In my mind my Husky was identical to John's plane at the old dirt strip east of us my pops flew Stearman biplane off of when I was even younger. My little Husky morphed into a giant white and black S2R Thrush. Damn that plane was cool. It was extremely odd to watch that Thrush go off to work on that dusty old strip outside of McPherson. It was not painted in the standard safety yellow "get out of my way" paint, it was a pretty bird of all white with black stripes and plus it was a Thrush the best crop dusting plane ever made. I knew it was because Pops told me. The two of us were only flying

23

in our imaginations but we would always observe our immediate surroundings and incorporate everything we saw into our flights. *Should I have learned back then?*

All the grand thought often run directly into that dark day. One of our hired pilots, Rick, was flying our beefy yellow Grumman G-164 Ag Cat/600 another great biplane when it started running rough. My pops told Rick to head back to the airport but Rick wanted to finish six long passes instead of turning towards home. Once back in McPherson airspace, he failed to get himself all the way to the runway before the motor stopped running completely. If he would have listened, all might have ended differently. The airplane touched the ground about fifty feet before an irrigation canal. One the wheels dropped into the canal at a fairly rapid speed and the damage began. Both the wings and prop of the Ag-Cat were twisted and destroyed. The landing gear ripped off. Although Rick was okay, the image of that crashed yellow plane off the end of that runway became wedged in my brain. He was so close to making it back. It was a learning experience about listening to wisdom of veteran pilots. I found it interesting that how some pilots thought their skill alone was the inherent confidence that stopped death from grabbing them. It was luck more than skill in my mind.

I remember it was clear to all others that death was giving him a warning sign. Not too long after the Ag-Cat, Rick crashed and totaled our blue stripped, Piper Brave. It seemed to me Rick was flying on borrowed time. Should I have told him? Would he listen to a kid? The canal just slightly east of the black runway held in its arms the bright yellow deformed airplane that day. The sight of the crashed plane brought sadness into my heart. My emotions were packed with the feeling of empathy for the destroyed airplane. I had completed so much pretend flying in it. Any crash brought the same feeling deep inside. It was always felt as a big loss. The pilot was my first priority for I needed to know the plane had protected him and he was safe. When the pilot was fine but the planes destroyed, I found myself mad at the pilot, not the metal flying them around. Trevor and I played silently in each Husky that day out of respect for the broken Ag Cat and smashed Pawnee. They would be missed. Rick would not be missed.

Hard to even count how many. Pilots came and left like the weather. Some quit and some got killed. Turnover is a common occurrence in crop dusting I guess. Trevor and I talked about how each pilot had their unique qualities. Rick had a great mustache that set him apart from the other pilots. We are talking a Burt Reynolds, Bandit, and mustache. My mind would drift into a daydream about driving my black Trans Am to the airport to fly all day. A Few great pilots remain clear in my head, as if I were standing outside right this minute, watching the wheels pop off the ground and their plane off into flight. One pilot Brent, a younger, muscle-bound pilot with massive arms is a clear memory. I always wanted his giant arms and sharp looks. If any man truly resembled a pilot, it was Brent. Not only did he have the swag he had the ladies in addition always showing up with a different one. Brent often did pull-ups on the prop dome hanging on the front of his Thrush. I found that inspiring. If he were flying the smaller CallAir, he would do a set of sit-ups to prep for flying. He was a good pilot as far as I knew for I only sat on my pop's leg or Bill's leg in the one-seat spray planes. It was strange, in the summer time months; my pops would go to work after dinner and fly all night. Trent, my pops, and Bill, would often team-spray large sections, while avoiding earthly obstacles in the pitch black of night. I could not imagine diving into a field in the pitch black of night to spray. Team-spraying a field is when multiple pilots spray the same field. One pilot gets a load of chemical at the strip while one pilot is flying back to the field and the third pilot is spraying. It was a fast and efficient way to attack large fields.

Such a dreaded thought. After flying a long night Bill, Trent, and my pops met up West of Howard, to team fly a 640-acre field. Time had flown by as it does when flying. After a few hours my pop called Bill on the radio, "Hey Bill, how is Trent doing?" Bill responded with, "No idea, he is not with me I figured he was at the strip with you." My pops explained he had not seen Trent for hours. Pops took off and climbed high to radio home base in McPherson and see if Trent had just flown home. It was an unpromising report over the radio that Trent had not returned home. Bill and my pops rapidly stated to search the surrounding area. Unfortunately, they found the yellow wreckage near the Arkansas River at the base of a high power transmission tower. Bill put his CallAir down on a narrow country road near the crash site then ran over to the wreckage site only to find Trent's sculpted lifeless dead body in the mangled yellow plane. It had been completely destroyed on impact. I had seen so many crashes already in my young life but what set me

26

back about that accident was the fact Bill and my pops had flown over the crash site for hours without seeing it. The thought of Trent raising his bloody muscular arm out the shattered windscreen filled my head. I pictured him pleading to a flying bright yellow plane to save him. The complete destruction of the plane provided a strange comfort that Trent died instantly. I know I had been around death too long when I found solace in instantaneous death versus a drawn out process.

My heart went out to his family but also to Pops and Bill. I figured they had to think about the maybes and what ifs after that experience. I know I would have. If they would have seen him sooner, could they have saved him? Come to find out, the answer to that question was no. He died from massive head trauma according to the coroner's report and passed almost instantly. Sitting in the grass next to the office, staring at each blade of green life dancing in the breeze, I found myself deeply thinking about the crash and wanting answers. While sitting there, I overheard to carefree pilots talking about the crash. They talked about how the fire department had to hose down Trent's dead body before touching him out. I could not imagine how the hose man felt doing it. I hoped that Trent still looked super muscular when they sprayed him down. Hearing that story caused a coldness deep inside me. Shivers ran through my core and escaped through my fingertips. It was incredibly rude to spray down a dead man. The pilot's next conversation was about the chemical being flown that day. Parathion was so dangerous four drops of undiluted material would kill a grown man. Understanding what an organophosphate was at such a young age was impossible, but there was darkness around that message. Knowing what that chemical is now brings understanding to the hose down. This was another learning experience in my make-believe flying world. I called a meeting with Trevor, in the back of the old dusty hanger to talk about what chemical we should never spray on. Trevor left me sitting in the big hanger pondering life. I knew that my crop dusting skill was so good I could get away flying Parathion but was not interested. Even with the evil darkness of death hovering around, I still wanted, more than anything, to be a real pilot there in McPherson. "Another beer please pretty lady."

Each day that passed reduced my thoughts about death and increased my passion for the air. Aviation was invigorating. When blended with the vivid imagination of two young boys, it became an incredible mental playground. "Trevor, this is crop duster I'm thinking it is time to call it a day and grab a beer, over." "Roger that Nick." When we would get done "crop dusting" each day, Trevor and I would go into the office, grab the key to the soda machine and get a cold, free soda. To us, the sodas represented our cold beers after a hard day of spraying crops. Sitting in the green grass with our sodas, we would discuss the day's flying. We always spoke as if we were having separate adventures in each plane. I am not positive, but pretty sure; we were comparing imaginations, or maybe stealing ideas for the next day's flight. Either way we were on top of the world and living great lives there in McPherson. I purposely held back information to make my next day's flight better than Trevor's. It was important for me to get as many hours of pretend flight time as possible before returning back to Montana to live my other life. My sadness seemed to amplify as the end of July approached.

CHAPTER FOUR
Retirement

At my young age there was one day that I hated. The dreaded day I had to return to Montana. Split custody is a necessary legal step in certain life events but not an easy event for a young boy to understand. In my situation, it was a massive hindrance to my flying life. I did love the cold winters in Montana but missed flying greatly. Despite getting to see my birth mom and friends, the return to Montana was a sad time at the end of every year. At my young age it was hard to understand all the mundane aspects of divorce, which to me, was nothing more than a drawn out fight that included the kids. Focus was directed onto the ugly parts of the process. Thoughts about the future where filled with confusion and wonder.

Divorce was just another convoluted path in my life already filled with strange adventures. Divorce had taken me my mom and sister on a bizarre trip to California. That time in life remains as fresh in my memory as flying the Cub with my Pops. My mom came home to get my sister and me. She told us we needed to take a trip with some friends. I was four years old at the time and Shannon was seven. My only concern was my dog and my toys. It seemed my mom had found healing through a random religious hippie community. We were loaded into a converted bread truck and drove across the country with a group of religious hippies. While they were all pretty nice, it was not a life choice I ever would have made, or will make. Even at four years of age I knew something was not right jumping into that cargo van on the sunny day in Montana. The van had beds built from the floor to the top. It was relatively comfortable. There was a lot of singing of hymns across each state on our way to California. After about a week of driving in that peculiar hippy filled RV, bread truck, combo, we arrived at a living compound in Aptos, California. Wow, to think about that crazy trip now brings madness. There was a lack of family feeling although they claimed to be a giant one.

I wonder where he is now. I remember it being a large area with cabin looking houses. It reminded me of my grandpa's cabin by the lake back in McPherson. It was a giant communal living facility, completely fenced in. At four, the fence looked as if it reached heaven for it was so tall. The fence came together at a gate in the front of the compound. There was one kid, my age, to play with. He was the son of a hippy couple and name was Sunny Day. Each time I call his name I chuckled inside. It was a puzzling time in my life. I remember finding myself in secluded areas of the compound alone trying to understand the whys. The dirt was so powdery under the steps of the hippy church but I found comfort hiding there. Begin so young, understanding failed me. I found myself lost and confused hoping for change. I needed to go flying.

While the strange memories lie and wait to be recalled, the grand events are there on the top for the smile and clip of happiness. One lucky day while walking across the compound, I looked up to see my Pops walking with his loaded 357 in his hand. I was beyond excited to see him. *This crazy crap is over,* I thought. He looked at me and said, "Get your stuff Nick, we are out of this crazy hippie house." I ran as fast as I could to get my stuff. When returning back to the dusty courtyard near the front gate of the compound, I could see my pops talking to my mom. His words towered above all other noise that day. He looked at her and said, "I'm taking my kids crazy lady, you can come to if you want, if not, who cares." In the middle of the strange world he had found me and protected me, as good dads do. Only this time it was from bell-bottom jeans, greasy hair, and long beards not flying. After a long, and mostly, silent flight in a Cessna 210, we ended up back in Kansas. It was when my feet hit the ground back in McPherson that I could finally accept that interesting hippie event was over. It was not too long after that when I was once again, separated from Pops and living in Montana with my mom. To this day, the word hippie has a negative connotation to me. Although sad to live in Montana, I was happy that Montana had a population of zero hippies. The divorce brought sadness and confusion for years, yet I pushed on with the one goal in life: to become a pilot. I would reach me goal no matter what.

Sadness crept into my brain often thinking about Trevor getting flight time, all winter long. Stupid divorce. I would only find myself learning feminine qualities from my mom and sister all winter. He would learn about Airplane while I learned about monthly cycles. On a positive note, I would utilize my winter in Montana as preparation for the next season of flying in Kansas. Christmas break I would fly out to see the other half of the family and always get a flight in with my pops. I never had to wait more than a few months before hearing the powerful word "CLEAR," just before another flight with my pops. I was that addicted to flying even at four years old. The thought of going to work with him filled my head months before the summer thaw started in Montana. As a young boy I could compare my next flight to a great Christmas present. Before long, summer would arrive and I would depart for Kansas. Soon back at the airport with a refreshed imagination for a hard summer of mind flying with Trevor.

On most summer days, Trevor and I would go to work with Pops at what we thought was the middle of the night. Driving to the airport in the dark with eyes half closed became our routine. Crop-dusters must go to work extremely early to kill the pests, not the bees that pollinate the crops. The bees are seen as the gatekeepers of the fields. If they were out, the planes are not. Pops would go fly in a Thrush or CallAir, and so would we, in our Ag Huskies. One particular day, in route to the airport I remember my pops telling us he would be flying out to an airstrip to spray all day. Trevor and I could just hang out there with our BB guns and pocketknives at the airstrip. That was as close to

Utopia as a young boy could get. To be around airplanes while playing in the dirt, shooting BB guns, and flipping knives created inescapable memories forever etched in my head. On the drive out to the airport that day, I wondered how all three of us were going to sit in the yellow plane with one seat. I knew my pops could handle it.

At the McPherson airport we saw Bill standing by his truck, helmet in hand. Bill and my pops had been flying together for years. Bill was a skinny guy that tried hard to grow a rick mustache but never reached its fullness. Looked more like an adult film star. Pops said, "Well Nick, your ride is here." Shortly thereafter, there were three bright yellow A-9 CallAir-235 airplanes flying in relatively good formation with Bill, Dave, and my Pops at the controls. The cockpits of two of the CallAirs had one great pilot plus a small boy with a smile pasted on his face. Looking out the window and seeing Trevor on Pops knee bummed me a tad. I later found that Trevor's ass was too big and Bill did not want his leg to fall asleep as it did the last time Trevor flew with him. He just needed the smallest boy with him, to be safe. Flying through the air in a yellow CallAir with the window down was about as great as it could get be. To watch the ground pass under the wings while feeling the strong wind on your face and smelling the exhaust from the engine created high level memories. Through my body I could feel each small bump in the air. As we flew through the air I looked out over the vast landscape of crops, then over to Trevor in the other plane only to see that smile still posted on his face. The checkerboard of colored vegetation looked so perfect and so precise. *Those farmers really knew what they were doing,* I thought. The bright squares of the vegetation underneath the yellow planes reminded me of Legos. With thumbs up in each cockpit, we knew we were the luckiest boys on the planet, and we both wanted that feeling to last forever. A few years down the road death returned to claim a token from our harmonious trio of pilots that day.

It seemed that death came to visit us too often in our little crop-dusting world. I wondered so many times why my heart was pulled so hard to aviation when the outcome always seemed to be death. Although death came so often, it was always a random surprise, when it did. I should have expected it to happen, but was surprised each time. There was now a solid understanding that crop dusting, was a dangerous occupation, but figured some pilots were just not meant to die. Seems those days are always first in my mind as I plan for my future. It seemed they happened so fast it is hard to remember who died first. Death came again to Kansas one particular dark morning to claim Dave. Dave was another pilot for Ag Air. HE was a good friend of my pops and a good pilot. Dave was a toe-head man with a vibrant sense of humor. If he were with adults you would hear the cursing and laughing. It was the same way with us kids. He always got us to laugh. Somehow Dave flew his Weatherly 620B into a cross-country transmission tower. As we found out, the smooth wing of the tan and yellow plane had logged itself into the crude grey metal of the transmission tower about half way up. The rest of the one winged plane plummeted to the ground.

I remember the sweet taste of Captain Crunch leaves your mouth when hearing about a recent death of a good friend. The moment I heard about Dave's death I ran out of the house to find a place to reflect about life. A farmer in the field adjacent to where Dave plummeted in had witnessed the entire incident happen. He rushed over to help but could not due to an intense fire. What is still most interesting about that crash, and his death, was the fact that Dave, while burning to death, was screaming "Mandy." As I was sitting on the trampoline in the backyard free of all dangers, I pictured him sitting in the cockpit of the burning wingless coffin screaming her name. That thought sends chills down my spine to this day. That crash randomly spins into my head without warning. That is one thought that I had always wished I could have wiped from memory forever.

Here I sit reliving every intense memory in my convoluted life, why. Will it make me better? Let's hope so. Mandy, was Dave's beautiful wife and obviously his last thought. I find that comforting that his true love was the final thought in his mind. I wondered if I would scream some airplane make and model in the same situation for I did not have a woman. His reaction represented the ultimate love, to me. Every time that thought created happiness in my heart the thought of Dave burning to death stole all romantic visions away. Our families often did things together. It seemed only yesterday I was strapping Dillon's butt, Dave's son, onto a wild bronco at the McPherson little buckaroo rodeo. It was truly sad to have to say goodbye to Dave. Death came like a thief and grabbed Dave in such a rude manner. I blamed neither Dave nor the airplane for that crash. It was merely the black covered reaper. I did not understand all of the aeronautic variables involved, but I knew he was a great pilot as I had hoped to be. His family's loss ate at my soul for weeks after the crude crash. For several days Trevor and I would walk almost silently out to our Ag Huskies. We each flew long flights in reflection of Dave separately. We would fly alone in our minds and in the cockpits of our Huskies. Dave would be missed and still is.

That call was proof that irony is real. Dave had called my Pops the afternoon before his fatal crash. He wanted my pops to know that he was done crop dusting and was going to move on to something else after the season was over. Hours later, he was dead in a burning wingless metal coffin. That would have been his last season crop dusting, but death came knocking and Dave answered the door. I wondered how it felt for the boys to lose their pops, but I was too scared to ask. I could never imagine the feeling of losing my pops. Although Dave was gone, the darn crops continued to grow so my Pops had to continue flying. Now every time he left the house I wondered if he would return. Death was hardening my emotions. A pilot would die one day and Trevor and I would pretend to fly the next day. We did find ourselves flying with respect and honor for those who had fallen. The acceptance of death did not alter my desire to fly for a living. The cycle of death was rapid in McPherson. I fully understood crop dusting was a deadly job. Something about walking the line so close to death created a challenge in my mind. I would be the pilot to tell death to piss off and live as the greatest pilot ever. In my imagination flights I focused on safety as much as possible. I knew that I needed to push through any negative experiences and focus on my overall goal of becoming licensed pilots as soon as I was old enough. Why did I still want to be a pilot for I had watched so many die, or come close.

CHAPTER FIVE
Time

Time flies, literally, when you are perusing your passion of flying. A blink or two and I found myself eleven years down the road on the same journey, Trevor and I had both finished our private pilot check rides. We were both considered legal private pilots according to the Federal Aviation Administration. I was able to see past all of the crashes and focus solely on my paths to that point. I felt greatly accomplished to have my private license. To still be in high school and have my pilot's license was beyond remarkable. I felt more complete with the license in my wallet. I thought I was a big deal. When Debra randomly walked up to me and said, "Hey, I heard you're a pilot now." I knew I had reached another level in life for she was so beautiful and had never noticed me before. Trevor and I knew all the ladies would like to go for a flight with us. Sitting in any classroom learning random stuff is when my mind traveled to the skies blocking out all incoming data. Thinking about the license in my pocket created a satisfied feeling wherever I was. Getting our pilots license opened the door for even more flying opportunities. *Damn, I was so proud.* At that age I cared deeply about the flying but also the ladies of course. I had hoped one passion would open the door to the other not caring witch one first.

I loved those winter nights. One crisp cool winter night, I found myself pushing the right rudder pedal to the floor inside the Cessna-172 Skyhawk to line us up on the centerline of runway two-Niner, in Great Bend. This was the same plane that I had used for my private pilot check ride. She was a great little bird of white with green and yellow strips. Her cockpit was dressed in stock green fake leather. To me, she was perfect. Furthermore, I was extremely comfortable in her. It was truthfully dark out there feeling each and every bump on the taxiway. Although I was a new pilot, I felt the Skyhawk had my back and would protect me. Practicing in my jet jockey voice into the radio microphone, "Great Bend area traffic, November three four Niner one Quebec is a Cessna 172 taking the active runway Two-Niner, for a straight out departure, Great Bend." It is hard to sound sexy like a jet jockey when your call sign has the word "Cessna" in it versus "Ghost Rider." We figured our brute pilot voices would develop over time with tons of practice. Or maybe it only came with F-14 flight time. Only we appreciated the jet pilot voice purely out of respect for the aircraft those pilots flew.

The girls could care less if we sounded like Maverick from Top Gun. Well some did care. At that time in life I was only hoping that one pretty blonde, Sarah, from Concordia would respect my professional pilot voice. She was a healer, on a roping team, and I respected that for sure. It is hard to explain how the speed of the horse with a beautiful girl on top, pulled at my heart. I definitely respected those tight cowgirl jeans she wore. I instantly noticed her hard curves and round butt in those tight jeans, followed by her blond curls. I appreciated her spunky attitude and warm personality. Sarah was a Cheerleader at Concordia High School, one of our rival schools. While I loved her jeans, that cheer uniform was also a tempting sight. Lucky for me, I soon found that Sarah was a great cowgirl, and even a better kisser. To hear the buzzer ring and to watch the shoot open to see that beautiful horse with sexy Sarah fly out at high speed was inspiring. She obviously wanted to know more about me because of my seductive Cessna fighter pilot voice. Whatever it was, it really did not matter, because she was a good kisser and because she wore those sexy reveling jeans. One thing I did not understand about her was her desire to taunt fate. She always wanted to make out by the milking barn. Only when her dad was in the barn milking the cows did she want to kiss passionately. Her lips were amazing and are still in my brain. Hank would have surely killed me if he ever found me kissing his daughter. Dangerous or not, girls, like airplanes, had to be test flown to see how they would react to me, or my goofy personality. Passing her flight test made me happy, as I was able to fly to first base multiple times.

It became apparent that death was a force near me where ever I might be, and the people I might care about. The darkness was close to Sarah as well. Roping alone is a dangerous past time, but that was not where death was waiting for her. Half of her cheer team and other friends were killed on Eastern Airline's flight 1717 out of Denver Colorado in 1987. The school had sent their Future Farmers of America (FFA) students to Washington DC for a conference. Sarah had a family issue which did not allow her to go on the trip. On the flight home, with a short stop in Denver, after weather diverted their flight, their DC-9 packed on ice. The investigation showed the plane had not been deiced completely. Therefore, it crashed seconds after it rotated for flight. The crash ended up killing 25 passengers and 3 crewmembers. It moved any flying job in my eyes into a dangerous occupation. *Why was death always near me?* While Concordia was competition for McPherson Christian High School, both were small schools, so we each felt the pain of their losses in that crash. The crash made Sarah's kisses that much more important to me.

She is still in my head. *Why, I did not know her at all.* I was shocked after reading an article about the crash. It appeared that one lady ended up on the runway, in her seat, upright, screaming at a destroyed DC-9 filled with death in front of her. She had the most amazing luck to be tossed out of a plane while crashing and ending up starring at it, not burning to death in it. The sound of the crackling fire was only squashed with the loud sirens of the emergency vehicles approaching the destroyed hulk of the DC-9. The thought of that lady sitting on the cold runway unscathed, still buckled in to her seat, and opening her eyes to a crashed plane, had to have been a life-changing moment, if there ever was one. She appears in my mind randomly without warning. Some twenty years later and she is still in my head. I spend too much time wondering what happened to the luckiest lady on the planet. I hope she is safe still. When I was in the Cessna with my buds, thoughts of Sarah were was always near. The thoughts about any sexy ladies were always around but flying brought them to mind. Thoughts about women are so easily intermixed with aviation. The defining process alone with hard lines and soft cushions filled with power under the hood. Taxiing out in the pitch dark of night with my buds always invited thoughts of pretty girls riding with us. Our conversations about planes often jumped into conversations about the ladies, then back to planes. We were normal boys in my opinion, minus already having our Private Pilot's Licenses. My flying adventures continued to grow as I did. *It was so long ago but feels so close.*

On the black runway in the dark of night there in McPherson in that Skyhawk, Trevor gave me "thumbs up" on my right. I hear Troy say, "All clear gentlemen, let's roll," from the backseat of the plane. Troy was close behind us with regards to his license. He was still building time and we all loved flying together. Troy always did have a respectful tone in his voice. Must have been something Phil had taught him. Trevor and I called Troy's dad, Zeek after some random donkey. I'm not sure who owned the donkey but it made me laugh so I jumped on the Zeek train. In all honesty, Phil was a great man and great father. We considered him another father figure in our lives. Troy's mom became my second Kansas mom as well. This was one of the many reasons we loved Troy Boy like a brother, he was raised just like us. With my best friends onboard, on that cool dark night, I advanced the throttle to the takeoff power settings and the Skyhawk came to life. It felt good to be the pilot in command on any flight. Knowing that Trevor and Troy trusted my abilities to keep them alive was empowering. As we picked up speed on the dark runway the marker lights became a constant beam of light running down both sides of the Skyhawk. With the rumble of the engine, at 25-hundred rpm, and the vibration of the tires rolling down the black asphalt, the Skyhawk was wide-awake and ready for flight. As the prop pulled us down the runway, the navigation lights on the wingtips created dim red and green patches on the dark ground. As I pulled back on the yoke to invite lift, the colored blotches absorbed into the darkness as we took flight. It was at this point that I tended to mentally pause and think about how incredible it was to be seventeen, flying that Skyhawk, in the pitch black of night with my best friends. That moment in my life could have lasted forever. It represented so many accomplishments and made me feel so proud of myself.

The question that came to my mind often was, how the heck did I get here and where exactly am I going? Some questions never need to be answered because they are so obvious. They still filled my head often. Flying was in my blood, pressed into my DNA, passed down from my pops. I was the son of a great crop-duster pilot, living in Central Kansas. McPherson was such a great town to live in as a young man, always something happening and loads of pretty girls. I had noticed almost instantly upon arriving in Kansas, the girl-guy ratio seemed to be high ladies, low men, compared to Montana. It was a perfect situation for a teenage boy, for me. Should anyone expect any other type of thought from a young man who loves both of his passions: planes and the ladies? It could only be expected, running around with two buddies that felt the same way about both girls and planes. My mind often filled with thoughts about pretty girls and beautiful planes. Still to this day people get confused when I'm talking about planes and the ladies. When I tell stories about one or the other I have to watch how I describe them. Both can have great "spinners" and curved lines. I was proud to be following my heart and this aviation path for most of my life, but I still could not believe I was there, actually doing it. Each flight brought the same questions, filled with the joy and excitement about being where I was in life.

My fingers were crossed that the snow bunnies would be as perfect as they were in Montana, at Zephyr Mountain. Kansas is extremely flat therefore we would load up our truck and head to Colorado for weekends of skiing. To my delight, Colorado produced twice as many beautiful snow bunnies. There I was living in McPherson, living life to the fullest without trying very hard at all. I did not consider myself that important but loved where I was. At seventeen I was a private pilot, a wide receiver for the football team, and a runway model for The Bon Marché. The Bon was a large department store chain in select states. One of my girlfriends, Liz, was a model for them and talked me into trying it. Liz was a tasty little thing so I had an obligating to try it. Trevor was a little reluctant to join me, but soon did. We heard that all the models changed in the same room and thought it would be a great place to hang out, and observe the ladies. We would strut down the runway modeling suites, then go into a changing area where the ladies were changing also. I found it truly amazing to be seventeen in a room filled with half-dressed ladies. I was almost late to every one of my sets because I was staring at sexy bras and panties. It made me laugh being a legal pilot but walking down a "runway" as a model.

If I was not at the airport flying or walking down a runway modeling suits, you could find me on a green field in the receiver position on my football team any Fall Friday night. My body was toned and chiseled because of it. I found happiness walking around shirtless in a slightly arrogant manner. I also enjoyed changing in the model room and flexing my abs. I was fast and dexterous enough to be a starting strong wide receiver and I felt important doing so. One particular night during the pregame warm up, I lined up against Greg for some hitting practice. At 132 pounds I did not find it fun to get pummeled by bigger players. I was there to catch balls and run fast only. Upon contact with Greg I felt heat intensify in my elbow area on left arm. "Greg there is something hanging off that screw on your helmet. Gross it's skin. Holy crap, it's my skin." Looking down to the gaping hole in my arm my knees grew weak and I was ready to pass out. Pops was there shortly and ran me to the emergency room. The words spoken on the ride to the hospital are locked in my head as well. My pops said, "Okay Nick, we will see if they can get you patched up and back in the game by half-time." I could not escape the terrible thoughts running through my head about going back in the game after stiches. Pops looked at me and stated, "Nick, the girls will love it, if you go back in." That was all I needed to hear and mentally prepped myself. Even after the fourteen stiches in my left arm I arrived back at the football field. Walking out to my team, I felt like a king with all of the attention from the girls and my teammates. My pops knew what was up to and I only had to swallow a little pain to make it happen. One week later Trevor received five stiches in his left arm during the football game. I thought it was a brother-bonding moment. Unfortunately, we went to get his stiches after the game. He did not get to go back into the game at half time and did not receive the same fame as I did. He did not get to make out with Susan in the camera dark room, after the game, like I got to. It was interesting to be walking all of those different paths at that age. *What an amazing life.* I was only focused on the outcomes. Flying and women were the only two paths I cared to follow until the end. It was an extremely positive time in my life and I appreciated every second of it. Some did not appreciate those paths as much as I did. Some despised them completely, and I found it to be sad. I miss my abs.

CHAPTER SIX
The Circle

My mom was, and damn still is, a highly intelligent woman. There is no doubt in my mind that she would have cut off her own leg just to beat me senseless if she could have at that time. She had a giant fear for aviation and never wanted me around it. She thought crop dusting was created by the devil and doing it tested God. Their divorce never left her. I was merely four years old at the time of the split. It was as if the divorce happened yesterday, not thirteen years previously, to her. She was left sad, angry, and somewhat bitter. After the divorce my father was always painted as a careless hazard, not the loving man he truly was. Somehow, the judge only gave him visitation rights. At four you don't understand all of the logistics of divorce. You just assume you did something wrong and that is why you only get to see your day in the summers. That is how I ended up in Montana with her during the winter months. Only on Christmas break and in the summers would you find me in Kansas with my pops and the other half of my family. I could not be raised in such a negative light. I could not have my dreams painted ugly twenty-four seven. Sometimes an escape, or fresh start, must happen. Often times I thought everyone, at some point in life, could use a balancing flight in a solid Cessna Skylane to make everything better and build some Synergy. Sometimes you must forgive and flush out the negatives in order to move forward positively. Therefore, the move from Montana was a necessary thing, be it legal or not at first. I felt that I needed it to grow into the man I am presently.

All of the custody hearings were needed to be legal. They served a purpose but are hard on the souls. Family pitted against family is never a good thing. Seating in an emotionally unbalanced courtroom looking at all caused ambiguous feelings of concern, guilty, happiness, and tons of sadness. Although the process was long and tedious, it worked for me, as I finally became a resident of Kansas year round. The court reporter for my case was royally pretty. I was nice to have that beautiful distraction from all the hatred in the room. *Keep doing your job nameless beauty.* I may have mentioned the snow bunnies were incredible in Colorado also and I loved to ski. I have never regretted following my heart and dreams. I loved being a pilot. My pops often said, "Nick you are a cranky ass today. Does someone need a flight to get happy?" Flying is, and always has been, my true passion. If I had to wait for more than a week to fly, there was a strong pulling on my heart, a weight on my shoulders, and a small tug on my brain. I felt pulled to airplanes as a need, more than a want, in my life. I

49

always considered flying a solid reason for me being here on earth. To follow my passion I had to focus completely on it and work hard. For it to evolve into my reality I had to move to Kansas and follow the guidance of my father and all of the flight instructors that worked at Precision Air. Working hard was a quality passed on from my father. If it is wanted, you will find a way to get it should be a family motto.

I remember wanting the feeling commercial pilots had as they strutted around each airport looking important. To merely have the feeling that you were needed on a flight. I wanted to be recognized as a legitimate pilot. Over the years of watching pilots at the airport, I could tell just by personality if they were important pilots with good jobs. I wanted their strut and their confidence. Trevor and I needed to log as many flight hours in whatever airplane we could get our hands on. Trevor was not simply my brother, but also my best friend. He was the guy anyone would want to be best buds with. Best friends can create healthy competition as a driving force in life. Trevor was two years older. I often wondered if that made him wiser than me. He seemed to be naturally good at whatever he did. Although, a great quality to have as a teenage male, it tends to piss some people off. That is why we worked so hard to build our time, to boost are abilities and look better than each other in a loving way. More flight hours in our logbooks represented respect from strangers and each other. We knew high flight time pilots were more respected than new guys like us and therefore we needed more flight time.

Fortunately for us, our family owned and ran the only fixed-based operation (FBO) service in Great

Bend, Kansas: Precision Air. The excellent reputation that Precision Air had created over the years proved the service was an excellent flight school and also an excellent crop dusting company. I had flown in the giant yellow beast with my pops at Precision Air so many years previous. I had traveled full circle to be flying some of the aircraft myself. It felt good to be part of history, while focusing on my future.

CHAPTER SEVEN
Pushing On

We had some many planes to pick from. Precision had six airplanes reserved for student instruction. One helicopter, a Hiller 12E, aka the "Killer Hiller," and giant beastly grey and yellow G164 Ag-Cat 600 dedicated to dusting crops. Being around airplanes daily was thrilling, to say the least. I needed to learn about each one of them. It kept me in a constant search mode, learning more and more about our airplanes and their limitations. The first day, I was introduced to a helicopter as an aviation tool I felt they were scary as hell and dangerous machines. They represented a girlfriend that you cheated on. She would find a way get even with you at some point, I thought. They were much like Mother Nature. Helicopters were new to me and I often thought about all of the moving parts wanting to fly off at the worst possible time. In a helicopter, anytime, would be the worst time for a part to leave the helicopter. There was something romantic about them but I had no desire to figure out why. They glide like a cannonball, straight down. Precision had five other planes were utilized for daily charters. I was in heaven working for the family company while building flight time for free with Trevor. There were eleven airplanes at our disposal on any night of the week in the winter.

The word free represented their availability, not their hourly cost to be out flying around. Pops would have wrung our necks if he ever found out we were putting flight time on expensive airplanes. Not only were we putting hours on the airplanes, we always made sure they were topped off with expensive aviation fuel after every night flight. We did not fully understand that airplanes could time out after so much flight time, meaning airplanes are considered safe for only so many hours, than major overhauls need to be completed. We knew deep down, Mom, and Pops, would both wanted me to build my flight time for the future. I might need to take care of them someday. My logic was a tad twisted by my goals to be a respected pilot. In a justifying manor, I would tell myself at least I wasn't a twin-engine rated pilot so I could not fly the super expensive planes.

The eleven airplanes at Precision could be reduced to six after we removed the Cessna 414, Piper PA-30 Twin Comanche, and the Beech 18, all of which were expensive sexy twin-engine airplanes. We had to remove the twin-engine airplanes off the free fly list, as we were not licensed to fly them. Not being able to fly them was bad but they were big enough to make out in was so they did come in handy with the ladies. I had hours of make out time in each one of them but could not logged. Neither Trevor nor I possessed a multi-engine rating on our pilot's license but I knew someday I would have a multi-engine rating. In addition to the multiengine planes, we stayed away from the crop-dusting airplanes because they only had one seat. I had no desire to let Trevor sit on my knee while flying. I learned from Bill that Trevor would make your legs fall asleep and I was not interested in that. In all, single engine airplanes with multiple seats were the priority and were available for us to fly any night in the winter months. This is not to say that I did not fancy the thought of sneaking a twin out for a short flight. I guess my nerves were not as big as our brains. Looking back, I found maturity in our decision to listen to our brains. We never took a twin out flying as unrated pilots.

In the summer Trevor and I both worked for Precision loading and flagging for our pops in the helicopter and other pilots in the Ag Cat. We worked for the crop dusting division of Precision almost every day and most nights of the summer. It was an extremely hard and dirty job, coupled with little sleep. Every time the helicopter made its approach to land, on a warm summer day, it would fill your mouth with dirt while coating your sweaty body with thick dust. The dirt turtleneck was out of fashion so I hated wearing one. I mentally quit that job at least 50 times each day. In summer my friends would be out chasing the ladies while I was living in a dust storm, loading dangerous chemicals into my pop's helicopter all night long. I hoped they were not chasing my girlfriends. It was common for us to lose whatever girlfriends we had going into those summer months. I knew that I needed to get my flight hours to get out of the dirt. Plus the ladies needed me.

Trevor and I sat down to devise a plan to build our needed hours of flight time. We decided that in winter we would fly airplanes after the office personnel went home. Mum was the word. We did not feel as if we were stealing the time off the planes, but rather borrowing the time for future use. The winter nights provided solid air and strong performance in the machines we were flying. The faster we built our time, the sooner we would not have to load that damn dust loving helicopter or work with nasty chemicals. Winter flying was a glorious way to build up our time. We knew that working was good for us and provided us with the means to pay for the snow skiing. Deep down we knew this company was part of our family and nothing could ever destroy that. I knew that someday I would be crop-dusting for Precision, helping to support the company, thus the family.

One particular warm summer night, Mom brought my little sister, Rya, out to visit us at our last job for the night. I love when it's Pitch black yet still 82 degrees. After the helicopter was rinsed out, Pops sent us on our way back to the airport and invited Rya to fly back with him in the Hiller. We were almost back to the airport when the radio lit up, "Trevor and Nick, I need you to grab the crane truck and trailer and head back to the last field." We thought the helicopter must have died. As we found out, after our six-year-old sister jumped in the Hiller and Pops pulled pitch to invite flight, one of those parts that "wanted to fly off," did. The five-inch tube either exploded or uncoupled about five feet in the air and the helicopter slammed to the ground and broke apart into a hundred or so pieces. That perfect weathered night was killed by deaths attempt to kill my dad and sister. It was there but failed but failed to take anyone. Neither my pops, nor Rya, was hurt, as the helicopter broke apart.

From that moment on, the word helicopter put a bad taste in Rya's mouth. She avoided all flights in anything with a rotor system. A good part of the following day was spent picking up helicopter parts out of that random pasture near Great Bend, trying to figure out the gist of it all. Although I did not like helicopters, this particular helicopter had become family to me. I found myself bummed out to see her so badly broken. Once again a mental pause was needed to reflect on the event of that dark night and find some understanding about it. There was none to be found. It was needed to give the broken down Hiller some praise for keeping my pops safe, for so long. Thanks to the Hiller was also needed for protecting Rya as well. Looking at our collection of broken aircraft there in Great Bend, I found myself getting increasingly angry at death. I hated it. Trying to kill my little sister was the last straw. I would not accept death.

CHAPTER EIGHT
Winter's Innovation

As time progressed Trevor and I began to appreciate our "brilliant" hour building idea as we started racking up the hours of flight time. Those winter flights were the best way to build our flight time and have fun while doing so. We both knew that we could help other pilots along the way also. We soon we invited Troy to join us and log flight hours. We all needed flight time. We flew at least three nights a week, off and on all winter, every year. The summers were reserved for the crop-dusting. I had graduated to the guy with the scary respirator mask on his face hooking up the big green hose in the scorching Kansas heat. The blowing dust in the Kansas summer heat did not spice up my imagination as it did when I was a young boy in McPherson. I spent hours in the heat and irritating dust, day dreaming about the flying soon to come the following winter. It was opposite from my childhood, dreaming in the winter about the summer to come. Although the dirt was bad and the helicopter was loud, I was still connected to aviation every day of my life.

When we flew in those winter months, Trevor favored the Beech S35 Bonanza V-tail N2931F for its speed. It was a slick and fast airplane with clean lines and retractable gear. The V-tail was a likeable airplane and I enjoyed flying it for the speed. The Cessna-182 Skylane N429 Bravo Scott was my first choice. The high power and high-wing configuration created optimal lift, making the Skylane a super solid platform to fly. The Skylane had more power than I ever thought I would need. Although not retractable, or that fast, she was a reliable aircraft. Precision completed multiple charters per week into the Colorado Rockies. The high-wing design was ideal for strong lift in the mountainous areas of Colorado. Colorado is where I started my backcountry training. Backcountry flying was an endorsement I wanted in my logbook. Learning more about mountainous flying I respected other pilot opinions on the best planes in the mountains, which always seemed to be the Cessna 182 or 206. To me, the Cessna planes were the loyal work trucks. The V-tails were the sharp little sports cars, in my opinion. It was fast and sleek with its retractable gear, but you would never find me flying a V-tail in the Colorado Mountains. The Skylane profoundly proved its worth on an intense flight with my instructor Aaron to pick up two deer hunters in Georgia Pass, Colorado.

Aaron and Scott, both flight instructors at Precision, introduced backcountry flying to me in Colorado. Aaron was a veteran of flying in Colorado and loved being in the mountains. It was so great learning from his vast knowledge and experiences.

Backcountry flying put my human worth into perspective as we flew though giant valleys in various aircraft from Precision Air. If we crashed into the side of one of the mountains we would not even make a dent. We were so small compared to our giant surroundings. When Aaron asked me to fly to Georgia Pass with him I agreed because I had never been there, and loved challenges. My love of learning pulled me towards Georgia Pass that day. The flight would teach me valuable information. We fueled the Skylane, and took to the air headed west towards Georgia Pass.

That day, like so many others, was great and locked into my head. Two hours into the flight my mind could not process what my eyes were looking at when Aaron and I arrived to the Georgia Pass airport. It was obvious to me, the landing at Georgia Pass needed to be perfect every time or you would surely die. There was no room for even the slightest mistakes. A power in, go around, would never work at Georgia Pass. *Holy crap people land on that,* I thought. The runway was positioned on a downhill slope with a right turn throughout its entire length. A small part of me was intimidated by the geometry of it but the other part of me knew conquering that crazy landing would rank me a step above Trevor and Troy. In addition to the curve in the runway, tall pine trees surrounded the entire length of it. I thought, *how great, a curved runway on the sloped side of a mountain engulfed in trees*. Aaron looked down at the dicey runway, then back at me. "Take her in for a normal landing Nick. Be ready with the power when the wheels touch down." Knowing that Mr. Aaron had extensive backcountry mountain flying under his belt left me feeling safe enough to attempt the landing. I radioed the surrounding traffic. "Georgia Pass area traffic, November four two Niner Bravo Charlie straight in for runway three five Georgia Pass."

Still find myself shocked by it. When on the approach end of runway three five, through the trees, I could see the entire runway sloping up to the right. My apprehension was only elevated as the turbulent air, rolling down the mountain, bouncing us around in the cockpit. Aaron said, "Nick, take her in for a normal landing. Remember, it's just a runway." Looking out the window at that runway, *there was nothing normal about landing on the side of a mountain.* When I flared the Skylane, below the tree line, for touchdown, I was mentally ready for whatever obstacles the runway held for me. As the tires touched the gravel I had to immediately increase power to maintain forward movement. I found it disappointing there was no chirp as the tires kissed the gravel. That chirps was a "we have arrived" noise. It felt extremely strange to need half of the throttle to get to parking at the top of the scary runway. Most rollouts are relatively silent minus the gyros spinning in the cockpit and the wheels rolling on the ground. The rollout at Georgia Pass was nothing but loud engine sounds as the Skylane moaned to get to parking. My nerves calmed when I accepted I was in full control of the situation. This was a strange landing sequence, but I conquered it without issue. At that moment, I felt completely capable in the Skylane. It would not only be put in my logbook as flight time, but was also a great memory filed under major accomplishments in life. In my brain, I felt as if the Skylane was just an extension of me on that approach my thoughts transposed into mechanical movements in the 182. The view from the parking spot was breathtaking. Starring out the windscreen of the parked plane, I could see at least fifty miles of beautiful mountainous country. The runway resembled a curved path to follow down the mountain, though trees, to home. I was proud of myself and wished everyone on earth could feel what I felt at that exact moment.

Aaron was impressed, going on and on about the "great" approach. That complement boosted my confidence. After conquering that runway in Georgia Pass, I knew I could accomplish anything in an airplane. The idea of regular pilots landing on wacky gravel strips was exciting to think about. *Only crop-dusters land on little dirt strips,* I thought. It was nice to see that normal pilots flew into insane landing strips. Aaron stated that once we got home he would endorse my logbook for backcountry flying. I was extremely excited to get that endorsement. Backcountry flying endorsement set my flying ability higher, or so I thought. I did know that neither Trevor nor Troy had it in their logbooks, so I would be one step ahead of my brothers.

Aaron was also one of our part-time crop-duster pilots. He ran a large section of the local sugar factory in town, while also instructing people to fly, when not making sugar or crop-dusting. Southeast Kansas is a massive producer of sugar beets. Therefore a sugar factory was a prevalent odor. Yes, because a sugar beet factory produces an overused outhouse smell for about three miles around it. Aaron would beat everyone to the airport daily to give lessons in an older looking Cessna-120 tail-dragger. That little 120 sounded like a

VW Bug when taxiing around the airport those early mornings. Walking in to the office as the sun was crawling up, you would hear Aaron's voice on the Unicom radio. Respect for his love and dedication to aviation was given every time I saw him. On that particular flight, I was getting ready to appreciate his backcountry instructor's endorsement way more than his love of flying, however.

Aaron, although a small man, was a skilled pilot in that tiny 120 and also in the giant six hundred horse power Ag Cat. At Precision Air Service, I was responsible for checking every field during the day and noting any hazardous obstacles the pilots should avoid while spraying them at night. It was a large alfalfa field just south of Great Bend that we needed to spray one night. I drove the thirty-minute drive, penciled all of the obstacles on paper that Aaron would need to avoid while flying in the dark. I pulled over for a power nap.

It was nearing 1:30am when I found myself back at the field outside twenty minutes south of Great Bend to guide Aaron in with my radio. There was no moonlight that night, only ominous darkness. From a distance I could hear a 1340 radial headed my way and knew it was Aaron in the Cat. Those round engines produce a distinct sound. "Nick, do you see me?" "Affirmative Aaron, north of you about a quarter mile, I'm flashing my strobe." "Roger that Nick, I got you. How are we looking down there?" "Aaron, this is a sixty-acre rectangular field. There is a small set of wires on the north end. Should be an easy job." "Alright Nick, I'll dive in over you and move west." "Roger that Aaron, be safe." The Cat made a gentle approach to the field and flew directly over me about fifteen feet. You could visually see the exhaust flame shooting out a foot or so from the engine in the dark.

The sound of a radial engine screaming low overhead on any silent dark night was riveting. Aaron flipped on his giant spray lights and keyed the radio, only for me to hear a scream of fright like nothing I had ever heard before. When the lights lit up his path through that field, they illuminated a large set of hundred-thousand-volt cross-country power lines with their giant metal transmission towers running through the middle of the field. The sound of the radial engine pushed beyond red line echoed profoundly in the silent valley. The tips of the prop were screaming as he pulled with all of his might inside the cockpit to avoid deadly contact with the wires or tower. I failed Aaron and darn near killed him that night. I had failed myself as well. Looking at the list of obstacles I had jotted down, I discovered that I had not drawn anything about the set of death wires in the middle of the field. Getting to the field earlier that afternoon I had written some stuff down before taking my short power nap. It was clear to me my lack of sleep had invited death to that field. Aaron almost hit the wires and only by pure luck and skill did he squeak by them.

"Nick?" With great hesitation I answered, "Go ahead, Aaron." "Get your butt home and go to sleep. We will talk about this tomorrow." He already knew the cause was lack of sleep. It was a long drive home that night and I felt horrible about the near miss. Although feeling horrible about the incident, I was relieved to be talking to him on the radio versus talking to a gravestone. Aaron trusted me to protect him and I failed him. I was glad he did not hold grudges and further glad he did not meet death on that dark night. He knew I would learn from it, as I did. Every other job that summer, from that night on, had everything listed, even gophers. The near miss increased my safety concerns tenfold. Being around crop-dusting it felt that death was always near. For a brief while I felt anyone near me was in death's sight, ready to use its grip to strangle life out. There was s feeling that death had a curiosity with me. For that reason, I went overboard on safety from that night on and I managed to find more sleep. To choose sleep over girls was a hard compromise. For a seventeen-year-old boy that decision was difficult, but the right thing to do. It was obvious that Aaron loved aviation and, better yet, had a big heart. For there I was flying with him in the Skylane even after I almost got him killed in that dark field outside of Great Bend. On a side note, my pops asked me several random times over that summer if I had killed anyone the night before. It is always better to laugh about things than to focus on the negatives in that occupation. Thankfully Aaron loved to instruct and was willing to take me on the flight to Georgia Pass.

When it was finally time to leave Georgia Pass, I fired up the O-470 in the Skylane and got us pointed down the runway. Pressing both feet firmly on the brakes was a must to maintain our position on the runway. Our two passengers asked if I was old enough to be a pilot. Aaron laughed and told them he would fly anywhere with me. Feeling honored with that compliment, I aimed to impress our passengers with a smooth takeoff. With the window open the prop filled the cockpit with the fresh crisp mountain air, mixed with 100 Low Lead exhaust. The plane wanted to start her takeoff roll without any power due to the drastic slope. When making my radio call I figured honesty worked the bact. *Georgia Pass area traffic, November four two, Niner Bravo Charlie is taking the taking the active one seven hard left down the mountain for departure, Georgia Pass*.

The takeoff roll only seemed to be about fifty feet once power was introduced. By far that was the shortest takeoff roll I ever made. Georgia Pass was the most dangerous airport I ever flew into or out of. The downhill slope was only one of the strange dynamics needed to fly into or out of Georgia Pass. The need to apply left rudder for the takeoff roll was also interesting. After the window had been closed, the smell of freshly killed elk filled the Skylane. The hunters talked about their time hunting. Then soon changed their conversation to the ten or so aircraft that had crashed at the Georgia Pass airport over the years. The conversation about the crashes built a stronger feeling of accomplishment.

At the moment the gravelly hum stopped filling that cockpit, as the wheels lifted into the air and we were stabilized in a positive climb, I felt completely safe in the Skylane. The rugged beauty of the Rocky Mountains was mesmerizing as we flew home. The rigid peaks and harsh valleys eventually turned into flat valley land of agriculture as we neared Great Bend. That landing and takeoff set a newfound respect for backcountry pilots and their ability to attack such obstacles as Georgia Pass. After landing and putting my bird to bed, Aaron put his backcountry instructor's endorsement in my logbook. It felt as if I had been knighted, Sir Skylane. I called Trevor and Troy to set up the night's adventure, and to brag a tad. Truth is, I called to brag and then brag some more. It was the same thing I had done when I got checked out in the Cessna 206T Stationair. We could all expect a call if something great happened to one of us in aviation. After a call, I would spend time trying to figure out how I could top their accomplishments. This drove all three of us to reach for as many endorsements in our logbooks while becoming better pilots.

Cessna aircraft continued to represent strength and reliability throughout my high school years. My pop's good friend Frank walked into the office at the airport in, and asked loudly, "Who gets to fly me home to McPherson?" Raising my arm I volunteered. Frank pointed at me and said, "You, Nick, are hired, but we need to fly something that I trust." What would he trust? He flew A4s in Vietnam how could any of these little planes compare to that jet with regards safety? Pointing at a yellow airplane through the office window, Frank stated, "There we go Nick, that Cessna 206T Stationair will do just fine." "Frank, I'm not checked out in that plane." "Don't be a sissy Nick, by the time you get back, you will be checked out in the Stationair." I was excited about the checkout but a little apprehensive, not knowing if Frank was an instructor or not. Figuring all of his Vietnam flying put him a world ahead of any of my instructors, I jumped on the plan. Soon we were loaded in the mustard-yellow Stationair lined up at the far end of the runway. "Great Bend Area traffic, November two zero six Delta Juliet is a Stationair rolling on the active two Niner for a downwind departure, Great Bend." It was important to let everyone know I was flying a Stationair. As I put the power to her I could feel that she was heavier on the controls than her little sister the Skylane. We rotated and entered a positive rate of climb in the big Stationair. Although the controls felt heavy, her speed and power balanced it all out, creating a beautiful synergy. Looking to the back of the plane I saw four empty seats not two, but four. That plane was a big Cessna and it felt really good to be pilot in command that flight.

It was a cool fall day as we sliced through the sky in the Stationair, headed to McPherson. The air was crisp without any turbulence. The Ground was peppered with the multiple bright colors of turning trees. It was perfect weather to be on a checkout flight in the 206T. The speed of the Stationair brought the Cessna 210 to my mind. I knew the Centurion had to be incredibly fast airplane and wanted to fly one, soon. On the flight to McPherson Frank and I chatted about football and school. On approach to McPherson Frank said, "Alright Nick, she will be heavy on the flare, do not let her drop hard." With my nerves riding shotgun, I was set. We came in on a shallow descent to the runway. I pulled power back softly and entered a smooth flare. Frank was walking me through the landing "Looks good Nick. Hold it, hold it, and chop power." I held it with all I had. The controls were so heavy. When I chopped the power she settled to the ground harder than anticipated, causing us to bounce twice. A rough landing for me was not common and figured I was going to need someone to come get me there in McPherson. Second-guessing myself, I figured

Frank was not going to let me fly that big beautiful plane home.

Frank asked me to pull over to an area where he could jump out. He looked at me and said, "Good job Nick. By the time you get back to McPherson you will be smooth as glass. Now get going before it gets dark." Shocked by his decision to let me fly out in the Stationair I was happy to do so. Slight embarrassment sat in the back of my head about the hard landing. The big plane turned around and we jumped back on the runway. "McPherson area traffic six Delta Juliet taking the active two eight for a straight out departure, McPherson." I wanting to say solo departure because I was proud of myself but did not. Before I entered takeoff power, my eyes traveled to where the Grumman G-164 Ag Cat/600 had been sitting, destroyed, in the sagebrush some 75 feet from my current location in the Stationair. It seemed only the day before, I was standing there in sadness starring at its crumpled pile of yellow metal. I missed McPherson. My memory soon changed to happy thoughts as I pushed the throttle forward in that Stationair.

As I rotated the big plane, it entered into a high rate of positive climb with strong speed. With five empty seats in that plane, the power seemed endless. The flight home was filled with childhood thoughts of flying with Trevor and all the crashes I had seen. It felt so good to be right there in that Stationair, flying over the varying landscapes. Happiness filled my mind as I thought about my aviation path in life. Before long I was downwind for the landing on runway two Niner Great Bend. Like Frank had stated, my landing at home was smooth as butter and I felt at peace about flying the

Stationair from then on. The next day, Frank called to talk to me about my landing. Feeling apologies were needed, I told him I was sorry I had bounced the Cessna so hard. Frank told me that most of his landings in Vietnam were on an aircraft carrier. Each landing was considered a controlled crash, therefore my landing, to Frank, was smooth as silk. We both laughed. Although I had been checked out in the Stationair and signed off for backcountry flying, I still needed more time in my logbook.

CHAPTER NINE
Almost Enough

To build more time, Trevor and I would hop onto any charter that had room, without being pests. If one of our instructors was the pilot-in-command on a charter and we could miss school, we would strap our butts in and go. We would grab Troy if we simply had to pick up parts, or airplanes, in other areas. We did miss a lot of school, but it was for a different type of education, called life. Troy was present for all flights not considered charters by the Federal Aviation Administration. All three of us were building hours at a good rate and doing it in a legal manner. Flights came and went like catching head colds in Kansas. We became regulars in the cockpits of charter planes at Precision. Life was good and always filled with positive experiences. One day I found myself flying co-pilot out of Topeka, sitting in the Cessna 210 Centurion with Scott, another instructor/charter pilots a precision. In the plane were a police officer, a convicted convict, and us. Precision had a contract to transport convicts throughout the state of Kansas. Even in handcuffs the prisoner had to feel a tad free, flying through the air in the Centurion. Damn those planes are fast like a 206 on steroids.

On a cool fall afternoon Trevor and I showed up to the airport for work to find yet another giant yellow airplane on the ramp. The plane was astonishing to me. It was as big as the Thrush but sleeker in appearance. It was so shinny the wings looked wet from across the ramp. The plane sat absorbing the rays of sun and reflecting them off the glossy paint. We saw an older gentleman wiping the pretty plane down so we both ran out to learn more. That yellow plane was not a spray plane at all. Actually it was a North American T-6 Texan. It was the number-one training aircraft for fighter pilots in World War Two. It had the same engine as the Ag Cat, a P&W 1340 radial engine. The owner of the plane, Sam, made a deal with us. He needed to leave the plane in Great Bend for the winter. Sam told us if we took care of his bird all winter, he would give us a good ride in the Texan. We both jumped at the idea and watched that plane like a hawk all winter. We washed it more than our own planes at Precision. It was amazing how that bright yellow Texan grabbed your eye first when pulling into the airport. The yellow stood in bright contrast to the gray concrete ramp it was tied to. That airplane represented freedom. Being tied down to a parking spot stripped it of its freedom to me.

When the spring came to warm the earth, Sam stuck by his words and set up a flight for both of us. Strapping into that piece of history was humbling, knowing that it had trained pilots for our safety back in the day. As Sam walked around the plan untying it I thought it was free now to fly, as it wants. When I strapped into the back seat, I felt safe, I felt protected. Looking through the window out at the wings my eyes were mesmerized by the millions of shiny rivets holding the wing together. Knowing that each rivet had held the metal together for over forty years created a feeling of strength in me. I knew those glossy rivets had saved someone's life at some point. The cockpit was tight, unlike the Thrush, giving me a fighter plane feeling. When the prop started its rotation and the radial popped and growled it became a fancy Thrush in my mind. The power of the engine made the aircraft shake and shiver. It was great that non crop-dusting pilots got to feel the power of a radial engine. It was something all pilots should feel at some point on their aviation path, I truly believed. We taxied to the end of runway two-Niner.

As we accelerated down the runway I could feel the differences between the two planes. The Texan was incredibly smooth and much faster. I found myself wishing my fighter pilot voice had matured enough to make a radio call in that amazing piece of history. That plane was slick and sexy. After achieving flight and putting the wheels up in the wells, located in the wings, we climbed to 3,000 AGL. Sam said, "Nick, the plane is yours." After a few turns Sam keyed the microphone to say, "Nick, the Texan was a fighter trainer. It loves to do rolls and aggressive turns don't be afraid. Nick, slam the stick hard right then level after one roll." I responded, "Roger that Sam, here we go." I slammed the stick hard right the sleek yellow bird entered into a tight right barrel roll. I leveled the stick out to stop our roll. It was thrilling to have the control of that amazing Texan in my hand. Furthermore, I was excited to tell people that I had actually rolled one. The visual out of the glass ceiling while inverted was captivating. All of nature's colors of the earth stood out more brightly than I had ever noticed, but then again I had never been upside down in a plane with a glass ceiling. I was on cloud nine for weeks after that flight. Random flights would always present themselves to us at the Great Bend, airport. It was only a matter of running into the right person at the right, random, time. The thought of the beautiful Texan makes me smile. "Excuse me miss can I get another?"

A few months after that magnificent flight in the T-6, Scott approached me about another flight with him. He asked me if I would help him on an ash-drop. An ash-drop flight was a flight to scatter the cremated ashes of a deceased person on a specific location chosen by loved ones. I was apprehensive at first but accepted it in order to be part of the flight to honor a wife and mother, who departed this world sooner than expected. I thought this would be a good learning experience for me not only in the air but also on the ground also. I needed to know who to deal with people in these sad circumstances. I needed to learn how to act, face to face, with loved ones. Her husband hired Precision to scatter her ashes on the family cabin in the Ozark Mountains near Buffalo City, Arkansas.

Scott was a busy over weight pilot with charters and flight training. He flew every day with his mangy dog. He brought his little raccoon-looking dog on all of his flights. Practicing stalls with Scott in N1314J was always fun. As the little Cessna 150 entered the steep stall, that little hairy dog would float up from the back area of the plane. You would often catch a paw on the back of your head as he tried to get back to his napping spot. That dog loved to fly, as did his owner Scott. Scott, the dog, and I jumped into N4343D, another 172 at Precision for the flight to the cabin area. The 172 was a good plane for this type of flight due to its good ferrying speed and its ability to fly slowly, for the drop. There was a crude cardboard box with a clear bag filled with death sitting on the floor between my legs in the plane. I wanted to put it in the back seat but did not want the furry mutt to mess with it. The ashes were waiting patiently to dance freely through the clean mountain air and onto the ground near the family cabin. As we got closer Scott explained to me how to successfully dump her precious ashes as he flew the plane.

As we approached the drop point, I took the bag of ashes out of the crude box. That brown cardboard box was not fitting for any dead. On Scott's instruction I opened my window to a rush of air and put the edge of the bag out of the window. The speed of the plane would lowly siphon her ashes away. It felt good to help Scott on this flight and to be of assistance to the family. In a random way, I was giving death some credit; therefore I knew we would be safe on the flight. Everything was operating smoothly. The plastic bag was about half empty as she continued flowing out puff-by-puff. My mind pictured what parts where blowing out as the bag emptied. This flight was enjoyable and I appreciated what it stood for. This flight represented respect for a past life here on earth. Everything was going smoothly when all of a sudden,

Scott's fat arm accidently popped open the window on his side of the little plane. The massive flow of air caused a strong whirlwind in the cockpit. Unfortunately, it was not only air whirling in the cockpit but rather a small tornado of cremated ash. Before I could get my mouth closed, it was filled with the ashy grit of death in all sections of my mouth. We both coughed and spit the dead dust out of our mouths. We had to get her out of our eyes so that we could see to get home. The only thing I could do was stay respectful. I wanted to start screaming obscenities but could not with Scoot and his dog there. *Holy crap my mouth is filled with dead lady ash. There is dead lady all over my body. The dirt turtleneck is out of fashion is the dead lady ash turtleneck in. Screw you death not cool.* Rapid thoughts filled my head. As rapidly as they ran in they left. Although I focused on staying calm, I was freaked out.

I looked over at Scott but said nothing, as his normally white hair was now grey with puffs of dust shooting off of his hair. The raccoon looking dog in the back of the plane was now a greyish hue. In addition, I could see her ash had coated my arms also and any free skin on either one of us was covered. I knew this was nothing more than a sick joke from death. It was a simple and understandable warning to me. We turned the plane towards Great Bend to get her ashes off of us. On the flight back, my mind danced with questions about what horrible disease might have killed this lady and how it might be affecting me, as she was in my mouth and I was covered in her ash while flying home. There was little enjoyment on the flight home. We landed and parked the plane away from the terminal in case a loved one was watching. To this day I remember Scott grabbing his gray dog out of the back of the 172 and putting him on the ground. The dog took about five steps before shaking a large cloud of burnt ash off of him. Although gross, I found that dog shaking to be humorous. Truthfully, it was super funny and I love to laugh.

I drove home in a rapidly with high speed to wash her dead ash off of me. Once in the shower, I looked down only to see the white tub now had a brownish grey hue of death in the water. After getting myself cleaned up I ran back out to Precision and sucked the rest of her dead ash out of the 172 with the shop vac. I walked over to the office and put the last little pile of her ashes to rest, in the flowerbed at the office. Making the decision to pay more respect, I prayed that she would rest quietly and enjoy her peace now. I also prayed that if she died of something highly contagious for me not to get it. I must have brushed my teeth for thirty minutes that night. I needed to make sure she was out of every crevasse in my mouth forever. I did not necessarily want her out of my mouth, but rather death away from me. On that convoluted day, ferrying the airplane to and from Arkansas, I logged almost four hours of flight time. As disturbing as it was, it became a great learning experience. Furthermore, down the road, it became a great story of what not to do on an ash drop and why it is important to watch your weight.

At school, you would find us boys in the lunchroom briefly checking out the girls and talking about the past football game or the coming game. All right, briefly cannot be used for checking out the girls.

All three of us were good looking and we often challenged each other to get more looks than the other for the hot girls on campus. We lied to look better. In addition to the girls, there was always a long conversation about our last flight. Daydreaming about any new Cessna or Beech aircraft coming out of the factory became a constant for me. Wishing I could somehow get the opportunity to fly the new planes. Even back in the huddle after running a post route during a football game, I would find myself thinking about planes. Never did I grow out of my busy aviation imagination. When your one of the company pilots picks you up on the fifty-yard line of the football field in a Bell G3-B1 helicopter after school, you fully understand how great aviation is and how fortunate you are, to be a part of it.

That day, like all the others, was unexpected and amazing. The memory of it is as clear as glass. Not only did randy pick me up in a helicopter, he had Nancy with him. Nancy was his totally hot girlfriend. She was incredibly pretty and had a toned build. She was the older woman that boys dreamt about having a meaningless sex with. I was on cloud nine, jumping into the Bell and sitting next to a beautiful woman. As I peered out the clear bubble, I was looking at the field where I had such great memories from football and track. This would be another awesome memory on that football field. Randy landed right where I ripped open my arm on Greg's helmet that night. As the engine and blades gained speed for lift off, Nancy's breast vibrated against my arm, as we were all three smashed into the little cockpit. That was one bonus to the little bubble helicopters. If you got to fly with beautiful Nancy, you

77

would get some boob on your bicep. It was totally marvelous to feel the excitement in my heart from the helicopter, combined with excitement in other areas as the perfect breast gently caressed my bicep. *Where is she now I wonder?* Three years of high school at Great Bend Christian high school, and that was by far the best day ever. With aviation in your life, each day holds both good and bad surprises. For the most part they were good, unexpected, surprises. Death was there on the sidelines. Precision still had crop dusting so Death waited patiently.

CHAPTER TEN
Through it All

That big blue beast will always be in this mind as a great experience. One cold winter evening after working at the airport fueling planes, I had the opportunity to fly freight with Grantham in the Beech-18 N22PW That airplane was amazing. Something about saying November Two-Two Papa Whiskey on the radio always put a smile on my face and made me feel important. That call sign made me sound like a professional pilot. Grantham was an instructor, therefore I could log the time and he would sign it off. I saw it as one step closer to the multi-engine rating on my license. That flight would surely rank my skills higher than Trevor's or Troy's. Unlike most Beech 18's, this particular Beech had a nose wheel, a Queen Air tail, with a long aerodynamic nose. The Tradewinds converted Beech-18 was much faster than a standard Beech-18. The tradeoff for speed tends to be weight in aviation. Our big Beech was fast and smooth in beautiful blue paint.

79

Grantham and I jumped into the big, blue, Beech yelled, "CLEAR," built a fire in both of the 450 horse power radial engines, then flew over to Hays to get our first load of freight. The Beech at Precision was already a great machine in my mind because it had two beefy radial engines. Not just one, but two strong radials. The freight was headed to Oklahoma City, Oklahoma, to be shipped out via DC-10. It was a clear evening, meaning the visibility would be good and the flight would be smooth. I found myself feeling important in this historic, powerful plane. Much like the T-6-Texan, the Beech had WWII history as a light bomber trainer. Flying co-pilot in this plane confirmed there was a lot to learn about twins, especially the older planes. Although this beautiful bird's conversion was relatively new, most of the standard parts were still forty years old, if not more.

The sun was starting its drop as we flew out of Hays with our first load. We were heavy on departure loaded to the top of the plane with freight. During departure the 985s were screaming in a high-pitched voice. Although the engines were healthy and loud, the Beech was climbing out slowly at 50 foot a minute climb. My mind filled with hundreds of questions but did not want to bug Grantham for I did not know much about twins. A few minutes later he asked, through the headset, "Nick, did you fill up the all the fuel tanks because we were getting low on the tip tanks according to the gauges." A tip tank is the outer-most fuel tank on each wing. I stated, "Of course." Grantham initialized the fuel tank change process. At 900 feet, the right engine began to pop and shutter, shaking us roughly in the cockpit. The blades of the big metal prop became visible as the engine shut down on my side of the airplane. We started to slow drastically as if a parachute had been deployed out of the back of the plane. My heart fluttered as I looked ahead where I thought the impact site would be. If the left engine also died, it would be game over for me and Grantham. As heavy as we were, the left-screaming engine could not produce enough power to back to Hays. It only had enough power to get us to the crash site.

The curse words flying out of Grantham's mouth became louder and louder. He pushed the nose over to gain whatever airspeed we could. We started a shallow dive. Grantham turned to me and screamed, "Nick did you fill the tip tanks?" I responded in a scared voice, "Yes Grantham, I filled all four tanks," getting nervous as the ground was creeping up. I was mentally preparing myself for the end conclusion to this tainted flight. The tension in the cockpit was thick as Grantham yelled; "FOUR…there are SIX fuel tanks on this plane Nick." Embarrassed and scared to death, I explained which tanks I had filled with fuel. We were running on the tanks I had not touched. It seems that while we were in Hays someone had loaded death onto that damn flight with the freight. Grantham was able to switch tanks and bring the right-engine back to climb power roughly fifty feet above the ground. With the little daylight left, at fifty feet I could see each blade of grass, dancing in the breeze below, waiting for me, on the hill that was intended to be our crash site. Death was standing on the piece of land with open arms, for us. Although I felt it there, with scythe in hand, calling me, I refused to accept it. As the right engine came back into full power a feeling of safety draped over me.

Minus the engines harmonizing loudly in perfect pitch, it was a quiet hour and a half flight in the cockpit to Oklahoma City in the headsets. I spent the majority of the flight staring out into the darkness reflecting on every warning sign death had given me over the years. It seems I had not learned from one near miss and continued to dance with the devil. The two round engines were harmonized in perfect rhythm, calming me. Grantham assured me it was not my fault because I was not a twin-rated pilot. His comment actually made me feel worse about that situation. If I had been a twin-rated pilot, this close call might not have happened. He claimed it was his fault, and not to worry it. He was sure it would never happen to me again. Grantham said he could still see the fear on my face over two hours later. He looked at me as we entered downwind for landing in Oklahoma and said, "Nick breath man you are white as a ghost still." I had never been so physically scared in my life the moment I saw the grass dancing. That was too close and, yes, I was scared that night. Grantham explained if we had been light, without any cargo, the one good engine would have flown just fine back for landing. Because we were loaded so heavy on departure, it should have ended disastrously.

On that long night flight, the crashed Ag Cat in McPherson popped back into my mind. A picture of the broken hulk of the Ag Cat sitting destroyed in the dirt so close to the runway, yet so far away. It was pleasing once again to be sitting in a flying airplane, not a crumpled-up pile of bent blue metal so close to the active runway in Hays. We ended up flying three loads of freight that night. I was elated to see the runway lights and land in Great Bend after our final flight and looked forward already to the night's endeavors with Trevor and Troy. I could not wait to tell them about the unsettling night I had just spent with Grantham and the big blue Beech. After that night, fuel became a major priority for me on each and every flight. Grantham was right, I did learn from my mistake. It seemed that learning from mistakes was a major requirement in aviation. I wondered if pilots don't make mistakes in aviation, how do they learn anything. Although it scared me to death, that flight was a good learning experience for me, therefore I did not hesitate to fly in the beautiful Beech again as soon as I could.

While maintaining grades and participating in sports, I always found time to fly. Still blows my mind thinking about this crazy ass life. Besides being a pilot, I was a fairly normal boy. One week after flying with death in the Beech, Trevor, Troy, and I headed down to Chadron, Nebraska, from Great Bend, Kansas, in the Skyhawk to pick up a Piper Cherokee PA-28-140 Cruiser that had been weathered in a few weeks previously. We had gotten into a habit of dropping altitude to about three feet AGL (above ground level) once we crossed the Nebraska state line and then flew terrain of the earth. Trevor and I figured this style of flying would help us later when we became crop-dusters. It was nothing other than small hills and valleys, no major obstacles. On that particular flight Troy was the pilot in command, PIC for short. About thirty minutes into the flight, we were flying low through the snow covered landscape of Nebraska. We had just followed a brushy hill down and started the gradual climb back up on the other side of the snow lightly covered little valley. When we reached the top of the hill, altitude about five feet, above the ground, we were instantly startled by a heard of wild mustang horses headed in the opposite direction at full gallop. The instant thought of death encompassed all three of us as we all screamed and thought we were going to die right there in Nebraska by a heard of horses. I knew without a shadow of doubt death was riding the lead horse.

Peering out of the front window at that particular second, I could visually see the solid black wet eyes of a weathered chrome mustang staring directly at me. It was a strange moment, sharing a fearful vision between both man and horse. The white markings on the horse's face and back were crystal clear as they stood in great contrast to the dark browns and blacks. Both that horse, and each one of us, in that Skyhawk were engulfed in fear. Death was becoming more of a constant existence in my life yet I failed to recognize it in its entirety. Unlike McPherson, where death came and took pilots away, it was merely a feeling, a presence near us. Troy immediately started a climb and hard right turn while Trevor shoved the power in, as if it had been rehearsed a hundred times. The right wing came within a foot of that scared animal. A single foot to the left saved our butts that day. It was not excellent piloting skills that saved our lives but, rather, pure luck. Each time I saw death close enough to fear for my life, I tended to reflect on it quietly. All three of us fell into the same pattern. It was nearly sixty more miles without one word from any one of us. We were getting used to this ritual of silent flights and strangely accepting of it. Even as kids we understood the silent flights had to happen, a silent flight of respect and acceptance as death came to take pilot friends away or almost us. We all knew that death was watching. We all knew how lucky we were to be alive in that still airborne Skyhawk.

After arriving at Chadron I opted to fly the little Piper home by myself and let the boys take the Skyhawk home. Something in me, needed to fly that simple slow-flight trainer, the Cruiser, to adjust my thoughts and put myself in check, all the way back to Great Bend. I sat at the end of the runway in the little Cruiser thinking about those horses before making my call, "Chadron area traffic Cherokee November five zero seven four Echo is taking the active one-one, crosswind departure, Chadron." Shortly after putting the power to the Cherokee, I found myself at 10,000 feet above the Nebraska prairies in that little trainer, just thinking about my luck thus far in this life. The endless rolling hills below me was perfect for a reflective backdrop. Sometimes a pilot just needs to slow down and appreciate each flight. A reflective flight would help me to center the compass on life and get me pointed in the right direction. The event with the horses caused a deeper appreciation for life. I loved flying, but I would continue to do it with more respect. That Mustang was too close. Our ridiculous altitude almost killed a horse and all three of us. It needed to stop.

On that solo flight home to Great Bend I had an epiphany about pushing my luck with death and made the mature decision to become a stronger pilot based on skill, not luck. I realized that day, that flying was not only something for fun but, rather, it was life for me.

All of my goals, effort, training, time, love, passion, and desire were tied directly to aviation. I had been logging tons of time with the night flights and all the ferry flights. It was truly a great experience and a major part of my future. I knew after that flight there was still a massive amount of learning to happen for me to be a great pilot like my pops.

Dang that was so funny. Some flights we would all talk in our best jet fighter pilot voices for the entire flight. Made us all laugh, but we were getting better at it. We thought if we could master the voice of a fighter jock, their flying skills might randomly appear in our flying. More than anything, at that point, I just wanted a true jet jockey voice to sound extra cool on the radio. Troy's voice was beginning to sound professional and military. We had a gaggle of friends that would fly with us, but only two other pilots, Troy and Sam. Most flights were positive experiences, just how aviation should be. The close calls were locked in this brain as little safety manuals to learn from. Every bad experience in aviation stayed close in my memory while the good, every day, normal flights left memory much faster. Only special flights would remain locked in my head. At that time in life I was due for it was a good positive flight for I had been on too many nerve-racking flights and needed one to back my love for it. It was not soon after that I found myself on another incredible flight.

That flight, on that night, is still crystal clear in my memory. One night a good friend Sam flew me and Liz, my girlfriend to Tulsa, Oklahoma, for an early breakfast. My pops would always come up with exciting aviation adventures to combine with our school endeavors. Prom was one of those defining events that needed something great to equal it. He was sure the two of us would enjoy the breakfast in Tulsa after prom. I was sure that I would enjoy anything with Liz above 5,280 feet AGL, as I did. Joining the "club" at such a young age just added to my Private Pilot Certificate and backcountry endorsement in my mind. I had wished the FAA had the Mile High Club endorsement for my license. The FAA did not care about the club as much as I did or as much as any young male pilot would. At seventeen I was knighted "Sir Mile High" in the back of a Cessna 206 Stationair. I was the President of flying, and the ladies, in my inflated world. While she was a beautiful girl in everyday life, in the back of N4671F she became the ultimate sky goddess. Being a young man, any sex was amazing. Having it in the back of Cessna created a euphoric unforgettable experience forever implanted in my brain. Sex, flying, and food, was always the best combination at seventeen. That particular flight required several silent reflection flights. Thank you Sam for the smooth flight that night. It was so great to find myself on so many random flights. All of them came as rich learning experiences because I was focused on that. That flight was extremely educational and I enjoyed every learning second of that lesson. *Why did I learn from that positive lesson and never from pushing fate around?*

.

CHAPTER ELEVEN
Still Just Boys

T hose damn trees where so tall. One half-moon night, Trevor, Troy, and I, decided to fly out and buzz Tina's house by the reservoir. We had all been on several great flights without death near us so we knew this flight was needed. With a pilot's license came the huge obligation to chase the ladies, so we all thought. I could see myself as a lonely self-confident pilot, landing at random airports around the country, climbing out of some old rag-wing bi-plane wearing my leather jacket and being hugged on by mysterious ladies. Of course my leather jacket had a backcountry and Mile High Club patch on it. All three of us knew where Tina's house was geographically located. We figured her parents would certainly enjoy the flyby at eleven p.m. Troy and I were inspired by the thought of her liking us. Something about her great personality, soft heart and, hopefully, lips, pulled us in. Brother Trevor was there strictly for the flight time. We blasted out of the airport around 10:30 p.m. in the Skylane.

Tina's house was about a ten to fifteen-minute flight southeast towards Cheney Reservoir. The reservoir was moon lit in the distance and served as a navigation point most nights.

Once over the reservoir, I dropped us to within fifteen feet of the cool, fairly calm water. Cheney Reservoir was where you could find all three of us any free, fairly warm day in the spring, water skiing. Any night there was merely a sliver of moon, the reservoir would light up brilliantly. Every time I saw the crisp water of Cheney Reservoir, in Kansas, I pictured myself cutting hard on my Jobe slalom ski behind our bright yellow jet boat. Trevor and I bought a beautiful yellow and white jet boat for skinning. It was yellow and not used for crop-dusting. I found that ironic. The chromed-out 460 sticking out of the back would push the sleek machine to almost 70 mph on the water. While it was fast, I appreciated it for the looks I received from the ladies when I started it. I had Trevor convinced I could not back down the boat ramp so that I could be the guy in the boat starting it.

As I brought four two Bravo Charlie into the proper vector for the low pass, I lost sight of the house due to the bright reflections bouncing off the water. We were fifteen feet above the reservoir, getting closer to her house by the second. At that height you could see each tiny ripple in the fairly smooth water. The fear of the unknown ahead of us caused nervousness in my shoulders. In the Skylane at that altitude the constellation was visible from above and below. The reflections of the stars shimmered off the water. The star reflections seemed to be a perfect mirror image on the water. There we were, fifteen feet above a dark reservoir in the black of night without the slightest perception of death. We knew death was watching us. I always envisioned death riding on the one of the wing struts. I knew it would always fall off before the airport. Positive thoughts of death not being there filled my head. We were too focused on impressing Tina, not living in realism.

A voice of concerned logic came from the back seat. It was Troy and he sounded a tad stressed. "Nick her house is surrounded by extremely tall trees, if you remember. You should turn the landing light on just to be safe." "Okay, Troy will do. Just relax back there." Troy always was a voice of reason. Flipping the toggle for the landing light to the on position was something I regretted almost instantly. The second the bulb illuminated its beam forward our vision turned from black night to a wall of branches and leaves. No time to even scream, only time to try and fix the situation. I slammed the throttle forward to max power. The engine moaned and the prop screamed as I pulled with all I had on the yoke. There was absolutely no understanding of how we did not hit a tree and why we were all unbroken in a still flying airplane.

It was evident at that point death was riding with me once again. I leveled us out about 150 feet above the ground and headed straight back to the airport in a rapid fashion. Minus the engine hum inside the plane, it was once again a silent cockpit as we flew back to Great Bend and landed the Skylane. Silence was my focus as I reflected back on all the previous aviation uncertainties and close calls again. My mind drifted back to Aaron. Thinking of him turning on his working lights just in time to see massive cross-country power lines in his path. It put Aaron's fear and that high scream into perspective. After we were securely on the ground we jumped in our trucks and drove home feeling extraordinarily lucky. It was strange that we did not talk about the flight that night. In hindsight, we were all relieved to still be alive once again. The three of us knew it was getting close once again, but we did not want to face the thought of death due to our fear of it. That was a dumb thing to do. Another cold beer presented itself in front of him as he slurped the remaining foam of the last one.

It was several weeks before that particular flight became our defining story. We talked about how we almost died by the reservoir in the Skylane. He pulled out another dollar to tip the beauty on the other side of the bar. *These don't come as easy as they used to*, he thought then found his way back to reflective thought. We were just cocky seventeen and eighteen year olds living a busy life. Each time the story was told, we were closer to the trees. In one of the covers, we had tree branches wrapped around our tires. We embellished that experience to the max but each one of us was internally thankful to be alive, telling the stories. Each of us knew we had cheated death.

It seemed strange to have grownup conversations with my brother but that night it was needed. Trevor and I had a long conversation about that near fatal flight and made a few decisions to protect the brotherhood. No more night passes over any girl's house. We were too haunted by those trees on that dark night. Or should I say, haunted by that monumental moment of stupidity. I never tried a low night pass again. I did fly a low pass at night with a girl in the plane. On the brighter side, I did make out with Tina a few weeks after the near death flyby. That super scary flight opened a tiny door to Tina's heart for about two weeks of make out sessions, a score, so I thought. I figured it was perfect payment for the stress I had gone through just trying to impress her. Her mom and dad were not happy about it, but they never found out what idiot was out flying around in the pitch-black night at the reservoir and why. Her soft lips canceled the fear of it all. Thank you Tina.

What was I going to be? Along with all this fun, there lived the grand reality that I would someday be flying for my occupation. Two jobs swirled in the mix, airline pilot and crop-duster. One would be a true path for me, but either would be amazing. When thinking about the two flying positions, I leaned more to crop-dusting because it had a "bad boy" reputation and more freedom to fly as I had been trained. I had thought the "fear of death" defined the level of a bad boy reputation in aviation. The bad boy term was heard multiple times as people talked about crop dusting. Personally, I was not a "bad boy." A ladies' man, yes, so I thought, but not a "bad boy" at all. Therefore, it did entice me more.

After researching both flying occupations I discovered one could become a crop-duster any time after being an airline pilot. On the flip side, not too many airlines would consider hiring a crop-duster to fly the jets of their airline due to "bad habits" and "cowboy" reputations. Both required upper-level flying skills but crop dusting offered more freedom in the cockpit. It presented itself as a lone-wolf endeavor. It felt as if I would be my own boss in the sky versus flying for a giant organization that lacked the passion for each and every plane that I had. In my mind crop-dusters where always pictured as lone cowboys crossing some vast prairies alone on their black steeds. They would then find some small country town, a beautiful lady, and have a strong drink. Cowboy reputation was correct.

My thought on the crop-duster's cowboy reputation might have been created in my brain after mixing my flying experiences with my past rodeo days in McPherson, Kansas. The haunting memory of strapping my butt onto a small bull or wacky bronco often danced round in my head with a giant question, why in the world did I ever do that. Although I did not really like it, I guess I'm glad I did it. Scared to death to jump in a shoot with a bucking bronco. The situation always seemed to relax a bit as I slid my chap-covered legs down onto the back of some restless bronco and then strapped my right hand in so tight. I'm guessing that strong beast was as scared as I was. Sitting on that uneasy animal I saw a small tough looking girl stare me square in the face and run her thumb from one side of her neck to the other. Her older brother, a professional bull rider I thought said, "My little sister is going to kick your butt when you are done riding that bronco." Not only did I have to fear the rocky ride on that twisted horse but also I would have to fight a manly girl. My pops looked down at the little snot-nosed girl and told her to "piss off." She ran away. Once again my protector was there for me. Thanks Pops and piss off little dude looking. I was a pretty good cowboy and took second that year for my eight seconds of glory. Knowing that I could ride a beastly bronco, I knew I could fly anything and defiantly hold my own against any rough looking cowgirls.

From that point on, flying was always in my head no matter what life had in mind. Flying was a wide-open path in my life. Therefore, for the next few years I flew whenever and whatever I could just to stay as current as possible in the sky. There was an understanding that reaching a goal in aviation required some form of sacrifice. There was always the lonely old man around the Great Bend airport who had spent all he had in life to become a pilot, but did not travel the path any further. I sacrificed money in my quest to fly, but mostly time. It's hard to consider it any type of sacrifice when you are doing what you love and following your life's complicated passions. Life was short, but I knew through my short life I needed to reach my highest potential. Knowing that I needed to be better tomorrow than I was today made me a better pilot. Only more flying would produce a better Nick tomorrow. It seemed I was always looking for ways to improve myself on the ground and in the air.

CHAPTER TWELVE
Dr. Cessna

That was the worst day ever. Even on random, non-aviation days, it seemed to me that death, as a chilling darkness, was near. Be it an impending crash, or mere happenstance, death was a force I thought about often. Over the years we had traveled down so many lonely roads only to find destroyed aircraft with, or without, destroyed pilots inside. With death looking for me, I could only find balance in the air in any type of plane. Flying proved to be a strong release for me. If anything upsetting happened in my life, you would find me in an airplane over the Snake River, rearranging my thoughts with airspeed. One particular afternoon, Trevor and I went to take our family friend Holly, out to lunch. We drove to her apartment and knocked on the door, but she didn't answer. *"Trevor she has to be here, brother, her car is parked in the back."* We walked around to the back of the apartment complex, peering through the sliding glass door.

To our surprise we saw her sleeping on the loveseat with her head leaned back. Trevor banged hard on the slider. She did not move. Trevor looked at me and stated, "Wow, she is sleeping hard; she must be super tired." I expressed that no one could sleep through that. What if it's worse, like a heart attack or something? You could have used a shovel to pick Trevor's jaw off the rough concrete. He already knew what we were going to find, but I did not. We opened the slider and proceeded to find her lifeless body with a self-inflicted gunshot wound in her chest. My heart twisted with disgust and sadness. I could feel the sweat forming on my forehead as I starred at Holly's dead body. The black gun she used had kicked about five feet when she pulled the trigger. It was lying on the carpet near the couch. I blamed that heartless piece of metal at that particular moment, not Holly, for I did not have any answers. Her dead body created a dark, gloomy feeling in that cold apartment. I could not shake the cold off my shoulders, while sweating like crazy. *Come on cold, be gone, you evil bastard.* We called the authorities and my step-mom. It was hard to watch my brother cry. He was always so incredibly strong but this broke his hard outer shell and proved he was human.

After the police and coroner left the frigid apartment, Trevor left with Mom to try and console her and help her any way he could. I jumped in my truck and headed straight to the airport. I grabbed the key out of the office and jumped in my Skylane, screamed, "CLEAR," and fired it up. The strong plane and I headed to the end of runway One-One, for a silent departure. The interior of the Cessna was blood red fake leather. I found it fitting for a flight to forget suicide. There would be no conversations that day. As I wiped away a single tear running down my cheek, I introduced full power and flew out to our airstrip at Wilson Lake. The Wilson Lake strip sat on a high bluff above Wilson Lake straight north of Great Bend. Thoughts were garbled in my head but clarity increased as the airspeed did. I had always condemned suicide and saw it as selfish and weak. Holly had taught me to fish. She was one of the least selfish humans I had ever known in all of my life. We all loved her deeply. Therefore, I was confused with her choice to leave us. I hated that gun and wanted to know where she got it.

With those thoughts racing in my head, I pointed the Cessna down, then leveled it out about three feet off the gravel strip at full speed. At the end of the strip, I yanked back hard on the yoke and cranked tight right. The airplane entered a sharp climb with a hard right turn. At the moment she did not want to continue her climb, we floated deep below the bluff until we were a few feet off of the water of the beautiful lake. The Skylane and I completed that maneuver, over and over, for almost two hours just trying to understand why death was by my side, watching me, and trying to get me. If not me, those I love. As sun started to disappear so I turned her towards Great Bend, racing against the black of night. Flying back I found myself with a clear head and empathetic feeling about her death. As the plane and I touched the ground, I felt better. Flying truly was my therapy. Although still young, I felt that particular incident had pushed me hard into manhood. The view of her dead body was haunting and chiseled deep into my brain, never to leave. The Skylane proved to be a good, inanimate metal friend as it came to my rescue like a good friend would.

The following day we learned the funeral had already been planned for the weekend in New Mexico. Pops was in North Dakota, running horses for the Bureau of Land Management in the "Killer-Hiller." He called frequently to check on Mom and the rest of us. I figured he needed a good flight in the Skylane but assumed the Hiller was his therapy. That night he told Trevor and me if he was not able to finish in New Mexico, early, we would need to fly the body to Zuni for the funeral. Trepidation jumped in my mind instantly, but I was willing to help. As twisted as it sounds, I was excited to do it for my family, her family, and yes the flight time. It would be a long cross-country flight and we would be helping Pops.

Molding negative situations, or thoughts, into positive outcomes was something I had practiced regularly. The only positive outcome for this death was the flight time. As we both thought, Pops could not make it back in time so Trevor and I had to "man up" and fly the body. We fueled my trusty Skylane and got it ready for the flight. It was a dark haunting sight to watch the black, lifeless hearse pull onto the airport tarmac and backup to my plane. The Precession Air mechanics had already pulled out the back seat and bulkhead so we could lay Holly peacefully in the back of the plane. This was one flight where I knew without a shadow of a doubt that death was on board with me. This was the first flight where we could physically see death in the back of the Bravo Charlie.

It was a chilling radio call at the end of the runway with a body wrapped in a sheet directly behind us in that plane. "Great Bend area traffic, November Four Two Nine Bravo Charlie taking the active, two-Niner for Gallup direct, Great Bend." During that flight, talk was about anything that would keep our minds out of the back of the plane. From weather to the paint colors on airplanes, we talked about anything and everything that would keep our minds busy, not thinking about Holly's lifeless body behind us. We did not talk about what we were physically doing at that very moment. We did talk about some girls, but in a respectful way since there was a woman with us.

About an hour out of Gallup, New Mexico, I was searching for my Kansas City Chiefs hat that had previously slipped off my head. I was flying with my left arm and feeling around between the seats with my right arm, blindly searching around with touch only. I then stretched farther back only to find a handful of soft, dead hair. The chills instantly covered my body. My mouth lost all moisture and became dry as sand in the desert. Cold death chills started at my fingertips and ran hard straight to my neck and then down my back. Instantly, I let go of the yoke and told Trevor, *"The plane is yours."* Although, there was nothing to fear, I found myself more fearful than ever. There was a cold darkness in the plane draped over my head as if death was taunting me. Trevor flew the rest of the flight then landed us in Gallup, New Mexico, where another ominous hearse picked up her body.

What a strange guy. Zuni, New Mexico was too small to have a mortuary, so Gallup had to be used. The driver of the death hauler was a nice, talkative man, bless his soul. He overheard Trevor and I talking about being hungry. The driver then offered to take us to a drive-through that was relatively close to the airport. Trevor responded properly with, "Thank you, but hell no. We are not driving in a hearse with our dead friend for food." We jumped in a courtesy car and went for food still in disbelief that he wanted us to ride in the death-mobile. After dinner we jumped back in Bravo Charlie after and flew the short hop to Zuni, New Mexico. Holly, along with the rest of her family was Native American. She needed to be put to rest on the Zuni Reservation in Zuni, New Mexico, and we fully respected this wholeheartedly.

As I pondered back on the entire experience, I felt I was close to what I considered manhood in those short three days, wishing it were possible to be transported back in time to the cockpit of my Ag Husky in McPherson. The simple thought of going outside to feed my cow, pet my dog, or fly in the Cub with my pops. It was truly important to have that Skylane in my life to help guide me and take care of me. Over and over again it had been there for me. Once we arrived in Zuni I felt the need to fly the death off her, but could not get myself to do so. Soon there would be flights in my life not tainted with death, I thought.

After the funeral and three days in Zuni New Mexico, it was time to head home to Kansas in the Bravo Charlie. This time, I would be flying it solo plus one passenger. Jimmy, Holly's son, would fly back to Kansas in the Skylane with me. I called weather and filed a flight plan for the flight home. Everything looked good for the flight. We jumped in the Skylane warmed her up and headed to the runway. I made my call: "Zuni area traffic, November four two Niner Bravo Charlie, taking the active three four, straight out, Zuni." The engine came to full life as I pusher the power to its takeoff setting. At 65 mph, I rotated and entered a positive rate of climb. Soon after, we were trucking along at about 9,500 feet (AGL). About an hour out of Zuni the weather started to change a bit.

The cockpit was filled with the monotonous hum of the motor and propeller. As we flew over the bright colors of the New Mexico desert, we suddenly found ourselves flying between cloud layers. One layer was about 100 feet lower than the other. Clear skies could be seen between the layers. A decision had to be made: land and wait it out, or push on. This cloud system was not reported earlier when weather was called but, nonetheless, it was there. Seeing the crisp blue sky on the other side of the layers, I made the decision to go for it. I soon realized it was a dumb decision. It was as if death was given permission to come into that plane and have a seat on the red carpet and kill us. The layers closed on us fast about halfway through. The brilliant blue sky in the distance became a hostile grey mass of evil, icy clouds. The fear level was not bad until Jimmy looked out his window, turned to me and asked in a panicky voice, "Nick, why is my tire all white? Looks like it is frozen, covered in ice."

We were packing on the ice in zero visibility. We had just buried his mother, now we were tempting fate. If we did not get out of the deadly situation, the next funeral might have been ours. Power was increased to max and my alternate static source was pushed in under the red panel. When the artificial horizon came back into full effect, we were circling almost straight down. Although spiraling down rapidly, we had no idea due to the spatial disorientation caused by zero visibility. It so astonishes how weather can play with your mind and senses. In that Skylane death was waiting patiently for me to come home with it. With eyes focused on gauges and my mind on death, I leveled out as best I could to slow the rapid descent. As Bravo Charlie leveled out, the fear of mortality became strong, for I understood it was near once again, super close. Shivering in fear, I grabbed the map in hopes of finding refuge close by. The map indicated we were within a few miles of Springfield, Colorado. In addition, the map indicated that we needed to find blue sky before 3,100 feet AGL or death would win this battle. At 3,060 AGL, directly below us, was the only large mountainous hill. I did not want to meet death up close and personal on the top of some random mountain in the middle of the Colorado prairie.

With two shaken men aboard, the Skylane slipped out of the clouds at 3,175 feet AGL. We were a little over 100 feet from the top of that random mountain. One hundred feet above the ground had never looked so low in all my life. My mind instantly traveled back to the big beautiful blue Beech-18 freight flight with Grantham and how close fifty feet looked though my scared eyes. At least in the Beech Grantham was with me. Two pilots work better in hairy situations. Although, we were a hundred feet up I could visually see every inch of the rough grassy terrain in front of us. We had enough altitude to swing hard right, fly down the side of the mountain and jump onto the final approach for runway three five Springfield. When the wheels rested the ground firmly I took a deep breath of appreciation. The Skylane was still rolling down the runway when Jimmy leaned over and hugged me. He took a deep breath and said, "Thank you for saving our lives Nick." I taxied the Skylane in to parking, pulled the mixture, and watched the prop move into stillness. Before it came to its complete standstill, Jimmy had already jumped out and physically kissed the frosty ground. With weak, nervous legs, the two of us walked into the terminal of the little airport. Inside, there was an older weathered gentleman behind the counter. He greeted us in a manner I will never forget. He said, "Well hello boys. Only a fool with a death wish would be out flying in this." I raised my hand, looked him square in the face and stated, *"Yes, I am that fool."* I sat down and reflected silently on flying with death literally to New Mexico and forgetting to kick him out of my plane for the flight home. Almost dying on the way home was yet another eye opener that there was still so much to learn in aviation.

Sitting in the weather building looking out the window I knew it is easier to blame anything other than you. While you know where blame belongs, you focus on saving your own pride and not looking at the idiot in the mirror. At first blame was on the weather report, not myself at the moment. Truth is, I should never have put us in that situation. *Never split layers man, you know better than that.* That thought ran over and over in my mind. Mom and Trevor were driving back to Kansas. After seeing the weather, they figured I had found shelter in Springfield. Lucky for Jimmy and I, they swung by the airport and picked us up. I was extremely happy to be driving home. I figured it was death's loss and it would have to wait longer. On the long drive home my time was spent daydreaming about the why's and how's of my life. Focus fell on getting my Skylane home to its warm hanger in Great Bend. After that flight, weather became a new area of focus on my aviation path. A better understanding of weather was needed to reach a higher level of aviation expertise. If not, I figured death would win its fight for me and I did not want that. Close to being done with high school, I wanted to be around for the future. *You told yourself that a hundred times but continued to invite death to hang out with you.*

CHAPTER THIRTEEN
Standing Rock

A Few weeks after graduation the family moved the company to Bismarck, North Dakota and transformed it into an air medical transport company. A Skyhawk would be with me, but the Skylane stayed in Kansas. I wondered if the little Skyhawk would be a great friend like the Skylane. After some time to getting things organized, I found myself living in Little Eagle, South Dakota, on the Standing Rock Indian Reservation with a couple of our pilots. It was a strange environment, being one of only a few white men on the reservation. We had the only airplanes on the tiny airport used solely for medical transport. We owned a Cessna 421 Golden Eagle, a PA-32-300 Cherokee Six, and a Skyhawk. Often I flew myself to Bismarck for instrument lessons at the local flight school. Damn that was fun. There would be no stopping my journey and I was extremely happy to be working in aviation still. It was odd to be so far away from crop-dusting. I figured there was a plan out there for everyone and I needed to look hard and find mine. I was building good time in the Cherokee Six weekly. It was a strong bird, as it was basically a low wing Stationair in my book. In addition, I was getting valuable flight time in the Golden Eagle. That airplane was powerful and fully equipped with all the bells and whistles. None of which I knew how to use.

Flights were random therefore we lived on call. Being there in Little Eagle was another great life experience beyond aviation and into cultural norms. To know that we were there to help made me proud. My first flight in that beautiful Golden Eagle was a night flight from Little Eagle to Sioux Fall, SD, then on to a trauma one center in St Paul, Minnesota, to get a man to the Burn Unit. A few days earlier a young man fell into the tribal burn pile when dumping his trash at the Little Eagle dump. He was burned over fifty percent of his body and was not healing fast enough in the Sioux Falls, hospital. We picked him, and his nurse, up in Sioux Fall, grabbed some fuel, jumped on the runway, and headed to St Paul. This flight was another learning lesson. A new plane so tons to learned in the cockpit of the Golden Eagle, trying to figure out all of the buttons and what they did. I knew death had already failed with this guy and that eased my mind a little. Except for the strange smells coming form the back, it was an exceptional flight of learning. Before I knew it we were sitting on the tarmac in St Paul unloading our patient. It was going to be a fast trip home in the speedy Golden Eagle. By the time we rotated, with wheels in the wells, the sun was partially up, highlighting all of the painted rock below in a magnificent manner. It was an awe-inspiring moment.

At that moment in life, I realized how much creative beauty God used when developing this earth. Sometimes it is breathtaking just to lay eyes upon it at certain times. Even in a lighting storm, you can see his creative beauty. So many different flights and so many experiences already in my young life, I felt blessed. At eighteen years old I knew there was something big waiting for me in life. So I would wait for it.

A few days after the flight in the Golden Eagle we were washing the Cherokee Six on the ramp, getting her ready for any flights we might need her on. Daily we would see a young man in a motorized wheelchair driving back and forth in front of the airport. He could not enter the airport due to a cattle guard at the entrance' but nonetheless he was there every afternoon. Jimmy, a local and employee, was with me washing the plane when I heard my pops yell over to me, "Hey Nick, go ask if he wants a ride." I was thinking, *the guy in the wheelchair?* Pops, without knowing my thoughts said, "Yes, Nick, the kid in the chair, go ask." Jimmy and I were on a mission for a flight. We dropped our washing equipment, headed out, to stop the young man. I asked if he wanted a ride in an airplane. With noises that did not resemble any language I had ever heard, we decided that he was saying Yes, for sure take me flying. It was obvious this young man was impaired both physically and mentally, but we I knew he would love a flight. *Who would not want one?* With Jimmy on one side of the chair and me on the other, we drove him to the cattle guard. As we drove him over the crude rails of the guard his head bounced uncontrollably back and forth. At that moment I was a little hesitant taking him flying and feared it could be illegal somehow. I

107

blocked any negative thoughts and pushed on. We got him and his chair to the trusty Skyhawk. Once at the door of the plane, Jimmy grabbed the lightweight, disabled young man and put him in the backseat and buckled him down.

Jimmy and I jumped in and started the plane. On the taxi to the end of the runway I felt that it was such a great flight I wanted to give it a grand radio call to celebrate it. Knowing that there were no planes around to hear it, I needed to do so anyway. I squeezed the microphone, "Little Eagle Area Traffic, this is Cessna eight two one three Romeo departing zero six straight out with special cargo, Little Eagle." Before I pushed the power in, I turned to check on our special cargo in the back. To our surprise his seatbelt had not been tight enough and he had slid almost completely out of the blue seat in the back of that Skyhawk. Jimmy looked in the eyes of our special cargo and said, "Sorry buddy, I got you." Jimmy used one arm to push his frail body into the right position and securely tighten his belt. With an all clear from Jimmy, I pushed the throttle forward to take off setting and away we went.

The Little Eagle runway is located on a small plateau of land that would allow pilots to drop off the end of it to gain speed for altitude. Large, beautiful plateaus surrounded the Little Eagle reservation, making it a great area to fly around. Tons of my time had been spent skimming the tops of the plateaus, then diving off the edges. Once I had gained some altitude with the special cargo, I picked a giant plateau to buzz and drive off. Deep down I knew our special cargo would love a real flight filled with excitement. There we were, about three feet off the dry top of the lonely yet beautifully colored land mass. I remember the sun was pulling the grand colors out of the rock life. When we reached the end I rolled her off the top in a sharp right turn, dropping in altitude about 400 feet. Jimmy looked at me and said, "So flipping amazing man." I loved how you could see the different colors in the different layers of the rock out the side window while dropping in altitude almost straight down. *That Skyhawk loved flying there in South Dakota.* After one more, Jimmy tapped me on the shoulder. He said, "Nick, our special cargo is foaming at the mouth." Turning to look, I saw Jimmy was not exaggerating. Our Native American passenger was foaming from his mouth. The Skyhawk was pointed straight back to the airport. We were getting that kid home safe as fast as we could. Death would not find this guy in my plane. After the touch down, I maintained a fairly high rate of taxi speed to get him to the safety of his wheelchair. When I pulled the mixture, to kill the engine, Jimmy jumped out to get the wheelchair and load up our special, sick cargo. We got him across the cattle guard and watched him wheel away. The rest of the day was spent waiting nervously waiting for the authorities to come and arrest us.

A few days later, while working at the airport a white sedan pulled over the crude metal of the cattle guard and drove directly over to me. A female tribal police officer called me over to her car, Jimmy followed. She introduced herself. *She was an extremely attractive woman and her uniform enhanced it,* thought. She looked at me and asked if I had seen a young man in a wheelchair around the airport in the past. My mind ran straight to jail. I could not believe that my suspicions were right. We were going to jail for trying to build some happiness in a broken stranger's life. She was there to take me to jail for taking him flying. I did not want to lie to her, and had not seen the wheelchair for two days. *"Yes officer, I have seen him a lot."* Her response startled me when she looked at me with a serious glint in her eyes and asked, "Did you take him flying?" I was lost for words and was scared I was going to jail. Jimmy spoke up behind me, "We took him for a ride in that airplane over there," pointing at the Skyhawk. I knew we were done at that point.

It was when a smile appeared on her pretty face that my emotions were completely confused. She must love taking people to jail, I thought. She said, "That is the greatest thing you two did. Thank you for doing that." She explained to us that although he is physically disabled he worked at the tribal office entering data on a computer with a mouthpiece, one letter at a time. He had gone to work the following day and typed in, "The greatest thing on earth happened to me yesterday. I went flying in an airplane and it was the best thing ever in my life." I was so happy to hear that. Chills of happiness flew down my back as the smile on my face was stuck. It made me feel that I had truly touched someone with aviation. I created happiness in that broken young man and I would not change anything about it. She continued to thank us and then said goodbye and drove off. I had given hundreds of rides but not one of them ever created the feeling I had inside right there in Little Eagle, South Dakota.

The flight of special cargo became a defining flight for me. Merely thinking about it created a deep feeling of accomplishment, followed with the positive feeling of being on the correct path in life. Any thought about that day still creates a grin of satisfaction. Little Eagle was filled with positive flying experiences, with death being absent in most flights. My little brother, Ethan, came to Little Eagle to visit a friend he had made in town. I got a call from my pops telling me to grab the boys and fly to Sioux Falls for dinner, with them. I was happy to do so. I loaded Ethan and his buddy up in the Six, and taxied out for departure.

It was a warm sunny day when I made the call. "Little Eagle area traffic November four one five three Hotel departing zero six downwind departure, Little Eagle. I pushed in the power and the Six started to increase her speed down the runway. With ten degrees of flaps in, she popped off of the ground close to where she always did, about two-thirds down the narrow runway. I put us into a positive climbing attitude. When doing so, the airspeed on the Six started to bleed off fast. As we got to the edge of the bluff I had to nose her over to maintain flight speed. Something was not right. Something was incredibly wrong. That Cherokee Six always had more power than ever needed. I made a 180-degree turn to get us back to the runway. Unfortunately we were already flying below it in altitude. We were too far below the plateau to even think about landing back there. The Six was not able to even maintain straight and level flight. My eyes looked nervously out the windows for an easy fix to the situation. With white knuckles and a dry mouth, I kept looking for alternatives. A million scenarios ran

111

through my head and once again death was in my plane. I was able to get her lined up on the road heading to out of town but knew the vegetation on both sides of the road would flip us over, killing us maybe. I made the decision to go for it and started my pre-landing checklist.

As we got closer to the ground Ethan was asking me a hundred questions about our altitude and about crashing. I did not intend on dying in a Cherokee Six that day. I had to mentally block him out of my head if I was going to save us. When we reached the critical altitude of fifteen feet I ran through the part of the checklist to inspect the magnetos. To my disbelief and wild surprise, I found the toggle for the left mag was in the off position, meaning we were only running on the right mag. At full power this bird could not maintain level flight only on one mag. I instantly toggled the left magneto into action feeling extremely stupid. We could feel the power come to full life immediately. The engine moaned loud while we were pushed back in our seats. Only fifteen feet kept us away from possible death that day. That is but a small distance for survival. If I could have, I would have kicked my own ass when we landed at Sioux Falls. I was so distraught over my near-death mistake. Once again, it was my fault much like splitting cloud layers with Jimmy in Colorado. It was my fault. There was no one else to blame. I remember walking into the bathroom at the FBO, looking at the stupid man in the mirror, and saying out loud, "You are a lucky bastard Nick, that was completely your fault. You almost killed your own brother." Fear had escalated into being my reality for the rest of that day. Once again, I found myself looking for areas to improve on in my flying. I turned my focus towards details after the Cherokee Six mag issue.

Minus a lighting strike in the Golden Eagle, all other flights in South Dakota were solid and without incident. Even flying the Skyhawk to Trevor in Kansas went without incident. Studying my faults in aviation would build understanding. My faults could not be used to define my ability as a pilot. It was a sad to drop off the Skyhawk to Trevor, but he needed flight time also. My friendship with, one three Romeo, ended the second Troy and Trevor stuffed the Skyhawk into a snow bank while flying low in Kansas with Troy's dad in the back seat. Trevor had told Troy to bring it up a hair about two seconds before the nose wheel dug in at 100 mph, putting the plane almost vertical on its nose before coming to a stop on the cold snow-covered prairie. Everyone on board was fine. Trevor explained that Phil's response was priceless. He reached forward and slapped Troy in the back of the head while all three were still buckled into the crashed Skyhawk sitting near vertical. I was glad my brothers and Phil were okay but frustrated they wrecked the Skyhawk, flying it low. It was a good plane and would be missed. With, one three Romeo, now crashed the flying in my life slowed. It seemed that as the flying slowed the days mixed together and time escaped. *Those days just mixed together.*

The years bled together and soon I found myself living in Iowa, working on my tail dragger endorsement in Waterloo, Iowa. Working towards my Commercial Airplane License kept my focus. Once finished I knew the commercial ticket would start my separation from flying for fun to flying for pay. Time was not spent talking about it because it was the direction I had always followed. At that point in life I just knew I needed it. Only a small percent of the population in the United States has a commercial Pilots License. Although, I enjoyed my time in Little Eagle, I was in Iowa to continue the aviation path that was started so long ago. I had learned to appreciate a particular Citabria N8MM as the ultimate training tool on my path. You can reflect back on mistakes, but I had found that you should not dwell on them for too long. Mistakes build learning, if they don't kill you. I just needed to stay on my path and focus on the learning needed to get me to where I needed to be. Now 21, I still couldn't believe everything I had been through in life. Loving life pushed me to by proud of myself for following my passion for flying and women and for not dying in the process.

CHAPTER FOURTEEN
Made It

We all have good and bad memories. Hopefully we all have the one stellar memory that is forever carved in our grey matter. There is always one memory that can invite peace and happiness always. Over time only two types of memories do so. Great exciting memories are always present, yet the stupid mistakes that became learning experiences stay fresh as well. They remain with us, crystal clear, for life. In our recollections they are as vivid as the moment they happened some place back in time. Some remain as instructional manuals we must follow in life to stay safe. Others represent escapable areas that we could mentally run to for smiles and happiness. Memories such as my first solo flight or my backcountry landing endorsement from Aaron at Georgia Pass represent an enjoyable place to escape to in my mind. Still young, I rated joining the Mile-High Club in the back of a 206 a top notch learning experience. Thank you Liz. Other flights, such as the

115

Holly flight to Zuni, the near death ice flight home, or that ridiculous flight over Tina's house with my buds, in the pitch black of night will remain as instructional memories. They persist in the "what not to do" manual for life. Flying into that death ice with Jimmy and finding Springfield so close will always take me to thoughts about luck. All of these remembrances have remained fresh in my brain, as if they happened yesterday. Although clear in my head, they could never compare to my ultimate of all memories in my aviation life. My day, we shall call it. All the flying, or girls in my life could never rank as high as my day.

With absolute clarity, I remember the second my eyes gazed upon her that morning. I pulled up to my beautiful yellow lady and jumped out of my truck into the cool, moist morning air. It seemed to be extra bright yellow that morning as the sun, barely up, gleaned off the dew-soaked giant yellow wings. I felt the cool moist air on my face. I took a deep breath of the dawn air, than stared intensely at the 600-horsepower yellow plane. On that particular morning every inch of the powerful radial engine engulfed my vision. The smooth curved chrome intake and grey exhaust pipes appeared in radical contrast to the rough metallic cylinders. Everything on this engine represented toughness. The plugs all connected to the engine with their bright blue plug wires. From a distance, the plug wires looked as if they held the engine together tightly while also making it look sporty with their bright blue color. I visually inspected the smooth yellow fiberglass speed ring, which hugged all of the cylinders and kept them tight to the core of this power plant. On the belly of the Thrush was a chemical pump. The chemical pump had a sleek small prop on it that controlled the flow of chemical with the speed of the airplane.

That little chemical prop was important to me because friend and aircraft designer Mr. Weatherly designed and built those props for use on chemical pumps. The thought of him designing the 620B that we had in McPherson so long ago brought understanding of what a small circle crop dusting was. His office was close to our office. Some twenty years ago he designed and airplane now working next to us building little aerodynamic props for little pumps. Crop-dusting is a small community. When something bad happens all seem to know. Looking at the little prop, that day, I realized how small the agriculture circle really was.

The S2D Snow looked identical to the Thrush Commander Pop's flew in McPherson and Great Bend. My plane only had 600-horse power compared to my pop's 800 ponies, but that did not matter. The Pratt and Whitney 1340 had then, and still do have a reputation for reliability and power. My pops used to wear a T-shirt that said, "Wright R-1300 engines aren't worth a pile of dung." The dark blue print on the bright yellow shirt was so bright, you could read from across a parking lot. We all called the D-model the "Thrush," not the Snow. Technically it was an early model Thrush named after its developer, Mr. Snow. It had the same round, beefy radial-style engine and yellow, get out of my way, paint job that most all Thrushes had. Wanting to feel more important and thinking Thrush was a stronger name, I called it a Thrush, not a Snow.

This was it, my day of reckoning. Years of flying anything with wings and a motor brought me to this monumental point. Could I call myself a grown man that day? Yes, I felt that I could. I was ready being older and wiser with regards to aviation. Hours upon hours of practice in the 115-horsepower 7ECA Citabria tail dragger with Chad had prepared me for this meeting with the Thrush...the ultimate crop-duster's aircraft of choice.

The big one!

The big bad boy!

The Thrush!

Yellow Fever!

The big nasty!

I could call it whatever but in the end, it was just my day to become a crop-duster in a 600 Thrush Commander.

It felt I had graduated from the little buckaroo rodeo into a professional bull rider. I was jumping from a calf called Citabria to an 1100-pound snot-tossing bull named Thrush. I was ready. I had daydreamed about that moment for as long as I could remember. At 22, my time had finally arrived. Six years previous I would fly anything that crossed my path to build flight time so I could get to this crossroad. Over and over I said to myself, *Holy crap we are here*! What a giant step. My first crop-dusting job and it was in a Thrush! Not a little Pawnee, Ag Truck, or a CallAir, but a big powerful 600 S2D Snow

Commander/Thrush. I couldn't believe it. I had taken all the appropriate tests to become a legal Iowa aerial applicator. I completed all the flying hours necessary to be a legal Commercial pilot in the eyes of the FAA. Wow, I was ready to complete my life's mission. At that moment, it would no longer be my reoccurring dream but, rather, my reality. Where was death that day?

I stepped onto the slick, due-covered wing, opened the cockpit door and slid in. The stick, gauges, pedals, and the seat—all exactly where they were the hundreds of times I had started this giant for my pops, as practice. Never had I started it with the intent of actually flying it. Appreciation was given to my pops for the opportunity to master the start sequence for this mammoth motor. Looking out at the giant metal wings from the cockpit I could not remove the smile from my face. My pops would stand on the wing and give me the hidden secrets while I was starting it on days past. Today he was strapped in a helicopter, working somewhere close to the airport. It would have been nice on that day as well, but I was ready. It was all me that day.

On any other day the starting motions were robotic. That day it was different. I was going to actually fly the giant beast by myself. There was not one robotic thing about that. On that day, I was going to strap all of that yellow metal on to my back and go to work. That day, I talked my way through the pre-start checklist and then double, triple, and quadruple-checked it out loud. "Nick, fuel to the top in both wings?" The butterflies in my stomach were real that day and buzzing wildly as they wanted to escape.

"Throttle full forward, throttle full back, once twice, okay mixture forward. Mag selector set on right mag, check." After priming the system, I leaned out of the yellow cabin with honor, and yelled, "CLEAR!" I then pressed the tiny silver start button. The prop started its clockwise rotation, followed by the cylinders firing one by one until the engine came into full swing. The quiver throughout the plane found its rhythm as the big metal prop fell into its synch with the beastly motor. It was a beautiful feeling. The giant prop shook the cockpit as the horses begin to gallop. The deep throaty engine started to purr smoothly as it began to warm. It was amazing how that big plane could find such a beautiful harmonic balance of sound and motion. Sitting there I listened to the huge prop slice the air and the roar of 600 horses trying to escape. I couldn't have felt any smaller that particular day.

I was eager to get into the air, but also another level of fear had entered my mind. My level of fear surpassed pretty scared by a long shot. Not scared of crashing the big plane, but fearful of doing something stupid like ground looping this giant tail dragger. Although I knew that the Citabria had taught me the proper rudder dance, this Thrush was 500 horsepower stronger and I knew it would want to ground loop. Furthermore, I was fearful of not being a good applicator like my pops. He had an excellent reputation. My first field that day was less than a hundred yards from our biggest chemical company. Chem-Farm Services provided us with the majority of our crop-dusting work. Needing to look like a stellar applicator was my mission because I represented the family business. I told myself, *"Okay man, shut your mind up, this is your day, focus and continue on."* The fear I felt reminded me of the butterflies I had the seconds before I kissed April in seventh grade. She had taught me tons, as I knew the Snow would.

Sitting in the cockpit and seeing the giant propeller rotating smoothly to the heartbeat of the powerful radial engine was motivational. The combination of the big motor and giant prop provided a feeling of security. The thump of each rotation felt inside my body was inspiring. I had felt it so many times but if meant more that day. I was going to be considered a crop-duster in a few hours. Although ready to fly it, I could feel the sweat building in my helmet the leather stuck to my forehead and top neck. I took a deep breath of crisp air and exhaust and closed the door. I pushed the throttle forward and the beast started shaking and rolling forward to the loading area. My mind traveled back to McPherson on my pop's knee at six years old in the big R Model Thrush. I picked up my first load, 240 gallons of chemical, and headed towards the runway. Despite the D having a 300-gallon capacity I purposely flew light on my first day for better control and maneuverability. Therefore, I was happy with 240 gallons. There is no need to push one's luck I thought.

I was focused on a thousand different things in the cockpit as we taxied away. On that day the beastly yellow Thrush screamed, "NEW GUY!" from every exhaust port off of each and every cylinder on that strong motor. Over, and over, I asked myself at least twenty times, *"You think they moved the runway Nick." It seems so far away this morning.* As I made the long taxi, I thought about the previous six years of my life, prepping for that day. I half expected to look over and see Trevor in a red-stripped Ag Husky, from McPherson, taxiing next to me. Knowing he was with me mentally was reassuring. The airport was extremely dead that morning. *Maybe it's always dead this early,* I thought. *Or maybe word got out that there was a new guy in the air today, so watch out people.* Getting to the end of the active runway three one, my nerves escalated. My time was close. The big bird was turned into the slight breeze to start the engine preflight checks. Looking straight out I see the engine beating in perfect rhythm. It reminds me of a heart. The wings of the yellow plane had never looked so large before. That day they looked as if they had been stretched out. Each of the million rivets popped stood out at me to remind me they were there to protect me, holding all the metal in place as they did on the Texan.

As the power increased for my mag check the cockpit shook to full life, and the growl of the engine echoed off of the closed hangers across the tarmac. It never failed that the sound of a beefy radial caused a smile to grow on my face and people to look. *Okay, we have a 100-rpm drop on the right mag and a 90-rpm drop on the left mag, all in limits, both mags on, so we are good to go. Let's do this, brother. I have faith in you.* A mental pep talk from oneself was nice, but not as reinforcing as I would have liked on that day. Through it all, I needed more than anything to be a good applicator in this giant yellow bird. It was much like needing to have an impressive first date. If you do, you will get more dates. If not, good luck in life.

I rotated my head in all directions inside the yellow cockpit to clear the area and taxied onto active runway three one in Waterloo, Iowa. I triggered the radio utilizing my matured 22-year-old manliest voice, "Waterloo area traffic, November seven eight three Echo is taking the active three one for right turnout departure, Waterloo." Once lined up the centerline of the runway, I stopped the plane on the centerline to say a quick prayer that God would protect me. Also, I prayed that God would help me be a stellar applicator. I looked around in the cockpit and said, *"Death, there is no room in here for you, so be gone."* At that point, the latch man looked at me while waiting patiently for my head nod. I was ready to ride the big bull. I looked at the latch man and nodded my head as I increased power. *"Let's do this Nick,"* I thought to myself, as I inched the throttle forward.

The engine moaned loudly as it reached its takeoff power setting, forcing the strong Pratt and Whitney to breathe deep, dig hard, and pull the big yellow loaded beast down the runway. Concentration was focused on my rudder dance to keep the plane on the centerline. The tail lifted at 65 mph and the mains popped off the ground at 105 mph. I was airborne in that amazing spray plane and, I was all by myself. It was going to be a strong friendship of trust and respect. I would respect this yellow plane and trust it would not fail me. I could not believe my day had come and I was in control of the big, powerful, loudly singing machine. Despite the noise being deafening on the ears, my mind was intently focused on the job at hand; it did not bother me one bit because I was in the air.

We leveled off around fifty feet above the ground and headed towards the field. The air was calm and solid as the wings sliced through it. A slight cool breeze blew in the cockpit against my face already sweaty. That morning, flying through the solid morning air, I understood why crop-dusters go to work so early. Soon, I was flying above a bright green rectangle field of soybeans. *Well here we go*, I thought as I pushed the stick forward to dive the plane down into the field. The feeling of control flowed through me. I pulled back to level off at what I considered a safe height above the crop and lowered the money handle to get the spray flowing out. The money handle was used to turn the spray on and off. Pops told us it was called that because you only make money when the handle is down and the spray is flying out of the nozzles. From my angle it looked as if the prop was merely inches off the ground. Pass one was completed, then pass two completed. As I lined up for pass three, I saw my pops in his little Bell helicopter. Wow, that brown Bell Tomcat was so ugly. Although ugly it sure packed a big load of chemical. Pops was parked at the opposite end of the field. Pass three was perfect. There was no altitude change and no drift worries. That created a smile of contentment on my face. Dropping an auto flag, or what we all called airplane toilet paper, I marked where I would start back up on return to the field. After marking my return spot I turned the giant plane back towards the airport to pick up another load of chemical.

After landing back in Waterloo, I taxied the yellow beast to the loading area. As I spun around for my next load, I saw the little brown helicopter landing on its helipad next to me. After landing, pops jumped out of his ugly workhorse and walked over to my plane. A pat on my back was coming and I was ready for my "good job son" talk because I did such a good job. Never had I been so wrong about something. *Damn that was funny.* "Nick, did you get a nosebleed at that altitude?" *"What the hell are you talking about Pops, I was on the deck!"* "No Nick, you were not on the deck, you were in the nose bleed section." "You need to get lower son." You were about ten feet in the air." "*Wow, okay*, I thought *I was on the deck on all three passes.*" "Nick, keep lowering the stick until the tires touch the crop. It will feel like a bunch of hands are grabbing the airplane. Nick, then you pull back a hair on the stick and you will be set on altitude." "Okay Pops, got it." *"Okay, get your head out of your ass before you suffocate and get this job completed."* Well there it was. There was no arguing with a crop-duster who had been doing it for twenty years and has a great reputation. The ugly brown helicopter took off and disappeared in the distance, I was ready to try what I had been told to do, for I did not want to suffocate wow! Although my bubble had been popped, I still wanted to be a great crop-duster and was willing to try anything to get there.

By the time the fear had escalated to its highest level, I took a deep breath then dove back into the field where the white flag was lying in bright distinction against the brilliant green of the soybeans. Little noises became sounds of learning. Pushing the stick forward for a dive would increase the boisterous sound coming from the six hundred ponies up front. As I leveled at ten feet, obviously the comfortable height, I continued to put forward pressure on the stick, with great apprehension. The airplane stared to inch its way closer to the brilliant green soybeans at 115 mph. There was an understanding for touching the beans but I was not excited about the idea of making contact with them at all. *That scared the crap out of me.* When the tires made the slightest contact with the soybeans, I instantly thought, *okay game over*, and for a split second I knew without a shadow of a doubt I was going to meet death face to face in a Soybean field in Waterloo, Iowa. It felt as if ten thousand people grabbed my yellow plane and were trying to pull it out of the sky. I physically slammed forward in my seat. My butt lifted slightly as my chest pushed forward against the shoulder harnesses. My heart began beating wildly.

Although, I had kicked death out of the plane, the goose bumps on my neck confirmed it was there with me. A split second after the tires had touched the vegetation my pop's directions popped back into my head and I eased the stick back just a hair. Like he had explained, the plane found her perfect height around eighteen inches above the crop. At 115 miles per hour 18 inches off the ground seemed extremely lower. With intense focus on the end of the green crop my breathing became normal and heartbeat returned to normal. After the initial scare, the plane found the same height above the crop for all remaining passes. The bright yellow wing flying above the brilliant green crop was mesmerizing. I began to feel the height and I was safe. My subconscious just knew where to put the plane on each and every pass. The last two loads were applied at the new height and the application was completed perfectly, in my head. I never had to push my tires into any vegetation again after that day. Thinking about that moment still makes the little hairs on my neck stand. I will never try that again nor will I ever tell anyone else to try it.

The fat tires screeched when the rubber kissed the stationary asphalt as if to announce, *Nick did it people, and he is back safely*. I exhaled a long breath upon arrival. Fear of the unknown subsided drastically my comfort height was found. Fear was still there, but only as knowledge. It allowed me to see other aspects of my flights. The feeling of invincibility flowed in my head and a feeling of being a pretty important dude was also there in my head. I could most certainly be called a crop-duster at that second, of that minute, in my life. Finally, I had made it. I taxied my yellow friend to its sleeping area with a giant ear-to-ear smile on my face. Before I shut it down I said to myself, "*Man, you are kind of a big deal now*." Reaching down my left hand pulled the mixture back and I watched the fat metal prop come to a standstill. I found myself in the cockpit of that beastly airplane engulfed in quietness reflecting on the flight. I must of thought a hundred times that I was now a crop-duster. My life goal had been reached and it felt amazing to be right there, right then. It felt complete. The crackling of the engine metal cooling and the smell of chemicals only built my satisfaction. I tide my yellow lady down then jumped in my red truck to go to the office. Looking in the mirror, as I drove to the office, I saw a confident commercial crop-dusting pilot staring back.

Although Pops was correct about my height and explanation of how to adjust it, I remember seriously wanting to punch him in the nose for scaring me half to death. Unfortunately for me, my pops has always been a bad ass, so I would never punch him in the nose without fearing for my life. The scare was needed for my education and was stored in my memory forever to remember. It was a deep, deep, learning experience that would enrich my skills. The thought of the little leaves on the soybean plants drastically slowing the strong fast plane down was a radical concept.

After my first official, spraying job was completed, I reflected on what I had learned that wonderful day. With legs of jelly and a huge smile, it was time to go home and sleep like a young boy who had just experienced his best Christmas ever. On the way to the airport the following morning, fear did not overtake my mind, but excitement did. After about a week or so, I felt there was still a copious amount of learning, to be had, but I truly felt more comfortable in the yellow Thrush. Trevor and I were at the same position in our aviation journeys. We both needed more hours to feel more comfortable and to be accepted by all the other pilots in Waterloo as working pilots. A trade off was needed for the both of us to gain confidence in the Thrush. We would fly every other day. One day I loaded chemical into an ugly brown helicopter for Pops, and the next day I would be applying those same chemicals on some random crop in my yellow lady.

I remember using any opportunity to build my hours spraying. Soon I was robotic in all aspects of the application process from start up to shut down. My height above the crop was also robotic and never needed an adjustment again. At that point I could feel a six-inch difference in height above the crop through the controls and how she was reacting. The one thing that could not be robotic was the passion I felt for the job. When you are in love with what you do, it is no longer a job it, is a must have in your life. As the yellow bird climbed hard at the end of the filed the retreating green always created the feeling of accomplishment to me. Not only did I fly with the skills of a well-trained pilot, I flew with a love for aviation. I flew with my heart as much as my skill. The passion, mixed with daily growing skills, brought a smooth routine into the yellow cockpit that could be seen from the ground. People often told me, "Nick you are the happiest man I have ever met." At that time in life, I was the happiest man on the planet.

I repeatedly asked myself the question, *how many people in the world get to fly a kick-butt airplane every day and get paid to do so?* Yes, airline pilots get paid the big bucks but their jobs seem relatively mundane. We often referred to airline pilots as bus drivers. To fly "Big Iron" was respected by every other pilot on the planet. The only exciting part of being an airline pilot for me would be the sexy flight attendants. That was the only bonus that pulled me toward an airlines occupation. I had often thought I would marry a flight attendant. Trevor and I had joked about how grand it would be if crop-dusters had flight attendants getting us cold Cokes while we were spraying then doing whatever to relax us. Yes, the term pilot came with several words that could help to describe them such as money, fun, women, and excitement. Never, did I grow out of the women and aviation requirements of a pilot. We seldom think about the true defining words for aviation, such as stress, responsibility, maturity, money, worry, and death. Another word to truly define a pilot is: complete. I felt complete flying in the big yellow Thrush. It sucks that mistakes are for learning because they hurt.

CHAPTER FIFTEEN
Learning Curve

I find myself thinking back on my journey to this point in my life. It was a tough, long, dusty road traveled down, but I traveled it nonetheless. Being pleased about where my life had taken me always put contentment in my heart. The flying continued, increasing my knowledge and experience daily. Love for my job was evident from the smile plastered on my face. At any given moment you could find me in my yellow office, eighteen inches above some arbitrary field at 115 miles per hour loving life.

One day the Thrush and I had just rotated for flight at full power, indicating a solid 110 on the airspeed indicator, when I heard a strange, disturbing, noise from behind that set me back. The sweat beads formed on my neck. Not knowing where the sound was coming from concerned me. I had never heard any tone of that nature in all my years of flying. My shirt became stuck to my back as the sweat accumulated rapidly. About ten seconds later, Danny's North

American P-51 Ridge Runner appeared next to the yellow Thrush at an extremely high rate of speed, about thirty feet off the right wing. The smooth silver tapered wing looked so small against the giant, rugged, yellow Thrush wing. The thirty feet that separated us looked more like three inches through my startled eyes. The strange noise was a pumped up Rolls Royce Merlin-V12 engine screaming after me, then right on by. A sound that will always take me back to that moment, yet also create a good feeling in my heart is the rugged yet smooth sound of a Mustang.

After the startle retreated, I took a deep breath of relief and reflected on how beautiful that airplane was. The brilliant paint and perfect lines reflected the morning sun as Danny rapidly pulled away. The bright red nose and tail reflected in stark divergence against the metallic grey body. A memory carved into my mind, never to escape, was the sight of that beautiful airplane flying away so peacefully and so fast. There is something about a North American P-51 that represents protection and freedom. I found it riveting that Waterloo was a home to several P-51 Mustangs. Ridge Runner Three, Straw Man Two, Iron Ass, Risky Business, and Merlin's Magic all lived there depending on the time of year. Based on their flight type for the day, you could frequently jump in with Danny, Mark, or Hugh. Not one of the Mustangs in Waterloo was a TF model. Meaning the back seat did not have duel controls. A passenger is all I was when flying in one. It was still breath taking to fly in such a rich part of history at 250 knots (nautical miles per hour). As the power increases on the runway for flight my back physically pushed back into the seat. Watching the shiny gray wing pull away from the bland black runway in such a rapid manor was breath taking. In a mustang, you can feel and hear the power it has both, on the ground, or in flight.

Danny came to the office later that day to tell me that he had been making machine gun noises in Ridge Runner as he lined up behind me earlier that morning. All in the office had a good laugh picturing Danny, alone in his cockpit, making gun noises like Trevor and I did as young boys in our Ag Husky/Corsairs back in McPherson, Kansas. A few years down the road, Danny's mustang, Ridge Runner Three, was featured in the movie "Tuskegee Airman." It was a historical movie about African American pilots in WWII. The movie was spectacular. To know that I had flown with Danny so many times in Ridge Runner Three made it that much better. Thinking about Danny dressed, as an African American pilot, was priceless. He was a proud Portuguese man.

Confidence in my flying was built daily. Often times learning has a curve. Sometime one must go backward to continue forward. Every time it rains I think about that stormy day. While flying out of the Williamsburg airstrip, I flew the Thrush through a phone line while applying fertilizer during a rainstorm. Crop-dusters apply fertilizer during rain to help break it down and get absorbed as nutrients. Before that day, I did not know that crop-dusters flew in torrential downpours, though I knew light rain was okay. It was raining so hard that day I had no idea I had even hit the phone line until I was back at the airstrip waiting for my next load. That day the rain hitting the plane was loud enough to hear through my earplugs and helmet. It seemed to be a warning noise.

The Williamsburg strip sits parallel to Hwy 80 in Iowa, south west of Cedar Rapids. Watching the traffic pass by while getting my next load of fertilizer was a common thing. I always wonder where they might be off to. Anywhere they were going was not half as great as what I was doing. As I sat in the idling plane, waiting for my next load, I looked over to see a Highway Patrol car splash off the freeway, pull by the fence and park. He waved me over so I unbuckled myself and jumped out of the Thrush, down the slick wing, and ran over to the officer. He had a stern smile on his face when I told him, "I didn't think I was speeding in my airplane officer." He then asked if I was okay and explained that I had just taken out a phone line on the field I was flying. My hand slid down my rain-drenched shocked face. I explained I was fine and had no idea I hit a wire. He said, "Well okay, fly safe. You crop-dusters are crazy as hell flying in this heavy rain. More balls than brains if you ask me." A simple smile appeared on my face, then I ran back to my soaked yellow plane to inspect for damage. The Thrush was in perfect shape, without damage.

I was sad and I still had to tell my pops what had happened. I did not want him to think I was a haphazard pilot. I figured it would be okay because nothing was damaged and I was still a new crop-dusting pilot. When I got back to waterloo, my pops and I had a lengthy discussion about wires, fertilizer, planes, cops, and the whys. Moral of the wire strike, stay high when applying fertilizer, fly low when applying pesticides. It is so easy to blame the rain when you are fairly new at it, but I learned how to correct it. At the end of that day I looked in the mirror and reminded myself I was not a journeyman pilot yet and I needed to slow down and be more mindful when applying chemicals.

The wire strike floated around in my head for a few days. I felt better about things as time moved forward. My head was clear until it needed to learn some more. Sometimes learning is not fun. A few months later, while flying a large field near Mason City the need to learn continued. Pulling up for a turn, there was a massive pop noise inside the Thrush. My heart jumped as I flew the Thrush through a set of thirty-thousand-volt power lines on a perfectly clear day. The power line ran parallel with the road next to the strip I was flying off of. The power line took a hard right 90-degree turn to the top of a small hill. As I pulled up to make my turn, it visually caught my eye a millisecond before a loud pop in the cockpit as the wire hit and broke the right side of the windscreen. Although, it can be described as a wire witch has a connotation of being small. It was the largest wire I had ever seen. On the other hand, I had never seen a thirty-thousand-volt wire from three feet. As the wire slid down the backside of the aircraft and wrapped around the tail, my butt physically came off the seat. It is way too easy to blame the pilot on a clear day. At least the Thrush did not get hurt too badly. Better yet, I was happy I did not get hurt when the windscreen broke the wire wrapped around the vertical stabilizer. I had never slowed down so drastically in the Thrush before. Death was standing in the green wheat below the Thrush with a lasso made out of high voltage electrical wire. That pop was so loud.

When the wire wrapped around the vertical stabilizer, I knew I was crashing into that green field of wheat. My fingers tremble as they tried to maintain control of the situation. As the plane dramatically slowed I pitched us hard forward and introduced full power to create more airspeed. A flash from the Beech-18 flight with Grantham popped in my head, right at that moment. I was low enough and slow enough to visually see the blades of winter wheat where I was going to meet my maker. Death was back with me. He was smiling and looking forward to the conclusion. The roar of the engine was intense at max power. The aircraft shook hard as it fought to maintain flight. It was letting me know that a crash did not seem like a good idea. The plane surged forward, snapping the wire. Once again I sighed with relief through my labored breathing. Focus man and get us on the ground, I told myself. I was able to make a hard 180-degree turn left and get us on short final for the grassy strip. I was relieved that the rude yellow wings were still flying above the green grass and not smashed in it. Fortunately, I was able to maintain enough speed to get us on the ground.

That wire strike was a harder learning incident because it was completely my fault. I fully did not understand how I made it back to the strip. I knew I was going to crash. I always wondered what went through a pilot's mind seconds before they crashed, and now I know. A million different things cram into your head creating a jumbled mess. It might be natural trying to trick the mind. I was so positive a crash was going to happen that I extended my arm to protect myself on impact. Once I got her slowed down my shaking hand reached down to pull the mixture and kill the power. My rubber legs got me to the truck. I needed to go tell the authorities, the power company, and my pops but first needed to sit there in the silence to calm my weary nerves. My loader was wound up from the wire strike, as he was so close to it. Sitting in the truck I could hear him, through the glass, repeat over and over, in a high-pitched voice, how it sounded like a shotgun blast when the thrush contacted with the wires. It did make a shotgun sound inside the bird when I made contact with the wires. After notifying all about the wire strike, I went back to the strip to wait for Iowa Power to come and analyze the damage. It had been an hour and my fingers were still twitching in fear. While waiting for the power technician to get to the airfield I found myself sitting on the giant yellow wing wondering how. My mind filled with thoughts of death and wondered again if it would ever win, because it was there always there, always close.

I was happy to see the Iowa Power truck pull into the strip. I should say when he tried to pull into the strip. That was merely an ironic balance in life. The driver forgot to clear oncoming traffic, and smash. With a loud bang, another disaster happened. The Power truck hit a loaded van head on. A few minutes later the people in the van started making their way out. They crawled out of the smashed vehicle one by one. Although death failed to get me, it was still there trying to get others. Once they gathered their feet under them and saw the green Iowa Power truck, they started grabbing their necks and moaning in pain. Although I was really down on myself for hitting another wire, I was shocked see this family trying to manipulate the system. While it was the Power employee that pulled in front of them, they did not have to pretend they were in massive pain suffering horrible. I shared what I had seen with one Patrol officer who had responded to the crash. It boiled down to what the police officer told me in a concerned yet stern voice in the middle of that grassy strip: "Boy, if you had not hit those wires, none of this would have happened." He put some truth frosting on my sad cake. I sat in the green grass next to the strip looking at my yellow lady feeling fortunate to be there alive. Later that night I found myself thinking about how death was closer than it had been in a long while; I saw it and felt it strongly that day. I was pretty sure I was going to join it. My thoughts about death were increasing. *Why did I continue?*

I considered both wires strikes to be massive learning experiences. Both were eye openers at different levels. The second strike installed a true fear about how a few simple wires can destroy a massive airplane and its pilot. My pops, on the other hand, considered them both to be critical hammers to the company's checkbook. I was around crop dusting my entire life, so part of me understood that stuff like this was going to happen but not to me. I knew I was beyond wire strikes. I simply pushed forward and erased any negative thoughts, or self-doubt, created by the strikes. *This is crop-dusting and that is going to happen*, I repeatedly thought. Like Pops said I needed to get my head out of my ass.

As I continued to grow deeper in my career, I remained in a constant learning vigil about the limits of my yellow plane and much more, my limits in her. Soon three hundred gallons became commonplace for me. If the chemical was coming out of the overflow on top of the hopper, it was full and ready to go to work. I would get to my plane as the sun glistened off her damp frame each morning. At the start of every morning I would have a conversation with my golden buddy. *Good morning yellow lady, are you ready for a good day of flying*? I asked these simple questions while sliding my hand down the cold, dew-covered leading edge whilst performing my preflight inspection of the giant wings. It was strange that I got into the routine of talking to the plane. It was almost a superstition or a good luck tradition. I knew God had my back but felt I needed to have her back. It was a small way to pay homage to the yellow lady for my safety and a way to keep death out. *"I see your wings are looking strong today. Let's get you into the air so you can stretch them."* While normally I would not have random conversations with inanimate objects, it was not normal for anyone to strap their butt into a giant plane and fly 18 inches off the ground at 115 mph all day. I treated the Thrush like a part of my family. I took care of it and it took care of me. It was a perfect familial balance of safety and security. I envisioned the plane as an older beastly brother, or a beautiful lady, in need of love and respect. I knew if I kept my focus on learning I would retire an old crop duster someday.

CHAPTER SIXTEEN
After Thought

A t the beginning of April, I was on my own. The walking pneumonia had plagued my pops and Trevor so I was in charge of all the flying. It was a bummer they were sick but I was more than pumped to be in charge. I felt pretty big in boss pants. My confidence jumped as my responsibilities did. It took some practice to manipulate my massive plane into the smaller fields. We called the smaller fields, helicopter fields, because helicopters are more agile and maneuverable in small, tight areas. Furthermore, helicopters can get into confining spaces if they have a pilot with the skills to do so. My pops possessed those skills and was the only helicopter pilot at Ag Masters. With pops out sick, it left me to attack those tiny fields with my big yellow Thrush. The yellow bird did not let me down, nor did I let it down. Together we attacked countless fields smaller than ten acres then flew home for the next day of flying. While I missed my pops and Trevor, it felt amazing running the show and covering all of the work with the Thrush. Merely getting out of my truck caused my chest to pump up and head swell a tad. The feeling of high accomplishment was there for sure at the end of each day.

On the 7th of April, the yellow Thrush and I had been out flying some fields when the wind in the area started to pick up. I called it a day and pointed us back to Waterloo. My taste buds were screaming for coffee. I was hoping to get a hot cup at the café and shoot the breeze with the other pilots at the cafe. As I walked into the office to drop off my paperwork the phone rang, as if someone knew I had just walked in. On the other end of the phone was good friend and customer Chip. Chip was a rough looking middle-aged man, thin in stature. Chip had been severely burned at a younger age and the scars remained present on his face. When Don P., otherwise known as the Snake, lost control of his dragster, it flipped over on top of Chip. Before farming, Chip wanted to rule the top fuel dragster world. Although he was badly hurt in that crash, it made him almost a celebrity to me for knowing the Snake.

When you find out the history of some, their lives are often filled with unbelievable stories that pull you in to learn more. We all knew Chip as a local farmer in Perry, Iowa. His house was the key to his mysterious life. It was a vault of amazing stories and artifacts, surrounded by famous people. Although burn scares remain on his face he always had beautiful women near him. The 1992 movie "Of Mice and Men" was filmed on Chip's farmland. I can look at the cover of that movie and smile knowing that I had personally sprayed almost every wheat field in that movie. More than a drag racer or movie man, Chip's blood was in farming, to his bones.

On the phone, Chip explained that the wind was calm on Joe's Wheat field and he encouraged me to head back to Fairfield, to get the job done. While I was mentally done for the day, I did not want to upset a great customer and good friend. I hung up the phone, jumped in my truck, and headed back out to the Thrush. *Okay beastly friend, we need to go back out and spray some more.* I jumped into the still warm cockpit, yelled, "CLEAR" then built a fire in the powerful engine. After warming the big radial a few minutes, I jumped us back on the runway for takeoff headed east. We had to get back to Fairfield before the wind truly got us.

I always loved the flight towards Fairfield. Most days you would see magnificently colored hot air balloons floating around the Oskaloosa area. I would always fly close enough to give a wave, to people in the baskets. That particular day, there was a brilliantly colored balloon with purple and black-checkers and bright yellow stripes hugging the checkerboard. The balloon was just carelessly floating west of Oskaloosa without a worry. It was the largest hot air balloon I had ever seen. The site of the brightly colored, beautiful, balloon dangling precariously in Mother Nature's home was stunning. The colors were mesmerizing against the mundane greens and yellows of the vegetation below. As the Thrush flew close to the balloon, everyone standing in the delicate dangling basket waved. I waved back, than felt the need to salute them. I was extremely proud of where I was at that exact moment. Seeing the people in the basket I wondered why anyone would put that much trust in balloon guided by Mother Nature.

A few short minutes later I arrived at Joe's wheat field. Joe was a hard working fat man. I wondered how much food he must have eaten to work so hard all day long and still have his own gravity field. It really did not matter because he always wanted me to fly for him. The field was a long section of north-south land, which had a small hill on the northern most side of the field. Flying over the field I made the decision to fly it in one direction, using north to south passes from the east end to the west end. That way I could avoid any turbulence rolling over the top of the little hill.

I saw Chip in his white Chevy truck on the east end of the field. That truck was a trademark for C & J Farms. If you saw it, you knew the man inside was there to guide you, but also to help in any way possible. Chip and big Joe were good friends and partners in the local feed store in Fairfield, Iowa. Chip jumped out to wave hello, then triggered his radio, "69 this is Chip. It is relatively calm. The breeze is coming out of the North at around three to four miles per hour. There is no drift concern here so let's give it hell." *"Roger that Chip, I'm starting on your side, so stay clear please."* "10/4 69 be safe." *"Roger that Chip."* I started north of the hill and flew down the south side of it. I leveled us off at my normal height above the wheat. My left arm extended to compress the money handle to get the chemical out. After completing the first pass the money handle back up to turn the spray off. I began a hard right turn followed by another, to get back to the hill and start my next pass. I lined up on pass two. The yellow plane and I flew down the hill and leveled out on the flat.

This style of flying is called one-way, or round robin flying, and invites more airspeed. I love round robin flying because I love speed. *She felt so fast over the field.* Peering down as my airspeed indicator I noticed in my turn above the hill I was carrying 105 mph and 115 mph on the deck, at spray altitude. After the completion of pass two, I kicked her right while keeping about ten feet of altitude above the crop. As I rapidly approached the little hill, I pulled back to avoid contact. It was always thought it was a good idea to avoid the ground when flying. As I started my final right turn, I wrenched my neck around to observe I was not going to make my target pass if I did not get the yellow bird turned tighter. With my right arm, I applied more backpressure to the stick to get us lined up on the next pass. *What's that? Are you trying to tell me something?* Something isn't right. Ah crap!

CHAPTER SEVENTEEN
Breathe it in

Contorted by the sudden jolt. The noise was deafening as the metal transformed shape from a solid to many. As the motion stopped the epicenter of pain was acknowledged as it radiated across my body. Deep breath only found shooting pain in all areas of my body. When focus became clear, I found myself shocked at the site of the control stick physically imbedded in my bloody leg. The pungent smell of burning plastics and oils surrounded me. Intoxicating smoke filled the air. Blood was splattered on the airspeed indicator, still indicating 112 miles per hour. Each drop of blood sent ripples in the growing deep puddle below. As my chest fought for breath, quivered twitches interrupted the steady drips of fluids coming off my chin. My heart physically hurt from a lack of fluid pumping in. Ninety-eight point six degrees is dramatically enhanced as the warm blood traveled down my face, over my lips and splattered into another red reservoir on the floor of the deformed yellow compartment. The heat from the fire is close. *Why can I see the tread on the bottom of my shoe*? Disbelief consumed as I saw the carnage. My foot was twisted completely around the right rudder pedal in a manner that's not physically possible. My foot had completed a tight 180 degrees wrap around the pedal. My stomach churned with sickness as injuries became visible. Even at a pain level that is indescribable, I thought, *Man those shoes where brand new, now junk. I wonder if the blood will wash off. Why the hell am I thinking about shoes?* I had been so excited to find those ugly shoes because they looked like boots and felt like tennis shoes. I knew I would be faster on my feet in the plane with those shoes.

I watched as bright red blood pooled under the deformed ankle, still halfway wedged in the new shoe. *This is bad, really, really, bad. Just breathe man*, I told myself. My head felt weak and empty. What was missing? My helmet was gone. *Where is it*, I wondered. The compartment I was in was destroyed. I wondered if I would be completely destroyed as well. *Where was I?* The strong smell of hundred-low-lead and of fire was leading me to the end of it. A feeling deep inside simply stated over and over, *Nick, let's go home. "God, if you can hear me, I am ready to go home,"* I prayed. Death was sure to answer, *"I am here with you and I have won."* Death was my final obstacle in life. Never wanting to physically be around when death came was a natural human reaction. Time was limited. The wheezing in my throat could not expand my painful lungs much longer. They fought for each tiny breath of smoky oxygen. *I need only one good breath and I will be fine.* Feeling my chest fold in and out searching for clean air without pain was effort wasted. Each little movement brought tears to my eyes. My chest quivered strongly as my weak body fought to pull in minimal air. Why me Lord, why me. Denial was in a mental battle with acceptance of what was yet to come: final death. I had cheated it for so long, it was now here to take me.

At that particular, moment, in all honesty, I craved death to escape the toe curling pain that each cell in my body felt. The mixture of blood and tears brought a salty taste to my tongue. *Just move man, get that stick out of your leg*. I did not know why I couldn't move. I was pinned to the wad of yellow metal surrounding me. The bent metal in the tight compartment invited claustrophobia. The feeling of being buried alive filled my brain. The combination of temperatures, smells, and visions in that strange golden metallic world encapsulated me into a value of zero. I was worth nothing and therefore I should just die. I felt so small in that achy world. I was lost, lost beyond the point of ever being found. *It's so damn lonely here. Where is everyone,* I thought? I was simply waiting crying, bleeding and begging God to take me. All sounds travel into a steady hum. The hum escapes into endless silence. *Someone please find me, I'm not ready*. As the pictures faded into a constant blur and the myriad of smells blended into emptiness, I could only wait. It was only a few days ago Troy, Trevor, and I, were flying anything in McPherson, building flight hours for this path. Was I building time just to get dead? My whole life was a hurdled convoluted path to reach death. My path never included such a dramatic ending, only bliss and happiness. I knew death was watching but did not truly believe it was so close. *He is sitting here watching me bleed out.*

What's that noise? I heard the faint sound of the Hiller in the distance. *Maybe it was the Killer Hiller and my pops coming to save me from this misery?* A red and white Aero Medical BO-105 helicopter flies over the hill on the north side of the green field. As the Aero Medical helicopter gets closer to the impact site the blade slapping noise becomes louder and louder. Cool air blows on the crushed hulk. A strong breeze brought coolness as it blew across the streams of blood flowing down my face. Vision started to strobe rapidly. I felt myself being pulled into the darkness. "CLEAR, stand CLEAR," in a muffled, distant voice repeated over and over. Someone must be starting an airplane. *It's so silent in the darkness.* It seemed I had answered death's call without picking up a phone. What path is the next path for me? *Hopefully it will be a path not filled with this pain.* Then it blackness consumed me.

CHAPTER EIGHTEEN
Confusion

Strange my path of pain morphed into a path of solitude. That pain was so real but now gone. *Where am I, and how the hell did I get here.* Sand was all that could be seen for miles in every direction. Each chapter this life has been so different and confusing. My confusion was centered on why I was there and what was happening to me. That crash dream was so real I hope I never have it again. I could actually feel the pain in my sleep. My mouth was so dry and I was so thirsty. Never in my life had I felt so parched. The thoughts of a single drop of water in my mouth would have been heavenly. Each dry step brought a light rain of sand to my crusty face and rough tongue. Although there was a breeze, the heat trapped within it was unbearable. My tongue stuck to the roof of my mouth created pain with each move. *Even the slightest moisture would help. To lie down in the lettuce section of any super market to feel the mister spray on my face is a euphoric at high-level thought.*

The reoccurring thought of cool mist landing on my dry face brought excitement to my mind. Just one drop of rain on my head would make a world of difference. How long had I been walking through that dry desert? Better yet, why was I walking there? How did I get there and what was the purpose of it? Those questions circled through my dry head with every step.

The splits on my parched lips burned with each breath. I fight the want to fall to my knees and cry in the dissolute wasteland. Everything looks the same, sand dune after and dune, never a change. Rays from the blinding sun pierce my red skin. It was so bright out here. Much time was spent motivating myself to stay focused on getting to water. *Man, you must find water. Just keep moving forward. Keep moving forward.* Upon reaching the top of what seemed like the hundredth dune, hallucinations had started as I saw a little store in the middle of this forsaken wasteland. With all of the power I have left in my body, I pushed hard to reach the store, illusion or not. To my disbelief and excitement, it was real, not an illusion. Twenty feet from the door I grabbed my wallet to find a crisp twenty-dollar bill. Andrew Jackson had never looked so handsome before. *Only water for this guy,* I thought. How did I end up here?

As I entered the store, I was surprised to find they only sold water, nothing else. I was mesmerizing to see so many brands of fresh cold water. The air conditioning was on the fritz. It was cooler than outside but still too warm. I couldn't wait to get water and continue on this strange path in life. As I reached my dry arm out for an ice-cold bottle of water I hear a strange voice came from behind, "You don't want that.

That is water is mine." *What the hell?* I turned to see a polished .38 Special pointed directly at me. I took a deep breath and with all I had forced my dry cords to speak, "*But I need this really bad.*" The strange man replied, "Well you only have about sixty more miles to the next store. I'm taking all this with me man." His cold, rusty voice caused shivers on my depleted body. My heart sank. I realized I had walked directly into a robbery in the middle of a desert. Sure enough, before too long all of the water had been removed and I had been tied to one of the hot shelves. At least the airplane dream came with an understanding. I sat there and thought about the luck of some, then faded off to a deep dark sleep in that insane hell.

My memory was off. I was mentally losing days at a chunk. It seemed strange to wake up on my bike just riding down the road thinking of my super-hot girlfriend. For the life of me, I could not remember how I got there but happy. The last memory before being free on my bike was in the middle of nowhere tied to a shelf inside that store. *Someday it will all be understood.* It did not matter at that moment for I was alive, riding my bike. The cool air flowing over me felt well than it ever had before. With the cool air refreshing me, my thoughts turn to my girlfriend and the strong passion that exists in our relationship. Her black skin so divine, so smooth to the touch like the curves on my beautiful Ducati, her curves invited me. *Why can't I remember her name? She looks like Halle Berry.* How does the name of a beautiful woman escape any mind? Her hard body sure does not. I can visualize every inch of her as I shift gears and build speed. Oh man, so simple, Sarah is her name. I still find it astonishing that Sarah's twin sister is dating Trevor. Riding my bike always invited thinking. My right thumb initiates the right turn signal and my foot right foot, taps on the break of my bright yellow Ducati 750 Super Sport. After slowing I make a hard right turn into the parking lot. I loved the way that bike sounded. I accidently entered the exit, which had metal shards sticking out of the ground. Pop, pop, both tires on my bike were flat. I limped the bike to a parking stall and called Trevor for help. It means a lot to have a brother always willing to help you. Trevor said, "Have it towed to the shop, we will get it fixed tomorrow." I called AAA and got my yellow bike picked up. I knew my yellow rocket was in good hands at the shop, but I missed it already.

The next day was laundry day. I remember we had to go to the gross Laundromat for our clothes. Never before had I used a Laundromat. I had always thought of them as gross, dank, and dark places. That damn city was so busy. Still could not believe Trevor and I had moved to San Francisco. All negative thoughts about that city tend to dissolve into nothingness as I thought about my girlfriend. Although I hated that city, her body made up for it. Even going to a nasty Laundromat seemed better because of her. It was strange we were the only two people in the gloomy place. That morning the sun was shining its beams through the front window, creating life in the dark, damp Laundromat. Looking at the traffic through the front window reminded me we were still in a busy city.

Randomly turning my head out the front window I saw a strange metallic green low-rider. It seemed out of place in San Francisco. Personally, I have never seen a good use for low rider cars. Not my cup of tea, but to each his own, I guess. It was dropping itself into a flattened stance in front of the big glass window as Trevor was putting his laundry in his machine. There was a dark male in the front seat who looked familiar, but I could not remember where I had seen him before. Then it came to me. There was a picture of him in Sarah's photo album. Strange that he happened to be at the same place her new boyfriend was doing laundry at in the big city of San Francisco. There was something in his hand but I couldn't tell what it was. Ah man, it's a gun. *What, is this crazy world coming to*? I freaked out when I realized it was a MAC 10. I recognized that gun because I had shot one with Trevor and my pops in McPherson, Kansas. I'm so far from home. *Why do I live in this crappy town?*

The strange man pointed the MAC 10 our direction. Then it happened. Pop, pop, pop, I heard, then saw, the recoil of the gun move fast up and down as the bullets eject out the short barrel. The plate glass window instantly turned to a shattered dust. That day, like none other, felt as if time had decelerated. The copper was traveling slow as it flew past me. Pop, pop. I knew I had to warn Trevor. I turned to Trevor only to watch a round pierce his right temple, creating a misty red cloud on the left side. In that same instance I felt a burning like no other on the right of my chest. Death was in this damn Laundromat. I felt helpless looking at Trevor's lifeless head bounce off the cold, damp floor of the nasty laundromat. The hot lead tore through my front side before ripping through my lung, then exiting out my back. Breath was gone the pain took it. I gasped for air but my effort was futile. I stumbled back a few steps. My legs were sluggish as I floundered around before falling hard on to the cold concrete floor. There was no focus on anything other than pain. The moist, dirty, cool floor felt good against my bleeding penetrated body.

In and out of consciousness, on that cold floor I waited for the finishing round to find me. My mind momentarily drifted to the movies. I had seen so many people get shot in the movies, I figured the pain would be gone shortly and I would be up on my feet. Each breath in, or out, causes more tears to form in my unfocused eyes. *Focus on your breathing man.* With each beat of my heart, I could feel the warm blood pump out of the hole in my back. Every cell in my body was letting me know they were ready to die. My breath is incredibly unstable and labored. As my hole-filled body lay on the floor of that dank, dirty Laundromat a large pool of warm blood surrounded me. I turned my head just in time to watch Trevor fight to inhale his final breath and then consumed with stillness. The thought of death in a dirty Laundromat there in San Francisco, was not a fitting end for two brothers, or two best friends, anywhere in this sick, dark world. The sound of a car screeching off filled the building. All sounds blended into a steady hum. I can't see Trevor, only darkness now. Was it death again I wondered? I repeatedly told myself that I was ready to go. Dying seems like the logical way to stop the torturous pain. I would do anything to get the burning lead out of my chest. Stillness consumed me as I waited for death to arrive and take me.

Death would have to wait longer. *I don't understand.* Life was so confusing and sporadic there was a space-time upset in my life. Feeling lost as my memory failed to make any correlation form one moment to the next. Time was completely blended, yet lost. I needed to get to the end of it but could never reach it. The end was out of reach. Once again I was faced with the question of, how I got there. More importantly, did it even matter? I was still alive. *What is this confusing day of death was about.* There I was, wondering if it was for real this time. I am so hot and thirsty once again. Memory was so convoluted and broken up without understanding. What was the next path? I was hoping it would be one less confusing. That hope was short lived. *Am I really tied to the ground?* Hundreds of questions filled my brain as I realized I was pinned down with what looked like fishing line. That took me back to the store that only sold water where I was tied down. Why this happening to me was running through my head. I've never hurt anyone. I need a flight in Bravo Charlie right now to clear my head. The heat underneath my body was so hot.

Squinting my eyes provided some clarity. Intensely bright sunlight was blurring my vision and causing tears to drop. *The buildings across the way look so familiar.* Is this the Omaha Airport? My body was tied down to the active runway in Omaha, Iowa and I once again there was no idea of how I had gotten there. The asphalt was scorching. Each little rock pierced the tender skin on my back and neck. *No complaints Nick, you are alive.* Confusion is becoming a good friend now. Answers to all this insanity would be appreciated. Mind whirls looking for a way out of the situation. Being tightly tied to the ground, I was unable to move. I cannot move my legs at all. I'm sweating so mush. The sweat beads roll into my eyes causing a constant sting. Reflecting back on the confused day, there were no explanations about it. Went to do laundry with Trevor that morning and then I found myself tied down to a runway. Never should have gone to that nasty laundromat. Just when I thought that day was the worst day ever, I hear a distinct sound of a 1340 Pratt radial engine flying overhead. I was tied down to the middle of runway one seven, Omaha. The giant paint strips down the middle of the runway dwarfed me in size. The heat radiating off the paint was intense.

Opening my blurry sun-soaked eyes I could make out a yellow Ag Cat overhead, downwind for landing one seven. I can feel the adrenaline pumping through my veins with force as I struggled to get off the scorching runway. The line is too tight for me to get out. I am so thirsty. The plane turned onto short final for landing. The screeching sound of the tires kissing the hot runway increased my anxiety of what was next, I hoped that he could see, and avoid me. *Please see me, I pleaded!* More screeching and I raised my head to see the plane sliding sideways directly towards me. Closing my eyes I wait for the pain to come followed by death. It feels like it is not going to stop today until it wins. The loud sound filled the air of metal bending and scrapping as it slid down the runway. This plane is going to be completely destroyed I thought as I waited for the horrible noises to stop.

Eyes opened, bright yellow airplane parts surrounding me, but I'm alive. My legs lacked all feeling. *Am I paralyzed?* Squinting my eyes for more clarity I saw the round engine popping little puffs of smoke out of a few cylinders. Fuel was leaking from the center wing section. I followed the trail of fuel to see I was lying in a small reservoir of hundred low lead aviation fuel. The feeling of the fuel wrapped around me took my mind back to the laundromat. The warm blood felt much like the fuel on this hot asphalt. The fuel soaked into each and every hole in my back. I lay tied on a runway surrounded by yellow metal crying like a child. I hate pain. I look back at the engine only to see a spark ignite the fuel to consume the entire site in fire. The pain entered a higher level at that point. I am burning alive in a ball of fire. I am in hell. My eyelids start melting off, dripping on my cheeks. My destiny was fully accepted, death in Omaha fire on the runway. I needed water more than ever right then. I raise my right arm only to see the skin on my fingers curling up and dripped off into the fire. There is no glory in my life only complete pain both physically on my body and emotionally deep in my soul. All I wanted in life was to be a pilot. Then consumed by hot black silence.

CHAPTER NINETEEN
Reality Hurts More

Nickolas, can you hear me? "Look, his eyes are open. I think he can hear us." *I was sleeping so good, why is someone trying to wake me up, and who is it? Where am I this time? Why is it so bright here? What the heck was going on and what is that annoying beep noise? Am I in a hospital? Oh wow, I'm in a hospital. Must be from either the gunshot or the fire?* I waited for my blurry vision to correct slightly. I was completely lost, looking over and seeing Trevor standing against the wall. It was so bright in there. It might not be a hospital. *No way, this is Heaven! I watched Trevor die, so it has to be Heaven.* Disbelief filled my brain thinking about the guy that shot us. Death was never an option for me yet there I was dead in Heaven. *Was it the gunshot or the Ag Cat fire that killed me?* Why was I talking to my dead self about it anyway, I'm dead. Why is someone trying to get my attention in Heaven? "Nickolas, you were in an airplane accident and have been here in a coma for thirty-two days." *I knew they were messing with me. No, I was shot. No...an airplane crashed on me.* My mind was full of questions and confusion but I could not get any words to come out. *When did I crash and in what kind of car, I thought.* They must be mistaken. *I thought that Heaven would not have an irritating beep in it.* I did not remember a crash but I do remember my Sarah's ex-boyfriend shooting me like it was yesterday, not thirty-two days previous. I could still feel the burning lead ripping through my lung.

The voice continued, "Nickolas you crashed an airplane." My brain entered a long pause of thought. I remember being a pilot, *so what happened?* A crash still did not explain Trevor standing in the room against the wall. Nor did it explain the annoying beep in the background. Was I in my Thrush? Words could not be produced but it was obvious my brain was working. Well I was awake therefore I must be alive. Happy to be alive but how did I get here and what is wrong with me? I wondered how much longer before waking up on another crazy path in life. Someone needed to explain to me about Trevor being there? Watching him die was physically painful and now he was here with me in this bright room. That beep is driving me mad. Wait a minute; following the patch of cords coming out of my bed to an electrical box thing, I realized the annoying beep was a heart monitor. I can handle that annoying noise, if this is real. It was a much better sound if it only beeps in rhythm to my heart. That meant my heart was beating. Which also means I am alive. Eventually we will get to the bottom of the crash stuff.

In the chaotic hospital, in my beat existence, sleep was off and on without warning as all the days bled together. There was an acceptance that each day would blend together with the next. I found myself looking forward to the next path in life because this one was not good. While I never knew what day or time it was, I did appreciate seeing people I recognized. There was one day that did not bleed into the next. I consider that to be the most important day to me. I opened my eyes one day to see my pops and Mom. I could not tell you the color of their clothes that day, but I could tell what a tear looks like running down my pop's face. Still, to this day, I can see that image. He was so excited I was alive, but it tore him up to see me, his son, in such a fragile state. Seeing that lone tear of sadness brought a deep reality to my crash scenario. There was still no talking due to a crude tube thing sticking out of my neck. For communication purposes I have to point at letters on a piece of paper in order to ask questions. During the crash, my glasses were beat beyond repair so my vision lacks clarity. Therefore, communication is hard. My mind wants to ask a thousand questions but I have to filter through them all to find the most important questions until tomorrow. When Trevor showed up one day, I used my finger to point to the letters asking about my yellow bike was. It was important to make sure he had fixed it. I loved that motorcycle. As I pointed out the question, I saw a small grin grow on his face. He responded, "Listen Brother, I'm not exactly sure what you have been through mentally, but you have never owned a motorcycle, much less a Ducati." All of the answers, to all of my questions, came with the same sort of results; no, no way, and I am sorry brother. I had accepted the laundromat incident was a dream, but not having my motivational bike took my mind back into a lost space. The airplane landing on top of me had to be real but lacked the vocabulary to ask. The Ducati was so real to me; I often spent hours thinking about riding it when I leave the hospital. Convinced this new reality was my personal hell, I started to mentally question everything and blamed death like it was a human. A no-good dirty, rotten, human.

"Nick you have a girlfriend. She is white and lives in Helena, Montana." Her name is Karen. Reality hit hard as I hear this news. Not a black woman but white, with short blond hair. *I know her!* Wow, I was dating Karen from Montana. Karen was a sweet girl that loved life. She was tall, thin in appearance. She resembles a model. We had worked together at United Express a few years back. I moved to Waterloo to follow my passion while she stayed in Montana for work. Working for United Express allows her to fly out and see me for free. *Where is she now,* I thought? Pops explained that Karen was at my side for weeks but then had to return to Montana for work. *Maybe it didn't matter because I look like ten miles of tank tread,* I thought. Hours were spent in thought about her while questioning all of the whys and wondered if Karen had forgotten about me.

My pops came to see me. I cleared my head to point to the paper and ask, "Do I still have a girlfriend?" I wanted to know if she had broken up with me because I was burned so badly on the on that runway. After he put all the letters together he started laughing hard. "Yes, son, you have a few of them." Pops continued to tell stories about girlfriends. "Nick, your memory is not strong yet, but when you were in the coma your grandfather and I were talking outside your room in the hall. I'm not sure why, but I looked down the hall to see the elevator door open and to my surprise not one, not two, but three of your girlfriends somehow had all jumped on the same elevator at the same time." Oh wow, I thought, three girls and all my girlfriends? My pops finished the story while giggling. "We each had to grab one and go in different directions. I grabbed Donna, your grandfather grabbed Susan, and Mom grabbed Karen. It was awesome chaos, but we pulled it off. I'm sorry I'm laughing, but it was truly great." Did I crush Karen, I wondered? I remembered the names of Kristy, Donna Susan, Tina, and Karen. Time was spent pondering their meanings in my life. I thought about the whole girlfriend situation but did not dwell on it for too long. My new path in life only had room for healing therefore I only focused on that. There I lay, a broken pile of bones that may or may not ever work the same. I needed to know how I got tied to that runway.

There is no way, thirty-two days of random dreams is my reality living in my head clear and with meaning. I was living them vividly. They are real to me. I physically know what it feels like to burn to death. The dreams were my direct reality. Looking out the door, of my bright room, I spent time wondering if anyone out there was as screwed up as me. More than anything I wanted to jump out of my bed and go find out. I was stuck there in that bed envisioning all my different realities. Not being able to communicate slowed the healing process I assumed. People would ask a question and I would have to run through all the different stories living in my head to find a reasonable answer. Giving one letter at a time for an answer. Soon I found out the complete truth about my sarcastically wonderful stay in the Trauma One hospital there in Des Moines. It was the Thrush I was flying. What Happened, I ask all. I had caused the Thrush to enter a high-speed stall on my last turn over Big Joe's wheat field. Guess I never should have answered that phone call from Chip and gone for coffee instead.

Trevor and Chip explained I had asked the Thrush to turn too tight and she couldn't. When I pulled back to tighten my turn, the angle of attack became too great for her to handle. She snapped left while I was turning hard right. The impact was straight in at full speed after completing a seven hundred and twenty degree turn to the left. The impact was so powerful the giant round engine traveled four and a half feet into a packed dirt road. With all that news, my mind raced with a hundred questions. How did I get to this hospital was first and foremost important to me. I could not get the letters out fast enough to ask. "Nick, Chip, the farmer, and Tony, an off-duty fireman, pulled you out of the plane. You cannot talk because you are on a ventilator and have a breathing tube in your neck. It's called a tracheotomy. The tubes below your armpits are chest tubes to drain blood out of your lungs and allow them to expand. Your lungs were heavily damaged in this crash. There was a long while that we thought you were not going to make it through the night because of Adult Respiratory Distress Syndrome. You are one lucky son of a gun Nick." After this news watching my chest rise and fall, without me breathing in or out, became a distraction. I have tubes everywhere.

It was hard to believe all of the damage my body had received in the impact. Yet there I was alive, in disbelief, yet wondering about the road ahead. The doctor, Dr. Sanders was a GQ handsome man. I overheard the nurses call him Dr. Mercedes at least 50 times. I figured he was their target. He asked me if I understood the gravity of it all because I should have died. *He chose the right word because gravity had already won this fight. So yes, I understand the gravity of it all.* I was able to give thumbs up, so I figured, at best, my arms were still okay. Hours were spent watching the steady drip of IV fluid just trying to fill in all the blanks in my impacted life. In and out were my thoughts and in and out were my days. How did I live through it, and better yet, why did I live. Each time I awoke, I had to remind myself where I was and how I got there. "Nickolas, your heart stopped beating eight times in the helicopter on the way here. They had to use a defibrillator to shock you back into normal rhythm each time." That explained why the word "CLEAR" had repeated as a muffled tone in my head for thirty-two days. *Not only did "clear" mean move or get run over by an airplane, it represents clear out of the way before you get shocked.* That word always takes me to the great flights in the Super Cub with my pops. The Cub was such great times in life.

"Nickolas you are truly a lucky man. You broke your left ankle, right knee, and pelvis." "Furthermore, every rib broke piercing both lungs. Your lungs looked like Swiss cheese when you got here. The scientific name for it is flailed chest. You also broke your left shoulder and nose." *That explained the intense pain of the bullet ripping through my lungs when I was supposedly shot in a random, dirty laundromat.* "Nick, your organs were so damaged that we could not feed or hydrate you properly. This is why you only weigh 115 pounds." At that point, I could start to blend true reality with coma reality and make a strong reality smoothie to drink to choke on for understanding. When I was informed that my temperature was 106 degrees for nearly three weeks I could piece together even more. Thinking about the intense fevers I understood the hot and thirsty dreams in my coma. I racked my brain about the motorcycle dream but am still not able to blend it to any reality. My Ducati was bright yellow and powerful, as was my yellow Thrush. Maybe color and power was the similarity that tied them together. It seemed each time I woke, more information about more injuries was explained. "Nick, we're not sure if you will walk again, and we're not sure…if you will be able to establish an erection." *Holy hell, you fixed my knee, ankle, pelvis, ribs, shoulders, and lungs but not my penis?* At that moment the crash got a thousand times worse. *We need to figure that out immediately. Without a shadow of a doubt, I know I will need an erection sooner or later in my life.* I could not fight the tears from welling up.

I knew Dr. Sanders saw the pain in my soul as tears continued welled up in my eyes. At that moment, I knew he was a man, not just a robotic surgeon. He looed into my tear socked eyes and responded to my pain, "Nick, I will bring in a smut mag once you are a little more together. We will see what happens then." That load of monumentally negative news pointed me directly towards a depressive slide, but I could not stand for it. I over thought every simple thought, to death. I wished I could have run away and hid. *Oh yeah, my legs don't work, crap,* I thought. My Occupational

Therapist Nancy explained that patents in my situation would often allow depression to steal their healing thunder. She was a great therapist with a warm invite about her. You could visually tell she was a therapist but I would have thought, physical not occupational. Her body was well formed. I got the feeling she wanted to get everything to work properly on me. I mean everything. After thirty-two days of sleep I was ready for things other than healing. Depression would not steal my healing power. Even energy at the cellular level would be used for healing. Doctors have been wrong before therefore I would continue to hunt for other solutions.

Lying in the sterile emotionless environment was overwhelming on my brain. *How will I get out of here and move forward in a positive manner.* That question found its way into my head hundreds of times each day in my lonely hospital bed. The hospital was both scary and comforting. The IV drips of life running down the line into my little arm are so comforting. It was a necessary, mind-numbing escape to watch it. To see Mom and my sister, Susan, each night was a blessing.

Mom had a high-paying pharmaceutical job that paid for her to fly out from Montana and be with her almost dead son. Each night they would come in, hang out, and pray for me. My fear was that they would run into my pops and it would become an ugly scene. They blamed him for the crash that nearly cost me my life. You cannot blame someone for helping another reach a dream, but both did. It was hard to imagine life without flying even with death always around. Honestly, I love aviation. The clear liquid running through my IV was pure of defect, as it healed my shattered body and eased my troubled mind. Never did I get past a sixty-drips without falling asleep. When my eyes popped open, my mind would dig for the next number, but for the life of me, could never remember it.

The fear of dying does not leave when you are in the healing environment of the hospital. The fear became a constant. The thought of living in death's house was always there in my mind. With that thought came the ideology that death could stop in my room to say hi whenever it wanted. Knowing that you are in a place that can save you, if you become critical, builds slight comfort. I was at a point of thinking everything would be fine when a nurse came into my room. "Nickolas, the doctor is coming to pull the breathing tube out of your neck in a few minutes." My thoughts instantly went flew to the hot Pilipino nurse that tried to remove my catheter a few days previous. She forgot catheters have balloons on the other end. I had to physically shove her away after the forth yank. Not only was I embarrassed; I did not want her to cause permanent damage. You never know it might work again someday. She apologized fifty times after another nurse reminded her of the balloon holding it in place.

My mind raced with questions about not being able to breath on my own after the ventilator is turned off. What if I stop breathing? My head flooded with nonsensical questions and fear. That machine had been breathing for me for so long it might be keeping me alive and I did not want to die. Not being able to talk was a giant hurdle for me. If I was able to ask questions about the procedure it might have eased my mind. Being a mute was part of this hated healing process. I knew that God did not save me from a massive airplane crash to let me die in the hospital three months later. It was time to mentally pump myself up before the doctor came in. I starred intensely at my IV for a calming constant but did not find solace.

The doctor came in sooner than expected. A week later would have been sooner than expected for me. The doctor might have been death in doctor scrubs. Even though I had talked to myself, I could not block the fear of dying. The single good thing about the breathing tube coming out is I would be able to talk in a month or so. That is if I don't die. My mind was addicted to the ventilator and it knew I needed it. The doc came over to me and said, "Nick, it's going to feel strange when I pull the tube out, but it will be okay." He continued to explain it would only take a second or two and the procedure would not be painful. *Oh wow, have you had a breathing tube doc? How would he know there would not be pain?* I pondered the obvious question at that point*, why did I have to crash the Thrush?* Two nasty chest tubes had already been pulled out. *You got this man*, I repeated to myself. A few snips with tiny scissors and he grabbed the top of the tube and asked, "Are you ready?" Still with slight tremble, I nodded my head.

Three, two, one and I could feel the inside of my windpipe flex as the doctor pulled what looked like long slimy squid out of my neck. A few seconds later I told myself, *all right man, breathe*. To my excitement, my body fell into a normal breathing routine. The only difference was my unfettered concentration on every breath and nothing else. The fear of dying that night was strong. I stayed awake until the medical staff gave me something to make me sleep. The thought of falling asleep, and my mind forgetting how to breathe put me in a fearful place. I was pleasantly surprised when I woke up the following morning to the wonderful sounds of the intensive care unit. Does anyone actually sleep in hospitals, much less an ICU? That could be a research paper. The question that I never got an answer to: why do they need to do blood tests in the middle of the night? I'm pretty sure that my blood was the same in the morning when I was awake. *Rested blood must be better*.

After two and a half more months, just shy of an eternity, of hospital therapy with Nancy and others, including voice therapy, I was released to my pops and mom's house, nestled in a forty-acre apple orchard in Waterloo, Iowa. Although I was ready to leave the hospital I started second-guessing everything, for I did not have the comfort of a nurse at the click of a button. The transition was a change and change was more than accepted in my mundane existence. While at the folk's I had to finish fourteen more months of massive therapy, occupational and physical, just to learn how to walk again and do little things around the house. My step mom was such a trooper to put up with my craziness. I found myself low in life and desperately craved answers about my future. There were no truths. I was proud at that time for reasons other than that of being a pilot. At that point I was not a rated pilot but I was proud that I could walk a little and communicate. I was proud to be living.

Days were spent in pondering my ability as a pilot. I frequently wondered if I sucked as a pilot. Why did it happen to me? I moved into a steady routine of therapy and avoiding depression for months. I had reverted back to a small child that needed to be taken care of. Although appreciative of the help, I felt useless and hated it. It was humorous each morning for about a solid month a woodpecker flew to the corner of our country house where I slept for a wake-up peck on it. That woodpecker still held his pilot's license, I thought. It was obvious the woodpecker did not remember it was supposed to sing in the mornings, not peck the wood on a house. While his noises were completely annoying, I pictured him saying good morning Nick, now get up and go do something in Morse Peck code. My younger brother Ethan, and I just laughed about it each morning. The simplest things could bring happiness to me at that point in life. Life continued as if I had a choice.

One late night I was awakened by a massive pain below my pelvis and feared another trip to the hospital was in store for me. Ethan woke up and asked if I was ok. I reached down to where the pain was focusing its rage. To my surprise and ultimate happiness, I found that I had an erection. It was a revisit from puberty, being so proud of what I had found and did not want to let it go of it. Only difference now was the massive pain like a muscle that had not been stretched you years. The pain was death's simple way of letting me know, I should be dead. At that very moment there was a bright light from heaven was shining down on me. Pop's deep voice traveled across the house. "Ethan, is Nick Okay?" Ethan responded with, "He's fine, dad just has painful wood." Voices came from all over the house. "All right, Nick, you're back." Sleep came more comfortably that night and I felt more like a man when I woke. It was a giant leap forward and a big move towards full recovery. My family loved me and realized the importance of the monumental development that night. They never teased me about it.

Physically traveling through the healing process is extremely more complex than merely thinking about it. Caution must be taken when walking down the healing road. Every step must be watched. The path is littered with negative thoughts and empty answers. I was happy to be alive but afraid of never reaching one hundred percent of whom I once was. I feared depression was sitting on my shoulder waiting to jump in and take over my mind. Depression was a personal battle that only I could stop from ruining what little I had left. This is but another reflection that was carved into my grey matter and will never leave. It is just a circumstance that defines me to this day.

My step mom was there for me without question during the airplane crash recovery. She made all appointments for me and drove me to them all. Bless her soul. She always acted like she wanted to, so I am pretty sure she did. Her everyday life was put on hold to take care of me. I am pretty sure it places her into the stepmother hall of fame. I loved physical therapy because we always stopped for hotdogs after. Once again, little things mattered the most. We spent a ton of time laughing about life. Some people are goal oriented, while some are not. Mom was definitely goal oriented. I was raised with the common sense to step up and take care of the ones we love always. It is the right thing to do. Mom must have been raised the same way.   There was never a feeling of me being her stepson, only her son. Thank you.

CHAPTER TWENTY
Embrace Your Path

Years came and left so fast I knew I would be an old man with white hair before my life resumed in a positive direction of my choice. Every minute, of every day, I recovered a little more looking for any open doors directing me to another path in life. Through everything in this unbelievable rocky life, I stayed focused on moving forward. I question my existence, often wondering why I was chosen to live. Most people never would have guessed that I had been nearly killed in an airplane crash. Most just people thought I had been born with a slight limp in my gate. Daily contemplation about my future as a pilot hovered in my head. I reflected on aviation and what it meant to me. Aviation was still me life. It severely bothered me not to hold the certificate of health that qualified me as a Commercial Pilot. My brother Trevor and Pops would head to the Waterloo airport each morning for spraying. Although happy to be among the living, I was truly envious as they backed out of the driveway and headed out to the airport to fly.

Flashbacks came to me often. They were not of the crash but of me alone in the cockpit of the Thrush, flying past a giant hot air balloon and remembering the happiness that filled my life then. My brain often thought during those long days in Waterloo, that I had let my yellow friend down because I destroyed it. She did not let me down for I was still alive. I wished all of the dead pilots that I had known over the years had been flying a D model Thrush for they might still be alive. Bits and pieces of the crash would randomly appear in my head. One minute sitting on a chair reading a book the next minute in a crumpled pile of yellow metal fighting pain while pleading for life.

Although, I walked with a cane, I was still alive and should be six feet under pushing up daisies. That airplane was completely vertical when it hit the solid ground. The first thing that hit the dirt road was the hub of the prop. The prop hub is the farthest forward part on any airplane. One report stated that the impact was roughly 23Gs. Meaning the impact was twenty-three times my weight, which was 170lbs. With math, the impact on my body was roughly 3,910 pounds of force. The calculation came from broken welds on the plane and my four-inch lap belt cleanly sliced in half. That explained my ribs breaking into shards and turning my lungs into Swiss cheese. Even at that time in life more answers about the crash and all the injuries arose. Floundering around in my personal healing hell, I still found love for aviation. Happy thoughts of flying with Trevor and Troy regularly popped into my head. Walking out into the orchard I would have simple moments of positive reflection. It is so amazing how all of the trees were different in the orchard yet looked mirrored down each side of every row. Sitting in a synergistic row of beautiful apple trees in bloom often reminded me of positive moments from my past. The air always seemed more refreshing in that orchard, when in bloom. The refreshing air helped to clear my cluttered mind.

Thinking about my broken ribs and four-inch lap belt ripping in half made me think of my good friend Jimmy. The day before I crashed, I was bringing the Thrush in from a day of spraying. Jimmy a good mechanic friend who restored old airplanes, jumped up on the wing as I was slowing taxiing by his hanger. He said, "Hey Nick, your shoulder harnesses look like trash. They are tattered and look really weak. I have a new set in the office so park in the back and I will replace them for you." That day Jimmy was an angel dressed like a mechanic. If I had not gotten those replaced, I'm guessing my ending might have been quite a bit different and a lot more lifeless. My shoulder harnesses were weathered and tattered before Jimmy put a brand new red harness in my plane. There was no doubt the fancy red harness had saved my bacon and lessened my injuries. Furthermore, their bright red color made me look a little more like a jet pilot. There was always the beautiful harness to help me look the fighter pilot look.

Another injury that I dwelt on was an extreme compression of four vertebrae, which resulted in a loss of height. I was upset about losing an inch, down to 5'11". The compressed vertebrae had the doctors concerned about me walking again. I had gotten to a point in my life where I had to accept what had happened to me. I would often look in the mirror and say, *Okay man, this is a hard path to walk, but it happened to us, so we better accept it.* There was nothing I could do to change it. I knew I needed to embrace it, learn from it, and continue moving forward. To grin and bear anything of that magnitude was a hard learning lesson to swallow, but it had to be done. The other path of sulking, combined with depression, was not a path I could ever step foot on. Completely owning the crash was necessary and I did not let it define my piloting abilities in my mind. There was overwhelming support in my life from all of my family and friends who knew, and believed, I was still a good pilot. I Understand that depression is a path that some are called to. I know it was not their fault. Depression was a path that I could never be on, ever. Fighting it becomes a task equal to fighting death all that time in the hospital. My depression never hit strong enough to pull me onto its path of self-destruction path.

Some might see life as pure chance or random happenstance. We continuously run into different paths that change our overall directions. Once again, at that time in my life, I was at a crossroads in my life. One path led back to an airplane, or death, as my mother so often verbalized. The second path led to the unknown. The unknown was the scariest of paths. The unknown was filled with millions of horrible obstacles and "what ifs." I thought that life was about taking a chance on life, or mundane boredom. There did not seem to be a medium with no risk. When I compared the paths for any type of selection, I could not use safety as a measurement tool. I already knew how safe flying eighteen inches off the ground could be. The overall safety of a crop-duster was fully understood. The safety of the job was my living reality. The main measurement tools to use were love and passion. Love and passion had the greatest impact on all of my decisions. Determining where my heart was with regards to aviation. Did I love to fly? Yes, of course I do. That question was silly to ask, for all who knew me already knew the answer. Friends and family knew that flying was my love and my deep seeded passion in life. No matter the number of girlfriends or ladies around me, my true love was aviation. Every time I thought of flying, the crash had to be nonexistent, only the power and beauty of airplanes was in my head. Such an easy answer, with every cell of my body, both healthy and damaged: yes, I love to fly and missed it greatly.

With love for flying clear in my head, I had to figure out a way to get back, if possible, to reach my new goal of climbing back into a cockpit. I might never be able to pass an FAA physical again with this broken body? I had three obstacles to get around. My first obstacle, in the line of obstacles was, me. Did I have the balls to return? Was I too inundated with fear to do it? The thought of flying created trepidation mixed with happiness. Any reflection on my crash only caused turmoil and second-guessing about my ability in the air.

The second obstacle was finding an open seat in a crop dusting plane. I needed to find someone who would allow me to fly his or her plane. Understanding how a family-owned company works, I did not think it would be appropriate for me to ask my family to accept my mission of returning back. They would need to channel their fears of me crashing another plane, thus hurting our company financially, or even dying. It was selfish of me to expect them to ever let me fly again. I would have to live with their decision, regardless of the answer. They might say yes or they might say no way. Family is family and there is no changing that. They had all been there for me when I hit rock bottom and needed them the most. I actually hit lower then rock bottom. I was four and a half feet below rock bottom. I would stand by their decision either way. Personally, I had to except the possibility of yet another crash, but I loved flying and felt the pull deep in my heart. The third obstacle was the Federal Aviation Administration. The FAA has medical requirements that pilots must reach to remain certified. A commercial license has stronger requirements with regards to health. I would never be able to reach the health goals of the FAA but I would work hard towards them. I know I am capable of flying again I just need to find a doctor that feels the same way.

With flying wedged in my mind again, I found myself reverting back to younger days, looking for any flight I could build some flight hours on and a few I could not. I merely wanted to get back into the air to see if my passion lived. I did not have a flight medical so I was only flying to refresh my skills. One day, I found myself in the right seat of a beautiful Lear-25 with Mark. Mark was a wealthy pilot surrounded by tons of women, and a wife. Mark looked much like stereotypical rich pilot. Hair always perfect, aviator sunglasses that looked as if they were built only for him. He defiantly had the woman prerequisite in aviation dialed in. We had flown together multiple times in his corporate King Air C90. That plane was amazing also. I mainly knew Mark from the crop-dusting circuit. We had bought the D model from him for Ag Air.

Mr. Mark found he wanting more out of aviation and needed to expand his operation into leather and jet engines. He wanted his role in aviation to be cleaner and more executive looking, not always dealing with pesticides. As we blasted out of Waterloo that day he looked over at me and said, "Nick, if anyone asks, you are type rated in a Lear 25" Still in shock from the massive thrust of that sleek jet, I replied, "Okay" and sat there trying to figure out how everything worked in the busy cockpit. It was a flashback to the 421 in Little Eagle, trying to understand all the bells and whistles. Unlike the Golden Eagle, the bells and whistles were nine times more advanced in the pretty Lear Jet. The Lear is one of the sexiest jets ever designed.

Mark told me we were flying over to a radio shop in Des Moines, so he could get some work done on the stack of radios inside the beautiful jet. Truth be known, we were going out to buzz some random properties Mark had accumulated over the years. At 250 knots, fifteen feet above the ground, you gather a better understanding and respect for, airspeed. When we entered into a four-point roll after buzzing some business in a Lear Jet, I started to question why I volunteered to go. Mark was a great stick and I had full confidence in his abilities to fly anything. The four-point roll freaked me out a tad. On the flight back to Waterloo, a low fuel warning light illuminated followed by a "make your hair stand up" buzzer. Mark assured me that we had plenty of fuel to make it home. I didn't know enough about that Lear to question him, I was not type rated in it, only sitting in the co-pilot's seat wondering if we truly did have enough fuel. Flinches caused by the buzzer, intensified my awareness of the situation. *Here we go again.*

My pulse increased as the loud and annoying buzzer of the low fuel warning system intensified. I was the co-pilot of a fast beautiful jet that I knew nothing about. Between the annoying warning buzzer beeps, I could hear choice words flying out of Mark's mouth and thought how grand it was going to be to survive a crash in a Thrush and die in a beautiful jet due to fuel starvation. *Maybe the thrush was not pretty enough to die in so we will use a Lear this time,* I thought. Death was there on that flight, sitting in the leather seat in the back sipping Scotch. A deep breath of relief came as Mark put the Lear on long final for three-six Waterloo. To our surprise, as we were on medium final approach we watched in amazement as a tiny Piper Tomahawk pulled out, blocking our arrival to runway three-six. As Mark throttled up for the go-around he said, "I sure hope we have enough to get turned around now," through the headset. My palms, moist and clammy as the crash scenarios began playing in my head.

At that moment my mind traveled back to Rick and the Ag Cat crash in McPherson, Kansas. I did not want to be that crash people would say, "They were so close and almost made it back to the runway." I was cursing death for taking something so enjoyable and trying to poison it. With the warning light flashing and the buzzer screaming at us, we returned to short final and put her down on the numbers of three six. Still with rapid speed, my breath paused when the number two-engine flamed out, causing even louder bells and whistles to sound in the busy cockpit. "That was a close one," Mark stated. We only had roughly forty-five seconds of flight left before both engines would have died from fuel starvation. It was such a close call. Mark jumped out of the Lear to get a tug and pull us to safety. He failed to turn the master switch off inside the jet, leaving his petrified co-pilot sitting alone in the cockpit of the Lear with a screaming warning buzzer inviting anxiety. Lear Jets were not for me at that point. Death had ruined the excitement. Part of me knew I would be okay because Mark was a crop-duster. That thought did not stop the fear and second-guessing, however. There was a need for me to start figuring out the entire scenario. I tended to get drawn into the look and power of a plane before the systems that were involved to make it fly or, more importantly, the systems that kept me alive.

I was in love with one of Mark's expensive toys. Believe it or not it was not an airplane or a girl. Mark had a Ferrari Testarossa. That car, much like the Lear, was all about style and speed. One afternoon Mark stopped by the office and asked if I would drive his Ferrari to the airport in Des Moines, so that after landing with his date, they could drive off in style. I agreed because I wanted to feel like Don Johnson from Miami Vice. Just sitting on the tan leather in that white Ferrari instantly made me feel like a celebrity. I jumped in the car an hour early that night so I could test it out a little. After reaching 60 mph in first gear, I knew this car had more power than I would need, really more than anyone would ever need. When I grabbed second gear and she got loose I remembered Mark telling me she was worth over $100,000.00. At that point I backed out of the power and drove more maturely. Only a small percent of the population in the world has a commercial pilot license. I figured less had driven a Ferrari Testarossa. Once again I felt like a lucky man. That car surly made me look good. I was starting to feel close back to normal. The speed in that car created the same adrenaline flow that my D model created.

I had flown with Mark in his King Air, amazing Lear, and with him in the back of Straw Man. Straw Man was another perfectly restored North American P-51D Mustang in Waterloo. I had not fully learned my lesson about flying in aircraft, which I knew nothing about, so I just continued on. Next thing I knew I was in the back of Mark's Canadair CT-33 Silver Star fighter trainer jet. He only had beautiful equipment. At least that bird had duel controls so I could fly it from the back. Several months previously, I had flown to Canada with Chad and Mark, in the King Air, to pick up the Shooting Star. Chad had a massive amount of King Air flight time flying jumpers for the parachute school in Cedar Rapids. Knowing that I was not 100% healed completely, I still found kept myself in precarious situations. It was on the way home that death once again came knocking. Chad and I were flying the King Air home while Mark was waiting for an instructor to fly home with him in the Shooting Star home from Canada.

When Chad and I transitioned back into the United States we landed in Bismarck, North Dakota, at dusk to pick up some fuel. All was perfect until the

181

airplane started traveling down the icy runway near ninety degrees from straight. I knew there would be no fixing this King Air as it was traveling at 70 knots of speed, sideways. The right wing was leading the way to the snowy berm at the end. Looking out of the window on my side, I was looking straight down the runway. Chad jockeyed the prop controls, straightened us out and stopped before we hit the large snow bank at the end of the runway. After fuel we jumped back in the King Air and flew home to Waterloo, Iowa without incident. Over dinner Chad and I laughed about sideways landings in North Dakota and how they should be required for check rides. I am *still so fortunate to be alive.* Once again, I was happy to land at home in a running airplane.

Once the new jet was home, Mark spent an astronomical amount of money turning his stock silver CT-33 into the pristine "Black Knight." When finished, the plane was by far the most beautiful Canadair CT-33 eyes had ever seen. If ever an aircraft represents a female in description, it was that jet. Her lines were so solid, yet friendly. The jet invited you over to meet her the second your eyes caught even the smallest glimpse of her beauty. Her paint was perfect, looking wet, as if you could stick your hand though the metal. What grabbed me most about the paint was the giant red maple leaf on the underside of her. Only when the gear was put up and speed breaks away could it be seen completely. It made flybys more important. The CT-33 had a serious make over and turned out to be an amazing jet. After a few months of it flying and getting all of the bugs worked out, it was my time in her.

Mark and I flew the CT-33 to an airshow in St Paul, Wisconsin. Upon landing in St Paul, the canopy popped open. This was standard procedure on the Silver Star. It acted like a speed break. I looked to my left to see a group of Blue Angel's ground crew standing in line saluting us. They were all standing in front of the Blue's majestic F-18s. I felt honored as chills consumed me, I saluted back from the gorgeous CT-33. Seeing the Blue Angel pilots that night at an air show dinner was spellbinding. Several of them had seen us land the Black Knight that afternoon and had loads of questions about the mysterious beautiful jet.

Lieutenant Johnson, a handsome pilot type wearing a flight suit all know in blue and gold, walked over to me in my Canadian flight suit. He looked at me and said, "Tell me about that sexy lady you two flew in on. That is one gorgeous bird. She caught my eye the second I saw that giant maple leaf during your mid-field break for landing." It was great to hear a Blue Angle pilot compare the Black Knight to a woman. It confirmed my descriptions of aircraft over the years. It was obvious Lt Johnson had a strong passion about aviation. The only difference was he flew one of the greatest military jets for one of the greatest jet teams ever. There were multiple Hornet pilots sitting at our dinner table excited to learn about the Black Knight. It was magnificent to learn they loved aviation as much, if not more than, me. There was nothing but pure respect for the pilots of those sculptured blue and gold Hornets.

We had a great time at the airshow mixing it up with the Blue Angels and other great pilots. On the flight back to Waterloo Mark wanted to practice 270 breaks in the CT-33. A 270 break is a 270-degree right roll to a left hand exit. It is basically a three quarter roll with exit to downwind in the pattern of any airport. Pilots in high performance airplane do this maneuver as they enter the traffic pattern of an airport to bleed off speed, clear the area, and to look super cool. I figured it was nothing more than a rich boy's maneuver to impress. Come to find out, Danny had mastered the 270-break in Ridge Runner so Mark wanted to master it in the Black Knight. It was breath taking to be upside down in the 33 and able to see the earth in such clarity from the polished canopy. My mind traveled back in time to the T-6 Texan in McPherson. Honor was in the air and I felt privileged to be in that old bird, flying her like she was designed to fly. After fifteen 270s we decided that Danny could have the 270 title, we did not want to barf in the Knight so we headed home to Waterloo. Without any little Pipers blocking our approach and plenty of fuel, we lined the Black Knight up on short final for three-six Waterloo.

When the rubber made contact with the runway Mark, in a concerned voice, stated through the radio, "No left brake! We have no left brake!" The jet rolled off runway at a fairly high rate of speed into the tall grass. I questioned my existence again and wondered *why, oh why, do I continue to test fate*? Knowing I would not die, for we were already on the ground, was a good feeling but I did not want to break any more bones if she flipped over. I was unbuckled and standing on the wing before the incredible Black Knight stopped rolling through the deep green grass. I had fought myself from jumping onto the thick grass as we slowed with me on the wing. Seconds were spent wondering if the tall grass would cushion my broken body enough. Mark turned back to see me on the wing and started apologizing immediately. Blame was not on Mark. I blamed myself for once again flying in an unfamiliar plane. After thinking about the incident, I realized I had not even considered the overall age of the Silver Star. While most of it was new with new parts, it was originally built between 1948 and 1959. Even now, that jet still brings a smile to my face when it pops into my head. The Black Knight was the most amazing thing I had ever controlled in flight and I felt honored doing so. Once again I felt that I was pushing my luck but could not find the way out of it. I had already had such a horrible experience with death but I could not stay away from my love. No matter how hard I tried, I was pulled to aviation from every direction. I was addicted to the air.

Time was spent searching for the comfort zone in aviation that I needed. I worked tirelessly on my skills. If the FAA ever decided I was healthy enough to fly, I would be able to. The thought of me flying again concerned friends and family. At that point in time, I am pretty sure that only God and my pops knew that I wanted flying back in my life. My life without represented an ugly divorce where I had to see my beautiful ex daily holding another's hand. In that scenario she was always drop-dead gorgeous. It was the equivalent to being type rated in Mark's beautiful Lear Jet but never flying it. Every time my eyes saw an airplane flying, my uncertainty grew, as did my desire to be in the air again. It's hard to explain that I felt terrified and anxious while, at the same moment, I felt a strong desire and complete passion about my future.

Sherry from Waterloo offered her services to help me in any way possible. Sex was never an alternative or motivator for flying. I was just great sex. Thank you Sherry. Do not get me wrong, with every logical thought about my future flying came with thoughts of another crash where I ended up in the ground in a casket. Death had been near me for most of my life, why would I ever think it was gone? It had already failed so now it had something to prove. Honestly, I think death was just hiding better. It seemed I kept inviting it to hang out with me in random planes. Knowing without a shadow of a doubt, I would not live through another crash, I still had to try. We fall in love with things as we grow up. It happened to be planes for me. From an early age we start to live life in our heads and the outcomes are always glorious. From childhood, I had always seen myself as the retired pilot hanging out at the airport talking airplanes to whoever would listen. Retirement from crop-dusting had already happened a hundred times before I had ever flown one hour. *This is my life and I fully embrace it.* Appreciation will always go to my pops for helping me realize my goals. I was never pushed, only encouraged to do what I love. An understanding was created with myself that I might find death in an aircraft. I did not want that but I knew there was a strong possibility, so I had to accept it to move forward, and I did.

CHAPTER TWENTY-ONE
Mission to Finish

Ag Air had morphed into Rotor Blade Air while walking down the long, lonely recovery road. Trevor had obtained his Commercial Rotorcraft License and soon would be spraying with helicopters. He had passed me with regards to flying endorsements but I did not care at that point. Although my crash caused some financial strain, the company was still growing strong. We had located a Hughes 300C in Fort Lauderdale, Florida, to purchase. The plan was for Trevor and me to fly commercially to Florida, grab the helicopter and fly it home. The flight would be incredibly long but I thought it would be fun. Although I still walked with a cane, I was excited for the adventure. The idea of doing that flight with Trevor pushed me a tad more into what I considered normal life.

We arrived in Fort Lauderdale on a Friday only to find the helicopter had not passed one of the inspections so it be would be worked on all weekend.

While bummed a tad, we wanted her to be tip top for our flight home. We realized to be stuck in Florida was pretty great, with so much to see. We spent our time at Kennedy Space Center, Sea World, and the Doll House of Fort Lauderdale. We remembered that Motley Crew sang about the Doll House in Fort Lauderdale. Our maturity snuck out as we opted to spend a copious amount of travel money on lap dances while tossing out singles. It made me feel even more human as the girls were hitting on my still skinny body. They were only hitting on the single dollars in my hand but it still felt good in my brain. The look in Trevor's eyes was one of pure love. He loved those strippers so he got more money. Thank you Trevor.

Our last day was spent resting for the long flight the next morning. We arrived at the little airport just outside of Fort Lauderdale when Big Dog Aviation opened up. Trevor test flew the Hughes and found it to be in good working order. Soon we were headed off to Iowa, in the little silver bird. I had complete trust in Trevor's ability because his flight training was completed in an identical helicopter back in Waterloo. In addition, Trevor was always better at reading sectional maps than I was. Trevor was a total perfectionist. He had planned out the first day of the trip to the minute. There was a high cloud layer that brought darkness to the horizon. Florida was an amazing place to be in but flying over it in a new helicopter with no clear place to land, made me wonder. It was obvious at 109 mph the flight was going to take a long time to get to Iowa.

We were about two hours out of Fort Lauderdale, just past Orlando, when I started noticing a change in the weather. My senses were relatively sharp on weather changes after that flight with Jimmy through Colorado. Appreciating Trevor bringing me on this trip, I did not want to be a right-seat "worry pilot" and said nothing. The next few words out of Trevor's mouth answered my unexpressed thoughts. "Oh crap, this is bad Nick." Looking out, I could see nothing. We had been completely swallowed by gulf fog in zero visibility. This fog was drastically more solid than any fog I had ever seen. The flight turned into an instrument flight (IFR) in seconds. Unfortunately for us, we were not IFR-rated pilots and the helicopter was not an IFR-rated ship. Instrument flying rules are another section of flying I had touched but not mastered or got licensed for.

Trevor could see a small patch of fogless ground directly out his side window and knew we had to get to it. The feeling of enclosure came upon me. I could only see about a foot out in all directions out of the little helicopter. In Trevor's mind he did not have time to tell me what he could see, or what he was going to do, and slammed the helicopter into a steep autorotation so we could make the tiny hole of clean air. In Panic mode already, when the helicopter entered the abrupt autorotation, I screamed and extended my right arm to brace myself for impact. My vision clouded in with the color yellow as I screamed out loud, "*I don't want to die again.*" My body was not in that helicopter at that moment. For about thirty seconds I was back in my Thrush seconds before the massive impact. "Nick, you in there? Nick! I need your help now!" As the yellow faded into the surreal grey of the present weather, I noticed we were hovering three feet off the ground, but rotating right. The Hughes was drifting in a right turn although Trevor had the cyclic hard left. Trevor screamed, "Nick, push on the left pedal now please." As my foot pushed the left anti-torque pedal Trevor was able to get us on the ground in some random pasture. There I was sitting in the, still running, helicopter in the middle of some field hyperventilating and only getting worse. Trevor shut her down and calmed me down enough to catch my breath. Trevor explained that our spare can of fuel had been positioned on the wrong side of the helicopter, offsetting the weight and balance. If I had not been there inside the helicopter, he thought he would have rolled over and crashed.

We found we were only a few hundred yards from the airport we were shooting for. Walking seemed like the best plan to me but Trevor explained the weather was clear enough for the short hop. When the skids of Hughes entered their small oscillation pattern on the tarmac of that airport, I was done. Completely done! Somehow, some way, death had found me again and had taken me to the point of a breakdown. Never had I ever remembered fear being as intense as the tears started to flow down both sides of my face. I found myself mad and embarrassed. Mad at death for always getting to me and embarrassed that I cried about it in front of my brother.

That was it I thought. I unbuckled myself and grabbed my cane. As I hobbled away from the silver death trap, I told Trevor, "I'm done. Get me a ticket so I can fly home please." He spent hours trying to calm me down. It was not until he told me how much that fog scared him that I started to calm down. At that moment he became my protector more so than a brother. He pleaded with me to continue on with him, and I agreed. We flew a few more legs that day, then rented a U-Haul with an auto dolly. We took the rotor blades off the helicopter and put them inside the U-Haul and loaded the helicopter onto the car dolly. We knew the drive from Mobile, Alabama would only take a little more time than the flight. With my fingers crossed that death hated U-Hauls. That drive provided two days of reflective thought on life. There was absolutely no way you were ever going to get me into a helicopter again. I am an airplane guy only. We were back in Iowa before I knew it and I still did not have life figured out, but it was time to get back to work in Waterloo for my next adventure.

Rotor Blade Air had replaced my yellow D-model Thrush with a big brother model. We bought the R-model in Texas and pops flew it home to Iowa. It was a little younger and a little bigger than the D, but just as beastly. It was just a newer, slightly bigger, version of the D-model I had destroyed. They looked identical from the outside and sounded the same. It was really inspiring to see it and think about Pops flying an R so many years previously in McPherson. Here was one in front of me and it still represented greatness, strength, and reliability. At that point in my life, I did not have an itch to jump in the R-model and go to work. Simply standing on the sidelines of the flying field, and observing, was my path. Life became busy, going to the airport daily to fix my aviation addiction. I was still strung out on planes. I had convinced myself that merely being around the flow of aviation would be good enough for me. Even with that, I felt the constant pull of my passion. A constant life battle of healing and future path selection was my reality. Although, I knew that my healing had stagnated to the point where most doctors considered it as good as it was going to be. I needed to know for sure that my healing had ended. Somehow I needed to figure out how I was going to further help myself grow both mentally and physically into what I considered to be as good as it was going to get.

My world was flooded with fitness and healthy living. While I had made great strides physically, I was mentally confused, questioning my existence daily. Looking down at my chiseled abs and sculpted torso I was still searching for who I was. Each day I mentally accepted that I was lost. I knew deep down my happiness stemmed from flying. Honestly, I wanted to be considered a pilot again legally more than anything. The medical certificate that stated Nickolas was medically fit for his Commercial Pilot License needed to be in my pocket. I felt that I would not be taken seriously if I did not have my flight medical, so I focused everything on that path. A goal, or path, in my life drove me forward. Completion of a goal, no matter how small or mundane it was, truly helped my healing process.

Three long years after my accident I started to jump through the tedious hoops that one must jump through to get a medical back after losing it. That paper represented my existence and I needed to find myself. I felt I needed that paper so people would know who I was and respect my title as a pilot. When you are going through the legal steps, you find a million reasons to think the FAA is out to get you. Truth be known, they are only trying to protect you, as much as others. That is hard to accept when you are the one trying to get your medical back. The FAA requested that I go to a shrink to make sure my head was still normal. Well okay, not sure my head was normal if you think about the profession I had fallen in love with. Crop dusting falls second under explosive demolition expert on the list of dangerous jobs. Fortunately, the shrink thought I was relatively normal and guess what, I still am.

Even after diving head first into that medical process, it took six more months to retrieve my physical so I could be considered a pilot once again. You will always hit hurdles along any convoluted path. If you look hard enough you will carve your way around the hurdles and remain focused on your goals. All of that time, I was in a fight with depression. I had to make sure it stayed its distance from me. Three years and six months after the crash, I became a rated Commercial fixed-wing pilot again. Much like the best Christmas you have ever had as a kid, it was the best life gift to me.

I needed my second-class medical certificate to completely heal my mind. When I lost my medical, part of my identity had been wiped off the Earth. Looking for my identity as much as my medical made that day even better. When I got my medical back, I felt whole and complete again but still lacked the title of pilot in my own head. In my mind I was almost one hundred percent healed. If I could take the controls of any aircraft for one minute, I would mentally consider myself a full-on pilot again. Life opens doors as we move forward in it. It is up to us individually to decide to walk through the open doors of life, or not. I would run through any door to get closer to aviation.

CHAPTER TWENTY-TWO
Crystal Clear

I was a commercially rated pilot again and I started to accept my new life with little flying. I put more effort into women. Knowing I could fly legally if I absolutely needed to completed me. According to the FAA, I was a legal pilot plus I was working in an aviation field that I loved being in, aerial applications. It helped me get through daily life and maintain my focus on whatever my next step was going to be, here on earth. I was ninety percent of what I once was. Living in my new body and overcoming most of the obstacles that came with all the craziness boosted my ninety percent to ninety-nine percent, in my eyes.

Kristy, one of my "four" girlfriends at the time of the accident often came to visit me after I returned to work. She figured it would be good for my soul and mind to make sure I had full use of everything. Being a legal pilot again I was obligated to have ladies in my life. Plus it was much needed. Kristy thought maybe she was the fix that would push me along. Thank you

Kristy, for the reassurance sex and help. Feeling that I was living at such a high percent now in life opened up more the doors in the world I needed to focus and walk through the best one. If one truly believes that they are at the top of their game, they will be. The power of the mind is real, completely real. I know that first hand after living though that crash. I have been changed forever.

As the company continued to grow, we decided to convert the R-model Thrush to a turbine Thrush, an S2R-T. That conversion requires a challenging engine swap from the beastly radial 1340 to a lighter, sleeker, yet less powerful PT6A-20 turbine engine. Marsh was the mechanic to accept this challenge. Marsh owned and operated a maintenance shop on the Waterloo airport. He was the crew chief for Risky Business, a P-51 Mustang converted to a race plane for the Reno Air Races. The name of the Mustang always takes my mind to the movie. Marsh was a cool cat and the ladies loved him. Besides being a good-looking guy he had a personality that would make even the straightest lace laugh. Being a mechanic for a WWII Mustang made him a better mechanic for the job than your average everyday general aviation mechanic. He knew how to make older stuff work better than new. That is a key skill for any crop duster mechanic, for they are always working on old tired out things.

After researching the conversion, I found that even with fifty less ponies pulling the Thrush through the air, she should be faster through tighter tolerances in aerodynamics. As I watched the R mold into a mean looking S2R-T Turbine Thrush, my desire to fly her grew strong. The conversion of the plane was twofold.

The R model got expensive upgrades and sharp paint, and I got my nerve back to fly. When we first got the R model we called it the Texas red neck limo. It had been painted at some point with a roller, leaving the paint texture on it. We knew the conversion would make it new so fresh paint was a must. The conversation was bought from Bill, off of one of one of his planes in Kansas. It was really neat to get that conversion from Bill after flying with him in a CallAir some 16 years back. As I was painting the turbine Thrush a beautiful yellow and black, I wondered when I would fly it. When the turbine Thrush conversion was finished we had turned a bulky S2R model into a younger, sleeker, more modern yellow turbine Thrush. It was now an S2R-T. The letter T stood for turbine, which stood for power and reliability in the minds of most pilots. The conversion also stood for reliability. We had pulled a P&W radial engine off and replaced it with a P&W PT6A-20 turbine. Pratt and Whitney was still a name that represented reliability and safety to me. After seeing the completed conversion, I knew without a shadow of a doubt I needed to test it, much like I had to test Mark's Ferrari. Life had opened a door wide for me and I was running through it as fast as my weak legs could get me there. That Thrush was so sexy.

On a cool morning I drove out to our loading area. I pulled up to the S2R-T and jumped out of my truck. I was immediately hit with the fresh crisp morning air. A big sniff of pure clean air and my vision filled completely with a new, beautiful yellow S2R-T bathed softly in the bright morning sunrays. It was an extremely clear moment for me, a deciding moment. Needing to fly that incredible airplane at any cost filled my mind. *Soon RT, soon, I will get in the air with you.* At Ag Rotors each day was filled with adventure and for a short moment in time, the S2R-T was filed in the back of my mind.

Each morning I thought about the long haul it had been to get me to who I saw in the mirror each morning. I could not believe I had recovered as much as I had. I felt confident in all aspects of my life. Through a series of trades, Ag Rotors ended up with a glossy beautiful Cessna 310. We had traded an older helicopter for the beautiful twin. She was dressed in white with red and gold stripes. I have always found Cessna 310s to be attractive planes with the most amazing looking tip tanks. So perfectly formed and aerodynamically tight looking on each bird. To me 310s looked as if they were flying 200 knots just sitting on the ground. They just look fast. They look like Mark's Ferrari, fast at rest. Although I would have loved to get my multi engine in her, we had to sell her to cover some expenses. Pops said he had found a buyer in Montana and the two of us would deliver her the following day. Pops had received his multi-engine rating fifteen years previously in Kansas. He had not flown a twin, as far as I knew, for about ten years but it was like riding a bike to him. Knowing that I had no desire to ever crash again, or think I was going to, I asked him if he felt confident enough to make the flight. He responded, "Nick, it has a yoke, wings, and two engines. We're good. Do you have any doubts?" At that point I just assumed all was great and knew that Pops was a stellar pilot and I fully trusted him with my life.

Before I knew it, we had the wheels in the wells, headed to Montana, smooth as butter. At 15,000 feet in altitude my pops asked if I had brought my phone and if so to call our friend back in Waterloo to get heading vectors to Montana. Both of us could fly but neither of us was very good with sky maps. Before I hung up, Pops asked me to ask Jeff how to switch fuel tanks in the 310. It was at that moment I realized that neither one of us knew anything about the plane. I had still not learned my lesson. At that point I could sense death in the back seat once again flying with me. As my palms began to sweat I was freaking out in my head. The silent freak out lasted until that right engine sputtered and began to stop. Then I was completely freaking out, in voice. Pops asked me to get the aircraft manual out and look up tank swaps. I was completely and utterly flustered. The information on the tanks in that book could not be found. Whatever, Jeff had explained to us had been lost in translation, somewhere along the line. In a steady dive to maintain airspeed, I gave Pops the book and took over the controls of the 310. He was flipping through the pages as I maintained 100 knots while thinking about our new passenger in the back. It's not fair to love something you can never have. This was going to be the crash that killed me I knew it. The curse words were flying out of Pop's mouth. There I was flying on one engine in eastern Montana wishing I had two engines. What truly blew my mind was the only mountain within a hundred-mile radius was planted right in front of us. With the nose down to maintain airspeed, we were pointing about 100 feet below its crest. How many times in my life would I have to stare directly at where I thought I was going to crash and die? The flight with Grantham in the Beech, the wires strike in the D, and now in a 310 with my pops.

The fright flight in the Beech-18 with Grantham was in my head as I was applying pressure on the yoke to maintain 100 knots and avoid a disastrous stall in the beautiful plane. We were approaching the mountain relatively fast. The stress level in the 310 was off the chart as we listened to that screaming left engine fighting to maintain flight by itself. There was a tree on that lone mountain and I thought how perfect it was. We would be the only people in the world who could crash into a perfect tree and destroy it, on some random-ass mountain in Montana. As I focused out of the window at the perfect tree approaching, I notice something out of the corner of my eye so I turned my head. To my surprise I saw the prop on that dead right engine spin to life and heard my pops repeat, over and over, "Holy crap we did it." Both of us were frazzled, but death had lost another fight. About an hour later we made final approach on Two eight Left Billings Logan International Airport. We had mad it.

We were both happy to hear and feel the tires meet the hot asphalt runway and even happier to pull the mixtures back and kill both engines. What we had failed to do, as pilots, was open the cowl flaps to cool the hot engines in the 100-degree temp. Upon inspection we had fried three cylinders by not cooling them properly. We knew the bad cylinders would reduce the price of the plane, but we would take it. Neither one of us had any desire to jump back in that 310 and fly her all the way back to Waterloo. We would take a lower price and fly home on an airliner and someday laugh about that darn mountain. Death had lost again, but I wondered if it might win some day and take me for real. What fascination did death have with me and why. I was excited to return back to Waterloo and see my yellow turbine lady.

No matter who was at the stick, watching the RT fly was always glorious to see and hear. The sound was completely different with the turbine. The radial produces a rough rude sound while the turbine produces and educated intelligent sound. Hearing the turbine produce 100% of its power on takeoff was awe-inspiring. Nothing can describe the smell of turbine exhaust. Mustering up the backbone, I told my Pops I was ready to move back into the cockpit. He told me that he already knew that I had made that decision without me ever talking about it. We decided that I would go to Michigan where our operation had expanded, in the summer months. While in Michigan, I might or might not fly. I would go to Michigan with my Father with no expectations by either one of us. If the opportunity presented itself, I might or might not make an application in the turbine. If anything, I would just fly it around the patch.

The feeling of appreciation was immediately replaced with trepidation and fear of the unknown. I wholeheartedly appreciated my family giving me chance. Death had been away from me for a few weeks then and I was not in a hurry to see it or feel it again. The fear was built on the fact that I had never flown a turbine and did not want to hurt it for she was too perfectly built. I flew her in my head continuously for weeks before we left. Things at home had changed since I last flew. For one thing, I was married now. I had found the one woman that could put up with my addiction. The second mental obstacle was the fact that Anne Marie, my wife, was carrying our unborn daughter. I was torn between my need to fly and my need to be a good husband and soon good father. I knew that neither would happen if life did not have a synergistic balance. I needed flying in my life therefore I pushed hard to complete my flying path. I said goodbye to my pregnant wife and headed off to Montana. I was the lone cowboy doing his deed for his family.

The next morning it was time for me to strap my butt into that strong yellow plane. Half of my brain was internally screaming: *"Do not do this man,"* over and over in my head. The other half of my brain was battling for peace and synergy by reminding me of my love for aviation. It also reminded me that I was fully trained and capable of flying this beautiful plane in a safe manner. In addition my little girl would need me to provide. My stomach never felt such pain before. The knots were real, causing wonder about my decision. It seemed the mental side of my choice was attacking the physical need for it to happen. My loader that day was my pops. He was there to load the plane with chemical, and furthermore, observe my first application in the turbine. That was my first application since that awful day in 1993. It was more nerve racking thinking about the turbine than my first application day. It can be expected if you have gone through something so life altering that you will tend to overthink everything and focus hard on the negatives. When your thought process is on safety, overthinking is okay.

Much like my first day in the D-model, every inch of this pretty plane captivated my eyes. The smooth lines from the spinner to the tail were solid. Her bright colors stood out in awesome contrast against the mundane colored sagebrush in Miles City, Montana. I looked for death but did not see him or feel him. I jumped in the S2R-T, flipped the battery switch on to hear the gyros start their spin. Leaning out I yelled, "CLEAR" in a proud voice and hit the starter button. The propeller started her smooth clockwise rotation with a high-pitched whine as the prop increased speed. The sound from that engine screamed power, but at that point it was only the starter. That starter had to be extremely powerful. At twenty percent, my left hand inched the throttle forward to introduce fuel for the starting sequence. As the fuel ignited the high pitch whine turned into a throaty jet scream as the power climbed up past 75 percent. With a hearty turbine sound pouring out of the pipes, I knew she was completely alive and ready for work. The chills traveling down my back assured me I was alive and ready for work, too.

The smell of the burning jet fuel getting pumped out of the turbine exhaust stacks was exhilarating. I wish every morning I could walk of my house to smell turbine exhaust. For me, the waft of burning Jet-A fuel coming out of a turbine stack caused me to take a heavy inhale of fresh morning turbine. Most truly it is a smell that I associate with strength, trust, and reliability. I taxied over to get my load of chemical. My loader, Pops, jumped up on the wing, "Nick, if for any reason you don't feel safe, just bring your butt back here. We are the only two crazy bastards out here anyway. Just

202

be safe, son." I nodded that I understood. Pops jumped off the wing as I inched the throttle forward, causing the turbine to speak up and pull us to the active runway in Miles City. The taxi to the active was relatively short but I spent every second of it talking to myself about safety. I knew death was around but would not accept it.

I knew it was there riding shotgun in this one-seat plane. The difference between fear and death is slim. I made the call, "Miles City area traffic, November Two Six-Six Whiskey taking the active zero four, Miles City." When Painting the beautiful turbine, I had purposely left a single 6 number off the side of the plane. I could not see any pilot flying a crop-duster with a triple six N number. The FAA was not as religious as I was according to the fine we got later. Big ticket or not I would do it again. I always tried to change anything that created even the smallest negative thought in anything I flew. A triple Six N number was a giant negative mark in my book. As I lined up on the centerline of two-zero, I inched the throttle forward. Once the turbine reached one hundred percent she began to sing the sweetest melody. The pretty RT began to rapidly accelerate twice as fast as the D model. About a quarter of the way down the runway we popped off the ground and, to my surprise, jumped up in speed to 150 miles per hour, about 35 mph faster than the D. Much like when I was young, on every takeoff, I would still watch the wing drift away from the ground. In hindsight, I was just saying goodbye to the earth.

The turbine was so smooth and so quiet compared to the beastly radial engine on the D model.

It had an era of sophistication. The field my pops set me up on was close to the airport so he could jump in his truck and come watch my application. We lined up on pass one and dove into the field. Fear was hovering in my head. Although, fear was in the cockpit with me, it morphed into concentration for the task at hand. It all came back to me when I leveled off above the sugar beets. There it was, the cushion of solid air that separated the thin boundary between life and death. Throughout that field, the farmer had places large bee houses for pollination purposes. That was common for the area and just another obstacle to avoid. I knew I was high but I did not care. I knew my pops would not care about my altitude as long as I came back safe. Going across that field I mentally processed my turning procedure that was to come at the end of the pass. *Not too tight Nick, just smooth like this amazing engine, nice and smooth.* My first turn at the end of the field felt giant but smooth and I came around diving back into the field, headed in the opposite direction at 150 mph indicated. That turbine Thrush was so fast. Although, I felt high across the field, I still had to pull back to avoid the bee houses. The RT was so smooth and so quiet. I was excited to be right there, right then. *Dude, you did it, you are here,* I said to myself. Although this turbine engine had fifty less horsepower than the crude radial engine, it felt more powerful. It was purely the physics around aerodynamics. This turbine was a lot lighter and extremely more aerodynamic with a pointy nose. My research on turbine conversions was spot on. The long pointy nose up front sliced through the air like a dart.

I completed one load, than headed back to the airport. Next, was the second most important part, and I feared it slightly. I feared ground looping the wonderful plane. My legs were slower now due to all of the metal that held them together. *Dance fast man, move your legs, feel this plane, you have this man.* Tail draggers require a rather fast rudder dance to remain happy on the runway. I was fearful that my damaged legs would not dance fast enough and I would hurt this gorgeous plane. As I lined up to land, I said out loud, *"Please let me make this a nice landing."* The main gear kissed the asphalt runway and I remained glued to the centerline. As the tail started to lower, I remembered the Beta function of the prop. Propellers on turbines have the ability to move beyond flat and into reverse so they push the air forward to rapidly slow the aircraft. This is the Beta function on a turbine propeller-driven aircraft.

When the tail wheel dropped and bounced off the pavement my left hand squeezed the trigger on the throttle control and eased it back in to Beta. The turbine's strong jet noise increased as the prop started biting from the backside, pushing instead of pulling. The airplane slowed dramatically and in a matter of seconds Beta had reduced the speed to 30 mph and I was fully in control. A smile presented itself on my face. At that point, I popped her out of Beta and back to 100 percent of forward pulling motion. We taxied to where my Father was waiting with my next load of chemical. He came walking over to the plane without holding the loading hose. *Well this can't be good;* I was not expecting a praise speech like I was on my first day of flying the D-model. He was going to ask about nosebleeds at my altitude across the field. I smiled grew as I thought about my last first day speech. Okay, let's do this I said to myself and opened the cockpit door. My pops jumped up on the wing and leaned into the cockpit. "Nick, you looked like a million dollars out there. It looks like you have been flying this whole time without a break ever." "You were about a foot off the crop and your turns were perfect." "Keep it up son and let's finish this."

There comes a time in life when a compliment carries you past happiness into a euphoric place that builds confidence. Appreciation for that speech was like none other. I told death to get the hell out of my plane and applied four more loads to complete the job. Almost four years had passed from the dreaded impact in the D but I again found the path in life where I belong. Staying focused and jumping through the door that was opened allowed. That door allowed me to reach my goal. I was once again a true pilot. I was not one hundred percent healthy in my eyes, but I was with regards to the FAA. A little fear remained with me to keep me safe. An energetic thrilled look was glued on my face as I drove back that day. I could feel it. Excitement was in the air and surrounded the great accomplishment that had just taken place.

I had just completed a spray job, in a S2R-T Turbine Thrush. The thought of crashing again was in my head but I would not let it guide me. Death needed to leave forever. There was no desire to orphan my daughter before she was born. On the other hand, I did want to be able to take care of her. It was a battle entrenched in present life, for the long haul. There was no understanding why a battle of life and death was there, so I just stored the thoughts of death in the back of my head. It was clear that only I could go through this yoyo existence with death. Anna Maria could not mentally understand the need and desire I had to be in an airplane. She has never fallen in love with aviation. Learning to live with this fear was normal for I was the provider and I loved to fly. With crop dusting, I could provide for my family while doing something I was born to do and loved doing it. Often we cannot project our love for things in a meaningful way. It takes someone with the same passion to truly understand what you are going through. Anna Maria could understand my love for her only because she shared the same love and passion for me. She could not process the why I had to fly. One can try to explain to those that do not have the same passion why, but one cannot make them feel it. A passion is felt throughout your body. It is a driving force that cannot merely be described to others and equally embraced. It is deep inside those filled with it and only they can appreciate the direction it pulls them. My passion put me back into the air in that beautiful turbine Thrush and I did not expect others to understand the feeling it gave me to fly again but wished they could all feel it.

That was the only aerial application I applied in Michigan. After a few weeks back home in Iowa, my pops asked me if I could go get the RT and bring her home, a flight from Michigan to Iowa. I agreed, thinking 4,000 feet above ground would be much safer than twelve inches AGL. The next morning, Ethan drove me to Michigan so I could fly the RT home. While in the truck, traveling through the wet lush wet landscape, between Iowa and Michigan, a different kind of concern presented itself in my head. It was different to fly a spray plane on a fairly long cross-country flight over the wetlands. The one thought that kept popping in my head was that there was no place that I knew to make an emergency landing. I had never flown a crop-duster above 500ft AGL. To me, an emergency landing basically meant to conduct a controlled crash. The thought of that did not interest me, or my broken body, at all. I would figure it out as I flew along.

Death seemed to be more logical now in my thoughts. I was not an invincible pilot any longer. When I got to the airplane in Miles City there was little peace as I completed my pre-flight. While all looked good, I could not get the Lake Michigan out of my mind. The thought of landing in the water and being okay seemed unrealistic. I jumped in the big RT yelled, "CLEAR," and pushed the starter until her pulse was strong. It was when the turbine fired to life and her jet smell filled the cockpit that I remembered the defining words I had created for that plane: trust, reliability, and safety. The smell of its turbine exhaust invited peace into my brain and calmed me. While apprehensive, I knew this plane would protect me as I lifted off the ground headed for Iowa. The flight was relatively long but uneventful enjoyed the beauty of the water below. I chose to fly direct, which put me over Lake Michigan for about an hour. There was no place to crash t=so there was no need to worry about that.

When the tires repeatedly hit the runway in Waterloo, Iowa, on the last of their four bounces my fingers were trembling with fear. Somewhere on that cross-country over the unforgiving lake I accepted fully that I did not want to die in an airplane. Alone in the big yellow cockpit, those few hours of flight time caused a deep understanding that I was not invincible and subject to death at any time. The flight over the lonely waters did not assure me of safety but allowed me time to ponder death, with all its variables. At that particular moment I was over flying for a living in my life. Spending so much quality time with the yellow RT on the long cross-country home put my luck into reality. There is no way I should be alive. I was the luckiest pilot on the planet, yet I continued to push fate around. I needed to find a different direction right then and there.

It was not for a few more weeks that I had to accomplish the hardest thing to date in life. Already, I had convinced myself that I was out, but I still had to tell my pops that I was done. It was an extremely painful decision because I still loved flying and because my pops had invested so much time and money in me. Not wanting him to ever think badly of me was important. *I am not a wimp*, I told myself. It was hard to articulate how flying over that lake scared me more than crop dusting did. Honestly I believed there was more safety at 18 inches off the ground. 4000 feet AGL would give you way too much time to think about your death as you fell to it. Shortly after thinking about that dilemma I ran into my pops. He asked me why I had not flown for so long. Taking a deep breath with a long exhale, I told him that I was done with the plane. To my surprise he said, "Nick, that's okay. Nobody ever expected you to fly again after that nasty crash." A giant weight immediately flew off my shoulders and I felt okay about my decision. My pops has had the same passion for aviation for about twenty more years then I

209

had. He knew without saying so how hard that decision was for me and I respected that.

As I walked out of the office to go home, I heard, than saw, our new Red Hiller 12-E helicopter on approach. The sound of those helicopters had always been considered bad to the bone, to me. It was a helicopter that sounded like a Harley Davidson on the ground. Being older, I understood their flying dynamics and took them off of my extremely dangerous list. Thinking of Pops flying the Hiller back in McPherson put a smile on my face. This time it was Trevor, and he was testing the spray system for work the following day. He had only had his helicopter rating for about a year and was already spraying with one daily. At that exact moment I had chosen my next direction without even knowing it. The sound of those blades slapping the air was exhilarating. Sound can pull you, a smell can lead you, but curiosity can change you forever. Therefore, I started to jump into any helicopter when I could to satisfy my curiosity and enhance learning.

As Rotor Blade Air continued growing we ended up with an amazing yellow UH-1B Huey for spraying. I was still finished spaying with the thrush, but fell in love with helicopters. The Huey was such a solid ship. Three hundred gallons of spray in a helicopter was an astonishing feat for us to see. She would be ready to spray the next summer. Iowa farmer were going to love us more. At that time, wet weather was in full effect in Iowa. The rain would not stop coming down. The fertilizer jobs were stacked twenty deep in the office. Roads were being washed out and areas were flooded throughout our County. I remember clearly the phone ringing that day looking for a rescue flight. There was a group of construction workers trapped by washed-out roads and rising waters as the heavy downpours continued. It was up to us to save them. While the Huey was being set up to spray, we needed it right then to save human life. For them to make it home to their families that night, and maybe ever, depended on us. The Huey had been used to fly people for snow skiing in Spain before we bought her so we knew she loved to carry people. We also understood the ethical thing to do was save the workers. We pulled all the spray gear out of the Huey so she could be used.

Trevor said, "Let's go Nick." There was no hesitation to jump in the rain soaked yellow bird. As the large blades started their rotation the cockpit oscillated back and forth in rhythm with them. Even with the heavy rain, I could smell the turbine once she lit off. It was raining so hard. Trevor got her up to 100 percent power, pulled pitch, and headed us out to an area the construction workers were building a winery. It is one thing to hear a Huey coming, but to be in one, and physically feel it beating the air into submission, was another experience needed for one to be fully immersed in in aviation. Looking across that massive cockpit to see Trevor at the controls to my far right, I wondered if he had enough experience for this flight. The Huey twitched to the sound of blades slapping the air as her yellow skin danced through the gray stormy clouds. That bird was so large and so powerful. It was raining harder than I had ever flown in and the Huey was relatively new to us. The thought of the great Huey flying through the massive rain in Vietnam eased my mind a tad. Death was on that flight through Mother Nature's power. We landed at the construction site and picked up five workers, all of whom were extremely thankful to us for saving them from a certain death, so they thought. On the flight back to the airport Trevor showed us where the main road had completely caved in and was now flowing down a rain created river. When we landed we reflected on the rain and the power of that beautiful helicopter. We were glad we had that tough helicopter to help people in our community. Sitting proudly on the ramp the strong body of the Huey reflected beads of light through the droplet prisms that rested on her.

It was our duty to utilize our resources to help humanity and we were honored to do so. The flight in that helicopter pushed my mind hard into the rotor-wing world. Needing to determine one hundred percent if I was truly done with the S2R-T Thrush. I thought about all my training and knew that I had already having been through the worst. Therefore, I had to know for sure. Being too close to a passion makes life-altering decisions really hard. More than anything I needed clarity. In order for me to know if I was truly done flying the Thrush, I had to take a break from the airport and concentrate on myself, and my family.

CHAPTER TWENTY-THREE
Apache Troy

To fully accept I was done flying the RT Thrush I had to completely remove myself from the aviation theater. I took a mundane landscaping job with the Cedar Rapids there in Iowa that required little thought and no fear of death. I would spend my day working in Cedar Rapids and then ride the train home to spend time with my little family. One day I received the call from Trevor. He called because he had just gotten off the line with Phil, Troy's pops. My stomach twisted when I was informed of Troy's death. Silence encompassed the room as I delved deep into depressive thoughts. We had gone different directions in life but had remained strong friends. Troy shared the same passion for aviation that Trevor and I had. We had chased the crop dusting dream while Troy had followed a military path. At one point he had come to Iowa to see if crop-dusting was for him, but decided it was not. He became a pilot for the Kansas Air National Guard. Not only did he fly for the Guard, he flew the

AH-64 Apache helicopter for them. The Apache is the ultimate of ultimate helicopters. The awesome look of the beastly helicopter was breathtaking. Troy had matured his jet jockey voice all the way to attack helicopter voice. We were so proud of him, but also a tad envious. There was nothing on my plate but respect for Troy, ever.

Troy was a great friend with a great heart. He had one of the strongest work ethics I had ever seen. I once found him cleaning the cab of his John Deer Combine with a toothbrush on the family farm in Scott City, Kansas. Needless to say, everything Troy owned or operated was incredibly well taken care of. Troy was also a ladies' man extraordinaire. Trevor and I often enjoyed the magnetism between girls and Troy. It is always beneficial to have a best friend who was both pilot and chic magnet. Troy was also a great hunter. Trevor and I loved to stop by his house for antelope burgers. He once sent me pictures of some elk that he located and was going to hunt a few days later. He told me the Apache was a great elk spotter. I sat down with the phone to listen to Trevor about what happened to our brother, from our other mother. I was worried about Gwyneth and Phil and prayed for them to remain strong. I knew his death involved one of the world's most impressive helicopters. We questioned how knowing he was a great pilot.

I found death was not in his attack helicopter but rather his little Piper Super Cub. I had not seen Troy for a while and it seems he had found love and was planning to get married. So it was not only his radio voice that matured, his heart did also. Trevor and Troy had bought a PA-28-125 Piper Super Cub and split time on it. Troy and his fiancé had flown to Idaho, from Kansas, to tell her parents about their engagement. On the flight home they crashed off to the right side of the Afton airport runway in Wyoming and burned. My heart broke hearing that story. Why had death taken Troy, he was a great person and will always be in my mind. The plane was not discovered until the fog lifted hours later. The thought about how they might have lived if not for that evil death fog filled my head.

November three two one Alpha was just another aircraft I had flown to build tail-dragger time in over the years. When I come across that tail number in my logbook now, my mind instantly travels to the great times I had with my great friend. Sitting at the end of runway one two in Waterloo, Iowa, and keying the microphone, "Waterloo area traffic November three two one Alpha is taking the active one two straight out departure, Waterloo." That was the last flight that I made in that Cub about a month before it became nothing more than bent metal and ash. It was a great airplane. Troy was an amazing man and will be remembered that way for life. Anna Maria and I decided to use the name Troy for the middle name of our son. We wanted to keep Troy with us forever. It represents strength and compassion. Most of all it represents both my brother and my son. Troy you will always be in our hearts. Love you brother.

CHAPTER TWENTY-FOUR
Path to Life

I s that another door for me to walk through? *Well, all right, let's do this.* It most certainly took a bit of time to find myself. Over the long haul, I asked myself daily if I was truly over the Thrush. With no solid answer ever found I kept busy in life to avoid the pull. The next six years were spent in an accelerated mode learning how to be a good husband, father, and provider. Deciding to finish my education was a much-needed distraction plus a great experience. Starting that journey so long ago at Billings Community College in Montana, I knew I needed to finish. I hoped to find something that could drive my passion as much as aviation. It was hard to even fathom that thought because aviation was life to me in a complete sense. As hard as I tried, I could not get aviation out of my head completely. I enrolled in Hawk eye Community College in Waterloo, Iowa then transferred to Iowa State University in Ames. At that time in life my son and daughter were at critical ages of needing me. My petite blond wife was always at my side, trying to figure me out while raising our children. It fit my pilot image that I had a pretty and smart blond wife.

I often pondered my life. I was a pilot, if I needed to be. Otherwise, I was a student, father, and husband. In my older fatherly years, okay at 28 years of age, I was extremely proud of my education. Was it a degree or a pilot license that made me who I am? What defined Nick? This was another reoccurring question in my life. I was born who I was. Education and licenses just added to the full Nick picture. Although I backed away from aviation for a brief spell, I could not leave it completely. In high school I remember thinking helicopters were dangerous. As I matured, I found myself intrigued by them. My love for aviation drove me directly into the arms of rotor-wing aircraft. I had been working on my commercial helicopter rating for a while before I had completely pulled back from aviation. I figured I had started the process therefore I needed to finish it. Pops did not raise quitters, and, furthermore, I didn't fear it. Most importantly, I needed to fill the empty hole in my life. Although I was fully entrenched in life without flying, I missed it drastically. To complete my life I needed aviation in it. Even with all the radical blind turns I had experienced thus far, I felt that I had to have it. Plus, in a goofy thought, I knew the helicopters that I trained in were too small to carry an instructor, death, and myself. I worked hard to complete my helicopter rating.

Irony seems to live in aviation. It seems always present, much like death. Next thing, I found myself in a Hughes 300c helicopter shooting a confined approach with a Federal Aviation Administration examiner on my Commercial Helicopter License check ride. At the same moment I was physically flying through my FAA Commercial Helicopter check ride in Des Moines, John, one of our helicopter pilots, crashed in the Bell Wasp outside of Waterloo. At the same point I was starting my helicopter journey he almost completely ended his.

When I called my pops to toot my horn about passing my check ride, the tone instantly changed when he told me about the helicopter crash that had happened only an hour before. I still cannot believe he crashed at the moment while I was on my check ride. He might have been trying to steal my thunder. The thought that came to mind, almost instantly was, *Okay well that was fun. I will never need this thing,* looking at my temporary license in disbelief. John was flying the Bell-47 Wasp when a pitch-change link broke, putting him in a vertical position ten feet above the ground moving at 30 mph. The saying, "what goes up must come down," came into full effect as the helicopter settled to the ground tail-rotor first. While the helicopter was destroyed, John was okay. John had to have felt Death's knock on the door of that battered helicopter. I am truly glad he did not answer it that day.

People who know what I have been through ask me why I have kept aviation alive in my life. The simple answer is, it never died. Only I had physically died, not my passion. Although I was done flying the big yellow airplanes eighteen inches over crops at 150 mph, I was not done flying. After I physically quit spraying with the Thrush, I never stopped flying it mentally. My mind often drifted off into a sharp yellow world. I felt slightly emasculated every time I saw a crop-duster flying. Thinking back on it, I knew it was a form of depression trying to attack me. Although no one ever judged me for not flying the yellow plane, I could not help but judge myself. While I knew that I had stopped spraying due to my fear of death and my young family, I felt that I needed to follow my heart to be able to truly embrace happiness in my life. Also, I needed to mentally run through every scenario of catastrophic failure to feel I was prepared to move forward. Each time a door opened showing a new path to me, death would find a way to kill the happiness and shut the door.

It was not too long after Troy's death that we heard that Bill had been killed air racing in Reno. Wow, was the only word in my head to describe what it felt like to have two good friends, two exceptional pilots fall into death's grip within months of each other. Darkness fell upon the room as the depressive spirit entered again. Before my head could get to the how and why of it, I mentally went back to my childhood and was sitting in the A9-CallAir with Bill, flying in rough formation with my Pops and Trevor, over some random crops headed to some beat-down old gravel strip. It was strange that Troy died at the Afton Airport where the CallAir factory was. There was now one airplane that stood as a reminder for two great pilots. Bill had more hours than all the pilots I knew combined. Well not more than my Pops, I was sure. The S2R-T Thrush conversion was designed and built by Bill and his pops, Stan. Bill had fallen in love with air racing in Reno, Nevada. The Reno Air Races became his hobby. Bill's race plane was a formula one Cassutt. It was so small I jokingly called it, the formula one casket. I regret ever referring to his plane as that, for that is what it became, his casket. His race plane was so small, just one man and speed is all it was built for. He named his plane, "The Rya" after my little sister.

I found it confusing that Bill would pick such a dangerous hobby, as he was a crop-duster by trade. His youngest son, Travis, like Troy, had been killed in a Super Cub. Travis died after stalling over a set of wires shortly after engine failure while checking a field. Dale and Mac, two of Bill's brothers, had already found death's clutch while crop-dusting. Furthermore, Bill had already been in some terrible crashes over the years. Every crash, he was involved in, should have killed him multiple times over. In one story Bill was flying by the river outside of Great Bend Kansas when he saw some women sunbathing. He performed a fly bye so the ladies could see him. He turned left instead of right into the side of a bluff. He had avoided death's grip until now. In another story, Bill had fallen asleep one night while in the middle of a turn in his turbine Thrush. Besides him being a great pilot, his Thrush was incredible. It was powered by a dash ten Garret Turbine. On the wing tips of his Thrush, "Suck and Blow Screamer" was stenciled in black on the Thrush yellow paint. Shortly after his power nap began that night, he woke up just to witness the impact of his Garret Thrush and the ground in the pitch dark of night. He was okay due to the shallow approach in which it hit but lucky he was not killed. After that crash, his wife brought him dinner in the middle of any night job. Good on you, Shellie.

Come to find out, on one of the tight turns on the fast racecourse in Reno, a plane behind Bill's entered the turn too hot. The pilot of the other plane was unable to slow down, or pull out of the way, before chopping off the tail of The Rya, sending Bill to his demise. I knew death was flying the other plane. It seemed aviation was still surrounded by death, but I could not accept it as fact. I needed to understand all the different scenarios that were involved for every crash. Then, and only then, could I move forward positively in aviation. The thought of becoming an accident investigator entered my mind, for I had seen so many. Unfortunately, there is no flight time in that job. You will be missed Bill.

I had to research the helicopter crashes that my father, both brothers, and our hired pilots, had been involved in over the past years. There were six helicopters completely destroyed while spraying, and not one pilot seriously injured. Well there it was again, crop-dusting was extremely dangerous and death loved aviation. John did need stitches after he crashed my favorite helicopter of all time, the yellow Huey. John was the only one out of all the helicopter pilots that needed to go to a hospital. I always had to consider my wonderful hard landing in the D-model Thrush and my lovely hospital vacation. No weight could be placed on my crash because it was, my crash and I was the one searching for understanding.

That intense observation day is just another memory tattooed on my brain. Pops asked me to go out and observe John on his first spray job in the UH-1B Huey. We all loved that helicopter. I remember it being perfect for crop-dusting mainly because it was painted yellow and was so strong. Yellow seemed to be the main color for crop dusting equipment. John was a great stick and that helicopter was beyond awesome. The Huey represented decades of reliability and strength. You could hear the sound of the blades slapping the air a long time before you ever got a visual of the big Yellow chopper. Each time I hear the unique sounds of a Huey rotor system, it mentally takes me to all the Vietnam movies I have seen over the years. Furthermore, it makes me think of all the unbelievable stuff my pops had gone through in Vietnam, at 17-years of age. On that crisp, calm morning I could hear her echo in the quiet valley a good three minutes before I ever saw her. The sound traveled faster than the strong helicopter and always created a show.

John got to the sugar beet field and flew the Huey down into the southwest corner headed northeast with spray on. Everything looked really solid. His height was perfect. John had been an instructor in Montana, so his smoothness was almost expected. He pulled up into his turn at the far end of the field when, to my surprise and fear, the giant tail rotor and gearbox flew off the back of the helicopter. There was nothing I could do at that moment but watch death take the controls of the Huey and try to kill John. As the tail rotor flew away, the helicopter started spinning hard left. The turbine was screaming loudly as the Huey hit the ground in an unpolished manner. When the Huey made contact with the ground the blades tore through the tail boom at the rear, splintering halfway off the helicopter. My perspective about parts leaving a helicopter was right on. Anytime a part leaves a helicopter, it's bad. There are over three hundred moving parts on your average helicopter, all of them wanting to fly off. When it all came to a complete standstill, the engine was still at full power screaming loudly at max RPM. The bright yellow hulk of a Huey looked a thousand times brighter sitting in the vivid green sugar beet field and missing so many parts. The engine seemed to be calling for attention. I could not believe what I had just witnessed in that field.

The sound of the screaming engine brought fear of an impending explosion. *They all blow up,* I thought. It was the sound of death screaming to me. The carcass of the Huey was a good two hundred yards away. I knew I would find death in the yellow metal screaming coffin. The thought of death consuming too much of my life ran through my head. I could not seem to find peace in aviation. John was a great man. I wished I could have run to the crash site but that damn Thrush crash ended that ability. *"Faster man, faster, he might be alive."* I walked as fast as my broken-down legs could carry me to check on John. As I hobbled across that bright green field, I pleaded with God for John to be okay, hoping that I was wrong about the impending explosion. Soon I was at the screaming, crumpled hull of the Huey and was thrilled to see John moving around. "John we have to go now," I screamed. He got out and looked at the crumpled yellow Huey sitting broken and singing loudly in the middle of that green sugar beet field. "Nick, did you see that? That was one hell of a ride." As upset as I was, to hear that come out of John's mouth put a smile on my face. I had never heard him say hell because he was a strong Jehovah Witness and never cursed.

Once away from the broken beast I noticed an almost perfect circle indented in red on his forehead and nose. John told me his elbow really hurt so I asked to inspect it. When he lifted his arm and bent it, the bone popped straight out of the skin and pointed itself directly at me. Instantly I felt worse seeing that bloody elbow mess. When we loaded John into the ambulance I thought about death some more. Jehovah Witnesses are not allowed, through their religious beliefs, to receive blood transfusions. I thought about John surviving that insane crash then dying from needing a little blood. He went to the hospital for stiches, then home the next day. We were all sad about the Huey but happy John was okay after the crash. As soon as we saw him alive and walking around, we each individually asked him if it was, "one hell of a ride?' He did not see as much humor in that comment as we saw in it. We discovered the circle imprinted on his face was caused when John's head impacted the airspeed indicator gauge. I asked him if he could actually feel how fast he was flying. He did not enjoy that humor either.

John scared me bad that day but he is still flying today in Billing, Montana without incident. Watching that crash still did not drive me away from aviation but pulled harder. With regards to other crashes, they were all able to walk back, or drive back to the airport, jump into another helicopter and finish their jobs. I was the only pilot at Rotor Blade Air within inches of not returning to life after a crash. I was the only pilot to dance close with death and be able to talk about it. Well, I did want to be the best at something. I guess I turned out to be the best airplane crash test dummy in the family. Sick way to look at it. I had to completely step away to see if it was possible, so I did.

CHAPTER TWENTY-FIVE
Lost Passion Found

Anna Maria and I had started an educational life in the Iowa. I became a high school teacher and Anna Maria a substitute teacher. It seemed right that we both fell into educational positions considering we had waited so long to finish ours. No matter what was happening in my unbalanced existence, a pause would happen each time I saw a helicopter and a smile would appear on my face. Being away from aviation for so long was extremely difficult as if I lost a twin brother or something extremely special in my heart. I replaced flying with education but it did not fill the vast void in my heart and soul. My first teaching position was at a charter school in Des Moines, teaching Aviation and Aeronautics. Des Moines was an hour commute from home so almost two hours each day on the road. I considered it two hours of reflection each day and it was much needed.

On the hour-long drive home from work one day, I saw a beautiful black and white helicopter right off the freeway at a tiny little airport off the road. Come to find out, my pops and Ethan had started another helicopter company, Silver Springs. They had a beautiful Bell OH-58 Charlie model, the military version of the Jet Ranger. It was relatively soon after seeing it that I found myself strapped in for a ride in N290HP, the OH-58, with my brother Ethan. Multiple things that day roped me back into where I needed to be. When Ethan opened his door to yell "CLEAR," it took me back to a hundred different flights instantly. The sound of the Allison looking for 100 percent power put me directly back into the S2R-T Thrush and the perfect Huey. The main trigger that pulled the hardest on my heart was the amazing jet smell pumping out of the exhaust stacks of the Allison 250-C20B. That smell instantly put me back in the air without even leaving the ground. I was getting hooked but I wondered if Anna Maria would understand.

Ethan had been working on his helicopter rating shortly after I stopped flying the turbine Thrush. It was in his blood as well. He was a great stick. Ethan asked me to make the radio call to make sure I still knew how to do it, so I did. *"Vinton traffic November two Niner zero Hotel Papa is a helicopter taking the active straight out Vinton."* About five minutes into the ride Ethan put his hands down and said, "She's all yours brother." I quickly grabbed the collective and cyclic and away we went. To my surprise, and to his, I was smooth on the controls. It had been well over a year since my last flight in a Hughes 300C for my check ride. When you let go of the stick in an airplane, it continues as it was, in straight and level harmonious flight. If you let go of the controls in a helicopter, dysfunction takes over and you had better get back on them rapidly or the helicopter will beat itself out of the sky. My helicopter instructor, Robert, explained to me that airplanes want to fly while helicopters want to crash. Deep down I guess I had always known that, but I had seen too many crashes where no physical harm had happened to the pilot. I knew they were safer than planes because they were slower, so I thought. Robert had been flying for years, all in helicopters, with not even a close call. If you look for Robert these days you will find him in a UH-1H fighting fires in northern California.

That OH-58 Charlie model was the most incredible aircraft I had ever had control of. It was so strong and felt so solid on the controls. While the Black Knight was the most amazing jet I had flown, that helicopter was a close second. I did not know enough about the Knight to ever think I could fly it by solo. It is hard to think about how it ended up. The Black Knight is no longer with us. Mark sold it to a man in Colorado. The new owner piled it in short of some random runway, destroying the plane, the owner, and his wife in the impact. That jet will always be a top-notch aircraft in my head. I treasure pictures of it.

I felt I could fly the 58C if I needed to. I would want my pops, or Ethan, to walk me through the start sequence of course. Something about flying a retired military bird created historical security in my mind. I spent time thinking about the hundreds of men who learned to fly in this helicopter at Fort Rucker and I honored that. Flying this helicopter brought back the same feelings I had in the Beech-18, P-51s, and the T-33. Protection and honor were always in the air. Death was not near me on that great flight, in that great bird. Over the years I thought death gave up on trying anything with N290HP. Too many pilots had cheated death in it already so why would death waste its time now? That moment is still so clear.

It was over at that point. I became completely intoxicated with helicopters. Flying that beautiful bird was the new life direction that I had been searching for. It was a new path to fill and my old addiction. It was the needle on the compass pointing to victory in my life. I knew that selling it to Anna Maria would be difficult but figured her love for me would accept it. Soon I was hitching rides in any helicopter to build my rotor hours. I reverted back to my past strategy to complete this path. I jumped in with pilots I trusted to build those dreaded hours. If every hour starts with a smile and ends with one, dreaded is not a word that can be used to describe glorious flight time. In the pitch black of night I would find myself flying slowly over crops to prevent frost accumulation with Ethan, Trevor, and good friend Bret. One night I jumped into a beautiful blue Jet Ranger owned Ethan. I jumped in and we pulled pitch. To my surprise the voice coming over the intercom was not Trevor's. I was so excited to go fly I did not recognize the pilot was not Trevor, nor a man. It was Trevor's ferry pilot Clara. She was a good stick and it helped that she was hot. I did not feel the need to tell Anna Maria I had flown all not in a beautiful helicopter with a beautiful woman. Truth is it was fun and made me laugh to think about but I was there for the flight time only not the sexy pilot next to me.

Frost control is another type of flying that helicopter pilots can do to build time and make money while saving a farmer's crop from freezing. Most of the frost control flying was completed in a Bell Jet Ranger. Much like the 58, those helicopters were solid ships and turbine-powered to boot. You can jump out of a Jet Ranger in the middle of the night at 32 degrees, get a strong whiff of turbine smell plus hear the powerful turbine screaming and all is good.

Trevor owned a helicopter company within an hour's drive from my house in Waterloo. Somehow, somewhere, he found a Bell UH-1E Huey to spray with. In that E model Huey I fell really important making the call, "Fairfield area traffic, November six one four Zulu is the white Huey on the ramp we will be departing south, Fairfield." That Huey was a mind-blowing helicopter. The strongest helicopter I had ever flown. It will always be rated high on the ultimate helicopter list in life.

While Joe's T-33 and Lear were the ultimate gorgeous ladies, Trevor's helicopter was the manliest helicopter on the planet. It smashed our B model in coolness. Just sitting in that bird with the engine running brought a feeling of importance to me. The E-model was a standard Huey with an AH-1 Cobra helicopter rotor system. Not only did it have the beastly smell and power, the Cobra rotor system amplified the amazing slapping sound of the blades. That Huey was strong enough to carry a full load of chemical, full fuel, and both Trevor and I. I was able to fly in the Huey with Trevor or Ethan building time doing so. I would be the pilot in command during ferry flights between fields. While the Yellow B-model that John crashed was awesome, the E model helicopter was beyond awesome and into awe-inspiring. When you fly the E-model Huey the only word that hovers in your head is power, followed with more of the same word. It was big and mean but flew like its younger brothers, the Jet Rangers. It was extremely responsive on the controls.

It was strange one day after flying the manliest helicopter I went to fly one of the smallest helicopters I had ever seen. That particular helicopter was missing the "manly" part of it. One day, after flying six hours in the Huey, I traveled to Iowa Falls, to fly a Robinson R22 with my friend Todd. Wow, that helicopter had some masculine issues. It is such a tiny little helicopter with a tiny little piston engine. The R22 is an extremely popular helicopter in the flight-training arena because hourly costs are relatively low. On the other hand, the R22 has no popularity in my world of flying no matter the hourly cost. It is too darn small. One thing that I needed to remember was that an hour in any helicopter was an hour in my logbook. Liking the helicopter was not a requirement, only time building was.

Passion was once again alive in me, filling my soul. Other pilots' help was needed to complete my mission. While I needed their help I did not want to be a burden on their busy schedules. Moving forward into aerial applications with helicopters was the next step. Round two, in life. I had arrived and I was ready. Round one was all about planes while round two was all helicopters. Every time I thought about my path, I questioned myself. Was I truly going to move forward in that occupation again? The simple answer was; yes, I was. Crop dusting was still considered ultra-dangerous, but I always thought about the crashes where the pilots' just drove back to the airport jumped in another helicopter and went back to work. The long time spent in education had created a distance from my immediate fear of death. Therefore, I knew it was possible to follow my passion again. In Addition Anna Maria was backing me wholeheartedly.

During the winter months of 2013-2014 you could find me strapped into a beautiful turbine helicopter flying slowly over some random crop in the middle of the night, preventing frost on blueberries. Those flights were excellent leaning experiences, not simply a way to build time. On the days not teaching high school students in Des Moines you would find me flying the Bell-47 at Bret's Flying Service. Summer was close, as was an open pilot's position in the Bell-47 G2-A1 from good friends of the family. Next thing I knew I was the new pilot at Bret's in N47GA. It was great that I was flying a Bell-47 with an N number that has a 47 in it. I flew on weekends plus any day off from teaching, which was never enough.

Bret and Larry had spent a copious amount of time teaching me their style of flying and the company's crop-dusting techniques. I had known all three brothers Bret's Flying Service for years and I knew they trusted me with their equipment, as I trusted them with my training. Here I was once again walking down that path with a permanent smile on my face, but also with a logical thought of flying into my death. Understanding death from a mature view allowed more concentration on my flying. If my focus was on safety death would grow tired of me. Summer was right around the corner and in my mind I was beyond excited to be able to fly daily and consider myself a full time crop-duster once again. At that point in my life, death was not riding shotgun with me, only safety was. Still I saw myself as roughly 99% healed from the plane crash and I knew helicopters were considered safer. There was something so nostalgic about flying a Bell-47. A helicopter designed so long ago, yet still such a solid platform. With all new parts, it was more like a Bell-2014, not 47. The same style of memories filled me when flying the 47. Much like my flights in the Beech, P-51 and T-33, the 47 was a nostalgic piece of history. Looking out of the polished bubble gave the illusion that you were just sitting outside. It was an extremely solid flying machine. I flew hundreds of hours in all types of helicopter to build my time and to gain respect as a pilot. To me, she was as solid as any other helicopter.

Besides spraying the crops and frost control, I had also been flying for a company part-time as a co-pilot in a corporate AS-350 B3 Astar with pilot friend from Cedar Rapids, Gary. He was actually from London so we all called him the "Limey." *There is just something about people from London that you have to like.* Gary was so polite and so proper. He was also a handsome man and a great pilot. *Younger handsome pilots get better jobs.* Much like the E Model Huey, I felt proud to make any radio call in that bird, "Cedar Rapids approach, November Niner one Delta Sierra is a Astar helicopter three miles out for landing, Cedar Rapids. The day I received my first co-pilot paycheck from the Italian family company that owned the classy Astar, I felt that I completely back and ready to take on the world.

The beautiful helicopter was painted in the colors of the Italian flag. The company was Italian so it seemed right. It was not hard to see a big green, white, and orange helicopter coming your way. In my mind she was perfect, for I had never flown a helicopter with leather seats. Often I would jump in the back while waiting for passengers to see what it felt like to be rich enough to fly in leather. It felt better to have the controls in my hands. Leather just moved me up a respect notch in my crazy aviation mind. At that point in life I was married, therefore I already had a woman in my aviation prerequisite covered. Meaning, I did not have to chase the ladies, leaving more time for flying.

That helicopter jumped me right into corporate flying, so I felt. The leather seats and the power of the systems were beyond incredible and created a feeling of security mixed with happiness. I wished that I could have called Troy to brag about the Astar. He had beaten us all already with the Apache, but I still wished he was here. The reputation of the Astar was strong around power and reliability. Getting my first check, I thought, *"I am truly back as a pilot for hire."* What better helicopter to fly than that rock solid one point five million-dollar Astar? While it was awesome, it was not my 47. I often wondered if I would ever want to go fly the Astar by myself. There was no desire to do so for it was worth so much. My Bell 47 was simple in its design and function. When I flew the 47 she felt like an extension of my body.

CHAPTER TWENTY-SIX
Full Steam Ahead

S ummer came, as did my new full-time flying position at Bet's Flying Service. It was good-bye high school students, hello bugs and weeds. At the start of the season, a simple hundred acres felt like ten thousand acres. Soon I had built up my physical and mental strength enough that I could fly three or four hundred acres a day without issue. The road had been so hard to travel with obstacle after obstacle, but there I was. I was a rated commercial helicopter pilot flying a beautiful Bell-47 and there was nothing better in the world. To jump up to 100 feet AGL heading to my first field each morning while taking in all of the vegetation was such a satisfying feeling. It always created happiness in my heart.

Safety was a constant for me. I was now in a helicopter, another high-speed stall would not happen. It had so many moving parts my safety focused on them. The 47 proved to be a solid workhorse. Helicopters were now completely safer in my mind. I knew death was still an enemy I hoped to avoid. Much like the plane, I did not want to do something stupid that would hurt this prestigious old ship. A Bell-47 is a solid chunk of aviation history. I felt so privileged to be flying one. I respected it immensely. Flying a helicopter that has a giant bubble as the windscreen creating visibility for what seemed like days in all directions. I absolutely loved going to work, jumping in my helicopter, and flying a good part of the day. When my alarm woke me, the first thought in my mind was my 47. On the short drive to the airport while listening to rock or country I would visualize where I was going and how I was going to complete the application. Thinking back on it, flying a crop-duster of any kind is dangerous and requires strong physical and mental strength. After flying a long day I found myself relaxed and extremely self-confident. I needed that more than anything.

It made me proud that my fourteen-year-old son, Jackson Troy, was proud of me and proud to tell his buddies that his pops, was a teacher and a helicopter pilot. Every day was different and every day was a great adventure. I was so proud of myself and wanted my family proud of me as well. No matter the outcome, I was a helicopter pilot and no one could take that away from me. I even bought a bright red French Gallet LH-250 helmet to protect my cranium. Man, I love my helmet, and damn, I look good in it. Best $1,800.00 ever spent in life thus far. Well, there was the wedding ring expense that was pretty important also. Putting it on my head each morning took me from average dude to Captain Nick.

I still understood the dangers but absolutely knew that I had graduated beyond crashing again. I completed all flights with maturity. Also, I lived a life of constant learning to stay sharp. If I remained in a learning attitude, I would not grow comfortable and stay focused on attention to detail. OCD about safety was a flaw this time around in life. Finally, I had found the place in this big, and what I thought, dark, world where I belonged.

This time in life represented total completeness. Finding synergy through all of life's turbulence was phenomenal. The turbulence had carved me into what I was and I did and not to need to be anything else. I was a complete pilot. A few things were off kilter in my personal life at the time, but that did not change the fact that I was on top of my flying world. I was so proud of myself and happy to have found my true purpose once again. I was so pleased that my passion had stayed with me through it all. That passion had kept me on course and, guided, me through life. With my passion I knew that I could get through anything in my life.

I love summers, always have. Summer is the season dedicated to crop-dusting. What I didn't like was time off. I found myself getting so mad at Mother Nature for producing wind or the lack of rain. Both wind and lack of rain affect the need for spraying. After a few days off that summer, life seemed so different. I realized we were in a drought but I had just found my path and now must wait for rain. Daily, I found myself over analyzing life. Overthinking about everything is what I tended to do for no apparent reason. Thinking back, I understood that I almost died once in this life already, making it precious to me. The ladies of the past would come to visit me in my mind often. Those were peaceful thoughts. One thought would ram into another thought and then twenty more would smash into that one. My thought process was extremely convoluted and over active during any free times away from my helicopter. That helicopter was the glue that held me together and I appreciated it. To just drive out and sit in it would clear my mind.

Often times the past would blend into the present, and the future was nothing more than a stressor that couldn't be avoided. I felt so free in the air that is why I hated time off feeling confined to the ground. The helicopter was my synergy and without it the crumples of life try to take over. Flying was my escape. Little thoughts became obsessive in my head: did I feed the dog, eat breakfast, or take my vitamins? Honestly, giant voids formed in my life, caused from days off were driving me crazy. I loved flying but it was becoming too much of a necessity for happiness in my life. *I need a beer with my buddies.*

Those days off created such cavernous spaces and empty feelings. I recalled bits of the past but there seemed to be holes in it for I was in my future already and I was complete. I knew I was smart and I have always completed my tasks without over-thinking every little mundane aspect of them. This thinking process is new to me. I needed to go back to work because I felt a tad crazy. One day while pondering the strange things in my life I heard a helicopter flying outside and became increasingly frustrated. I remembered I am really handsome. Not stellar GQ handsome, but I remember looking in the mirror each morning at a self-confident person with a great smile. I found it strange thinking about my looks. Then it transformed into my persona. I remember putting my helmet on and transforming into Captain Nick. The blank holes in my crazy head were still blank. Pep talk time, something I was getting used to with all this time off. Honestly, I thought if I did get back to work soon, I would be deemed crazy by the FAA and put in an institution. Why was that time off so difficult? I loved days off from teaching to be home with Anna Maria.

Time off was not the same when you fly for a living. A day or two off from teaching was amazing but days off from flying were willed with sadness and confusion. I missed my little Bell 47. During this short time off, I found I needed to boost myself up a few times each day. I needed to randomly pump myself up about simple things. I would tell myself, *okay, man, time to focus on the here and now.* I tried to alter my negative thoughts and focus on what I could change and what in life truly matters. Depression from the first crash was on my mind. Something was missing again in my life but I could not put a finger on it. Daily I had to tell myself that I was a helicopter pilot, so that was not missing. Each day felt like another week off. Time was spent in my head thinking about how many days I had been off and how the stupid drought was hurting the crop dusters so badly in Iowa. I needed to get back to work.

It was going to be another scorching summer day. It seemed eastern Iowa was turning into a desert. Would it be 101 degrees in Waterloo again, a question asked each morning. The grass around town had transformed colors from brilliant green to strong golden, dead yellow. In addition, I could see the millions of cracks in the parched soil under the yellow brush we used to call lawns. I could not believe I had enough time in my everyday life to make observations about grass. The weathermen were serious about the drought in Iowa. They are wrong, so often, but they were dead on about the drought. Gazing out the window at the dead yellow back yard, the temperature 7:00 a.m. already distorts my vision as the clear beams of heat radiated off the parched ground. I don't remember it ever being this hot. Then again, I don't remember ever having this many days off between both teaching and flying. My memory was not as sharp as it used to be. Maybe it was an age thing. Never would I have thought, forty-four years of age would hurt my mental acuity. *Least I'm still sexy as hell*, I thought. Those days off were definitely a strange time for me. Something was so off and I needed to gather the solutions. I needed to get back in the air. Was that the sound of another helicopter outside? I popped out of my chair at least ten times a day looking for a helicopter outside.

Seemed life was about thinking about things but never understanding it. It was so irritating. Too much time off leads to too much thinking. I would often lye in my bed contemplating my educational journey and wondering if it would ever change my future. In what aspect would my education guide me and in what direction would it take me, if any. It was a petty and shallow way of thinking. It ran through my head none-the-less, almost continuously, on those days off. How did I get here and why was that question asked daily? What does this world want from me? I should be dead from the dreaded plane, but I am not, I am here. I felt no different from the individuals that ran those pedantic questions over and over, who am I and where am I going? Running through my education to see if there was something I missed in life. I might have needed to find another path if the flying did not pick up soon. Hating time off became my constant. My head never shut up and seemed to work overtime about stupid stuff. I asked multiple times a day, *what is going on with you man?*

So my A.S. is in Instrumentation and Process Control with a focus on Cisco Networking from Hawk eye Community College. It seemed weird that I went tech when I love aviation. I remember it sounded good to me and interesting at the time. My children were little and would soon need a good provider. When I started community college, it sounded amazing. At that point in life, I was creating a new Nick and that sounded pretty good. After completing the AS, the bright idea of never working with automated systems came to me. I then transferred to Drake for my bachelors in Engineering Management. The best part of that Engineering path was taking Calculus and making the glorious move in the business direction. The two programs were an oil and water difference. Calculus resembles a strange foreign language, a mixture maybe of French and Alien. I still remember I had to ask my Asian buddy how to turn on my own calculator. So Calculus was not for me, but I have the ultimate respect for those who live in that busy world and speak that alien language. I loved Drake University. Wait, do I have an EMBA? Yes, I do. It sounds important and flows good on paper but what am I ever to do with it? Executive Masters in Business

Administration from Iowa State University sounds presidential. Driving for that schooling every flipping weekend for eighteen months was not so bad. What doors did that open? I am a pilot and love it. But I am a teacher, and a helicopter pilot. I remember thinking that I had better get my head on straight or the FAA will come and take my license away.

The EMBA opened the door for teaching high school and I had always wanted my Masters. So I also have my teaching credential. Holy crap, I have so much education. I wondered why it had consumed my life when aviation had always been my first passion. I'm in love with aviation but somehow ended up living in education. That must be why I'm working on my Educational Doctorate at Grand Canyon University on line. Doctor Cantrell sounds pretty great. An educational doctorate would really solidify a love for education but I only have a ninety-two-page dissertation on the barriers to Islamic finance in America. I cannot believe I am so close to it though. Finishing my doctorate is a must. I just need some simple motivation to get me there.

I wish my house smelled like the old Cub's cockpit way back in McPherson. It was so motivating. Did something happen in my life? How the hell did I get here and why won't my brain stop asking about it? I saw the deep hole I was in every time I looked at the empty man staring back at me in the mirror. I knew who he was. He did not seem to recognize me, however. I had to keep asking myself these questions in order to stay focused on the present. I thought about going to the doctor and getting some answers but feared they would take my license. It was so difficult to get back after that stupid crash. I had worked so hard to get back. It was scary stuff. I was ready to get out of this funk and get back into the air.

Finally, the call came to get back to work. It felt like forever since I flew. July 2014 and I am going to work. *Boom, finally I get to fly her.* Loving the start of each flying day was common. Getting to the shop at Bret's Flying Service, picking up my work orders, and heading out to my pretty, aged lady, Miss 47. I toss my helmet in the bubble and start my preflight. I would always take a deep breath of fresh morning air? Each morning, of each day, was the same. A routine was important so that I didn't miss anything. Thank God I'm back. The helicopter preflight inspection is beyond visual. It also incorporates a physical aspect. To feel the solid smooth helicopter metal against the skin of your hand confirms there were no cracks the eyes had missed.

Physically touching the helicopter builds a sense of respect and appreciation for her, I thought. She needed to be touched. Feeling the fuel level with your fingertips and seeing the oil level builds comfort. I loved the cool mornings before work, breathing in the crisp air, the quietness only interrupted by a distant moo. Out on the ramp area you would see the 47 and I bonding before flight. After the preflight was completed, I would jump in, on the left side. My pops and Bruce, a cowboy family friend, taught me that you only get on a horse from one side. I figuring it was another respect thing that I would follow, therefore I used it for most things. I only got into Miss 47 on the left side. It just so happened to be the pilot side of the helicopter and I was the pilot.

I jumped in the helicopter, reached down with my left hand to roll the throttle full on, full off, three times. My right hand flips the battery toggle to on. I yelled, "CLEAR" then pushed the starter button. As much as you need to hear the engine fire, you need to feel every twitch and shake as the old bird came to life. The blades start their spin simultaneously as the cylinders start their throaty growl. The blades increase in speed until they create a solid, yet transparent, disk above my head. Looking out in front was necessary to make sure the blade track is tight, with no separation. Then I would run her up for a magneto check. After all the checks were finished, I was ready to go to work. One wrong twitch or strange hiccup and I could just shut her down to investigate. That bird always ran strong. It all balances out and becomes smooth as rotor and engine RPMs marry up to the takeoff power setting. My left arm would twist the throttle to increased power then pulled vertically on the collective to invite lift into the rotor system. Up on collective, a little pressure on the left pedal, and slight dance on the cyclic with the right arm to maintain smoothness. It fascinated me that a helicopter requires both legs, both arms, both hands, with both eyes moving in perfect synchronicity with the pilot's brain, just to hover. With a slight pull on the collective the landing skids become loose. The helicopter pops off the ground, and we're on our way. I picked her up and inched us forward, then headed hard right to get to my first field. It felt so great to be back to work, it had been too long.

Straight east of the shop that morning, I arrived at a new field. Well, new to me, Bret had flown it several times over the years. I had not flown this field before and thought that odd because I had flown so many. It looked wide open, free from any serious hazards. The proximity of the field to the county Airport was close. You could visually see the entire runway at a hundred feet AGL. Approaching the field from the west I made my visual safety observation. I flew around the field in a giant 360-degree counter-clockwise circle. This was the typical way I would check for any hazards that may affect the safe application of pesticides. Sitting on the left side of the helicopter, without the door on, gave me a fantastic visual of my target crop. At this point, I was looking for wires or objects that could hinder the application. There was a set of wires on the north end but they posed no hindrance to the application. The power lines were high enough for me to fly under, make my turn, and return the opposite direction. The field was twenty-one acres, so I would complete the job with three loads of chemical. This was only the second field of corn I had flown in Iowa. I landed on top of the loading truck to find Garrett waiting for me with the first load of chemical on the backside of the field. Garrett disconnected the loading hose and gave me his traditional thumbs up and I was good to go.

Miss-47 loved flying off that truck with a load of chemical. She was so strong and loved to work. I rolled in the power and pulled pitch. With 90 gallons loaded up she would jump off the pad like it was nothing. We applied the first two loads of chemical on the corn. Felt so go to be back at work in my helicopter. It was a relief when first two loads were completed smooth as butter. Flying north and south lines moving from east to west. Having a GPS in the helicopter was so much better than the "airplane toilet paper" auto flagger used in the Thrush back in Fairfield. The north end of the field had that high set of power lines that I flew under, made my turn and return in the opposite direction back under the wire. The 47 turned so tight and strong. I knew she was happiest up in a turn where all could see her. Each turn following each run provided me with an excellent view of the surroundings. When you get to the top of the turn and reduce power to invite a left turn, the engine sound reduces a hair as the blade chopping noise increases. It was seen as a beautiful harmonic balance of metal and power. I was happy to be at a point in my education on the 47 to notice the slightest noise changes. A 50-rpm rise or drop would get my attention immediately.

After completion of the second load I flew us back to the loader truck for our third and final load. I picked up some fuel and told Garret to head to the next field. Garrett gave me double thumbs up as I departed the truck. When I entered the field I was headed north on my third and final load of chemical, diving the helicopter down on the south end of the field and flying north. Next thing I knew, I was finished with the job, and headed home for a nap. Loved my job and thought it was the greatest thing ever. Love flying so much.

CHAPTER TWENTY-SEVEN
Flash Back

D reams are such an epic part of my life. They defined my existence in my coma some twenty-one years earlier, clear as day still. To this day I cannot believe how real they were and how I was living them as truth. "Nickolas, can you hear me?" Seems like yesterday the doctor was asking me the same question. Wait a minute. *Where am I, and who is asking presently? Come on man open your eyes more. But my nap had been so good. Is that Anna Maria over there*? "His eyes are open." *Who is standing with her and where the hell am I? It looks really familiar but I can't place it. Come on man, this is freaking me out.* Wait, this is yet another dream from the Thrush crash, right? I couldn't believe how real they still were. Okay, *man wake up. Dude, this is the longest nightmare, ever.* I decided to go with it and see how real this one was. It seemed strange that I had aged in this damn coma dream.

"Nickolas, I am Dr. Wong.   An attractive healthy Asian woman came and stood next to me. You were in a bad helicopter crash. You have been in a medically induced coma for forty-five days." *What? That is total craziness.* Oh man, I'm in Santa Clara Valley Medical Center once again. *Why was this dream so real,* I thought? She did say helicopter crash, not airplane? *Furthermore, did she say forty-five days not thirty-two? Was that a real Anna Maria over there? All right, I remembered her name and I was pretty sure I was awake.* Anna Maria then came over to me.

Anna Maria moved over to my side with tears streaming down her face. She leaned over and hugged me. As her tear-covered cheeks touched mine, she whispered, "I'm so sorry honey. I love you so much." In less than a second reality hit me like a hammer and I knew it was present time and not another flipping dream. I completely imploded. I could physically feel my soul sink to a low level that I did not know existed. Looking without clear vision while feeling the burn of disbelief, life had changed once again. The pain from the crash was not there at that moment but the pain from the disbelief radiated throughout my entire body. The how, why, and what, questions were coming out of my mouth at rapid speed. Yes, I could speak this time but really raspy. Why is my voice so raspy? Dr. Wong told me to slow down, just breathe. "There was a breathing tube inserted through your lower jaw for a while at the other hospital." *What have I done to myself?* A blanket of emptiness draped over me. My smooth breath was gone, leaving only a hyper breathing rhythm. A heavy weight sat on my chest as my heart sunk to a dark lost, world of loneliness. Seventy-seven days of my life has now been spent in a coma thus far. The coma was considered a total waste of time.

Why?   Why am I here again?   What have I done so badly in life that I ended up back on a lonely recovery road? I had already walked on a painful road for so long in this life. *Why did I need to hike the path again?   Was death flying with me again?* Although I had not noticed him he was there and I avoided succumbing to his final wish once again. I am going to be the guy that dies some stupid death. I can hear it now man chokes on sweet pickle and dies. How did it miss again? *Come back for me. I am ready, death, just flipping take me.* I needed to put it into perspective that I could understand. I had finished the field and went home for a nap. That would have been great, but it is not a logical scenario at all now. So what really happened and why?

On the third and final load, I flew directly into a randomly placed, and hidden, guide wire. The guide wire is a three-quarter-inch, woven steel cable, designed to provide strength and rigidity to power lines. We have all seen them sloping diagonally off the end of power lines. This wire was sitting at 12.5 feet above the ground between poles three and four. The 47 hit the cable in the middle of the bubble, at 55 mph. The cable folded the helicopter in half, with me along for the ride. Bleeding in a crumpled pile of a burning Bell-47 in in the middle of a sweet potato field next to the corn I was spraying. Why did I live? Was death playing with me because it could not kill me? I'm destined to die of old age. The fire was intense and the destruction complete. *Why, why me?   Death, are you flipping kidding me? You suck at your job, Death.*

To hear that two random strangers pulled me out of the burning hulk was pleasing. It proved to me there are still good people in this dark world. Mr. Shepard was playing with his daughter when he heard the impact. He ran out, assuming I was dead after seeing the destruction. When he arrived at the hulk of burning twisted metal he saw my chest expand as I fought for air. Mr. Shepard, along with another nameless individual, pulled me out and laid me aside until emergency personnel could get to me. As bad as the helicopter was burned it was obvious they saved my life. I hope someday to repay the deed somehow.

It was ironic that I was the first medical flight for the pilot of the RescueOne Bell-407 helicopter. I already had two hours of flight time in a Bell 407, which made the EMS flight better. RescueOne is one of the largest helicopter air medical companies in the United States. The thought of getting destroyed in a helicopter crash than saved by another helicopter is pretty awesome. Helicopters serve a great purpose but, unfortunately, they are not cable proof. Once again I felt horrible for destroying Bret's Bell-47 and putting me back on a twisted recovery road. *I can't believe I'm twisted up again. Really, I need to know, what I have done so wrong. I was only following my heart.*

My injuries, while bad, were not as physically ruthless as with the airplane crash, but then again I was only flying at half of the speed of the Thrush. An open fracture of my left humorous and a broken shoulder caused major bone injuries. A few fractured ribs, fractured face and, worst of all, a traumatic brain injury. My jaw had been wired shut to keep the new metal in my cheeks and nose stationary. The left humorous tried to leave my body during the impact but the doctors were able to screw and plate it back into position. This body now has two skeletons. The original skeleton that God had created for me and a man-made skeleton that was holding God's together.

The physical injuries failed in comparison to the mental. In my book there is nothing worse than a head injury. Over thinking everything and second-guessing myself until I was out of breath became the norm. There is no smell and no taste in life now. My vision lacks left peripheral in both the right and the left eyes. The blank field to the left has a strong resemblance to my existence now, dark and empty. It could also represent my future, blank and without shape. I had to push on again. I had to start a third path in this life to find myself.

All that time off felt much like a head injury coma dream. Now, I truly understand how depression attaches onto the soul and guides people to evil places. I was situated in life once more wondering what was real, and what my mind had designed for me to live now. Another rocky path of healing verses living. *Will this be years of my life again?* How could death have missed again, and why? *Don't be a chicken, death, come back and get me now. I am over this path in life. I'm still in the hospital so stop my heart. I am ready.*

Once again, I was excited to see friends and family as my mind started to remember things. Ethan came into my room one day. It was odd for him to ask me, "Are you here Nick?" He was looking straight at me, so I thought it was pretty obvious I was there. "I'm just making sure you know you are in Iowa and not still flying in China." I didn't know how to respond to that.

251

"Nick, last time we talked you were flying special operations for the Chinese government." I responded, "Ethan, I have been in a coma for 45 days. So no, I was not in China." Ethan informed me I had been talking to everyone about wild crazy things for weeks in my coma. I had been dreaming out loud during this coma. All visitors got versions of random stories concocted in my coma sleep. I was flying a BO-105 under special assignment in China. It was hard to accept that as truth.

Listening to all the different stories that I told while in a coma it was obvious my passion for flying had remained strong though it all. My memory had massive holes in it. For the life of me, I could not remember what my house looked like or where it was located. The dreaded head injury would be the end of me, I was sure of it. Doctor Holms, my orthopedic surgeon explained that he had come to see me five times, not to check on my arm and shoulder but to see where I was in my stories. I could not imagine I had talked to anyone without remembering it. Loving to talk is my thing so it seemed like a waste of my time not to remember great stories. I wished that someone recorded me or written down the important facts of my crazy coma dreams. I figured it would have made a great book.

CHAPTER TWENTY-EIGHT
Final Round

Now living chapter three, in this hard as hell, yet amazing life. I know I am blessed to be here but I question why, each day I wake up still breathing. Death has failed on its mission to devour me again and again and I would love to know the reason. I must be on some kind of a mission that needs to be completed before death can win the battle. Still, I lack both smell and taste. My loss of left peripheral vision drives me crazy. I can accept Dr. George's negative, yet realistic, assessment, "Nick, you will never get your flight medical back. You will not be a commercial pilot again." He is not only my general doctor but also a Federal Aviation Administration Medical Examiner. He knows what he is talking about with regards to aviation. His honesty was much appreciated. He did not hold out, an empty balloon of hope, for me to chase forever. Am I done dealing with death? Let us hope so. Will I fly again? Realistically, probably not is the best answer to that question. Still, I am pulled to aviation hard but think I can accept my new path of only living. I am passionate about life also. Can the question be honestly answered? No, I think not completely, because I lack the crystal ball that holds the answers. Maturely the answer is no, I will not fly again. Yes, that hurts to say, but maybe I'm not mature enough to follow through.

It does not matter how many chances I get on this earth. It does not matter how much healing must happen, both physical and emotional. Succeeding in a productive manner must include a clear path to focus on. One should always continue to focus on life and moving forward. We all need to be fully committed to finding our next path after one implodes. Could I ask for more out of life? Sure I could, but why. I am alive and I need to accept that as an amazing miracle. I will continue to give and receive love from family and friends. It is a blessing to have two great children who are wholeheartedly strong motivations and positive lights in my cracked' dark life. When finding my next path of focus, I will consider more than just personal wants. Will there be flying? Most would say no but they cannot predict what will happen. If that door opens, I might hobble through it again, or I might turn and walk away on my battered crash torn legs. I was not told after the first crash that I would not get my medical back. Therefore I worked hard until I got it. Dr. George is a medical examiner and he is pretty serious that I will never get it back. I need to remember I'm not twenty-two anymore and healing is a longer dusty road with age. It seemed a small eternity to me.

It has been nearly two and a half years since I lay bleeding in the crumpled shell of my helicopter in the middle of a green sugar beet field in Iowa. I think back on the crash as if it was my last stand in life, much like Custer at Little Bighorn. Never a time before that crash had I felt so complete in my life. Ethan called one day after being home around four months. He told me he was spraying a field relatively close to Waterloo and I should come visit. About twenty minutes later I was connecting the seatbelt ends in the Bell 206 Jet Ranger, AKA the "Red Rocket," at a field I had sprayed twice two and half years previously. There was no fear, only peace like none other, in my mind, for the small 5-minute flight. As the skids lifted off the ground my pilot skills fell back in line as my eye locked onto the gauges while scanning outside. My shoulders calm and without tension of stress. I fell right back into love.

Three helicopter flights now since the crash. Each one was important and each one showed me different things. One showed me peace. One showed me respect. The last showed me that my loss of peripheral vision as ruined my ability to hover smooth. While great to be in the air my loss of ability created sadness. Although, I know my days of flying are over, I really wished I had retained my piloting skills. I found it interesting that two flights in the Jet Rangers, the "White Knight" at Bret's and the "Red Rocket" at Silver Springs, did not have the duel controls installed in the helicopters. Without the duels I was unable to physically control the helicopter, much like riding in the back of the P-51s. Although Bret and Ethan both had good reasons to have the controls out, I had a suspicion it was to protect me, and my family, and to restrict my passionate drive for aviation.

If they could have stopped the pleasant scream flowing from the Turbine engine it would have worked better. Lucky for them I cannot smell. Therefore, the intoxicating exhaust aroma pumping out of the stacks did not grab me. The thought of never smelling turbine exhaust again is depressive. The sound alone from the turbine brought smell through memory only. Memory can bring back strong emotions. I was mature in my approach to my new life if not who knows what would have happened and where I would be now. Maybe I would not be sitting here pondering this strange life of mine. More than likely I would be milling around some little airport trying to score a ride in a turbine. I will relish that smell in my head for the rest of my existence on earth. I have accepted my loss of smell and taste as a payment for a great part of my life. Both flying experiences were great moments in my life and I plan on others to follow, as a passenger only. I do not feel like I am pushing my luck, only satisfying an itch, to feel human, completely.

In the Robinson R44, you cannot remove the duel controls because the cyclic is one unit for the both pilots to share. The T handle cyclic control is odd in an R44. Looking at the weak cyclic control took my mind back to the wimpy R22 with Todd. "Iowa Falls traffic, November one three Sierra Gulf departing straight out runway three two Iowa Falls." In a strange way making the radio call on departure helped with my need to feel like a pilot once again. Ethan knew that I never cared for the R44s because they are so squirrely. When he said "Okay, Nick, she's your bird now." I put my right hand on the cyclic and my left hand on the collective and flew us to our destination. It was just some random crop, fairly close to the airport in Waterloo. At the field I jumped out to let Ethan get the spraying done, then jumped back in for the flight home. At the controls, I felt complete peace, comfortable and relaxed on the flight back. Looking down at the checkerboard countryside of vegetation was inspirational.

Ethan had me shoot the approach for landing into the Waterloo airport. It was such a positive moment for me. I took us to about three feet above the runway then passed the controls to Ethan. While the overall experience felt right, my lack of left peripheral vision made my hover feel bad with a right drift. Although the hover was not solid, that flight helped me realize that my days in the air might be over completely. During my hover my fear was hurting Ethan or the helicopter. Ethan was excited, as was I, but not like before. The passion was still there but lacked the hard drive that it had previously, my mind came to the conclusion that I could fly if need be in an emergency, but I don't have to fly to feel complete anymore for I am alive. My confidence was bent a little after that flight. I know I can fly but not with the precision that I once had. I think if I keep myself confident about my abilities I will believe it. Just to know that I could fly a helicopter was satisfying and answered my curiosity. We both laughed as we talked about me applying for a blimp pilot position with Goodyear. "You would be the only pilot in the world to crash a blimp, spend 100 days in a coma, only to continue living," Ethan stated.

We have all heard the cliché saying that life is a deck of cards and you never know what hand you will be dealt. True words, but it is important to remember I

257

have a heavy influence on the dealer of life. Meaning, it is my life and only I have the power to persuade the dealer to produce a great hand for me. Life is short. It might be ugly, but it is our life to make the most of. This is not some egotistical, self-centered way of saying life is not fun. Even with a dreaded head injury I can influence the dealer in a positive manor. The path chosen in life should be a no-nonsensical, deepening path for me to grow in. With the correct path in life I found love, respect, understanding, belonging, and happiness. In addition, I found pain, despair, broken bones and heartbreak. Yes, I am fortunate to be alive and no, I would not change one thing of my battered existence, for it made me who I am today. I miss being in the air but appreciate the ground on a deeper level now. There is still so much understanding needed so I shall keep searching for answers with Anna Maria by my side.

CHAPTER TWENTY-NINE
Continue on

I could spend every minute of every remaining day that I have left on this beautiful earth trying to figure out the phenomenology behind my existence. Be it religious or scientific, I honestly feel that no person will ever be able to figure out the logic to my tattered existence. There is no human that will ever be able to explain how and why I have lived through not one, but two, horrible impacts involving earth, metal, and death. If no one can understand it, how can I? Truth is, I feel, I don't need to understand it I only need accept it. It happened to me, therefore I will own it and move forward as strong as possible. One day I will find it, an open door to walk through. If I keep my eyes open to see, my ears open to hear, I will find the next path to jump on and continue to move forward in this crazy, obstacle-filled existence, to my highest potential.

It is like a lost love to me. There will always be a craving to find her and fix her. There will always be love and passion in my heart for aviation. Blame cannot be placed on an airplane or helicopter for my near death experiences. Nor can I blame myself for I was following my dreams. They did their job, as did I. A shout out, of respect, goes to all of the sexy airplanes and helicopters that I have flown over the years. Special thanks are given to all of my instructors and knowledge providers thus far. Empathy goes to the yellow Thrush and Miss 47 that I destroyed. A special thanks is given to all of my supportive family and friends. I have put you through hell Anna Maria but you remain here. Thank you. I know it is hard to stand next to a guy that could be gone from this earth, never to return, at any moment, but you did. You stuck by me. Tears well as I sit here thinking of all the strong and meaningful support I have received. A big thanks goes out to God for having pity on my battered soul and bringing me back to existence here on earth. I would like to give a special thanks to all the women who have taught me their secrets throughout my aviation years. Any pilot should learn that there is no prerequisite between women and aviation. I was just a horny young man. It is important to remember not all dreams end as mine did. Some dreams can be realized without the fear of death following shortly behind. While sooner or later its grip will catch us all. I hope I have time to look death in the face and say, "Okay death you finally won, bastard," when it finally finds me.

These days I often find myself at Bret's Flying Service starring at the smashed existence of my helicopter, Miss 47. She is sitting on two pallets on the backside of the property behind the hanger where she used to sleep. When I'm standing by her crumpled cockpit amazement fills me to think about how, through this deformed pile of death, I maintained life. Over my lifetime I have seen more crashed aircraft then one could ever image. This one is by far, the worst pile of parts. Not because I was the pilot. It is just broken beyond anything I have ever seen over the years. With that, I give thanks to Miss 47 for somehow allowing me to live. There is not one time I see the twisted metal that my mind does not run fast to those great days when I was on top of the world. Even with the amount of tragedy involved in this crash, seeing the 47 sitting sad and lonely on those pallets makes me wish I could fix her back into a flying machine. I wish I could jump in and go. My passion has lived strong though all. I'm sorry I destroyed you Miss 47, but I am not sorry I love flying. *Well crap, I need to go for a ride. Has anyone seen my yellow Ducati?* "Your cab is here mister too many drinks for you to drive. Go home and sleep off all of these memories and remember you are still alive for some reason and young enough to do anything to make a difference." "Thank you for listening to me, good night." The stoic man grabbed his flight jacket and walked out to the waiting taxi for the somber ride home.

True passion can never be killed. It is the leading force that marries our dreams to our reality. Search hard for your passion. When you find it, hold it tight and never let it go.

~Bryan Wesley Cantrell~

The following three pages are dedicated to the aircraft that filled Nick's life with joy mixed with the fear of death.

Aeroca Champ
7AC

Weatherly 620B

Cessna 210

S2R-800 Thrush

Cessna 150

Hiller 12E

A9-CallAir-235

Cessna 172

G-164 Ag Cat

PA-25 Pawnee

Piper Arrow

Cessna 120

F4u Corsair

Cessna 182

Piper Aztec

Cessna 188 Ag
Husky

Cessna 206

Pa-31 Navajo
Chieftain

Beech 18 Tradeinds

P-51 Ridge Runner

BO-105

Cessna 421

P51D Straw Boss

Bell UH-1B Huey

PA Cherokee Six

Piper Super Cub

S2R-600 Thrush

7EA Citabria

Lockheed T-33

S2RT Thrush PT-20

600-S2D Snow

King Air C90

Cessna 210

Bell Tomcat

Learjet 25

Hughes 300C

Formula One Cassutt

Bell OH-58C

Robinson R-22

As350 B3 Astar

McDonnell Douglas DC-10

UH-1E Huey

Bell Jet Ranger BIII

Bell 47 G2-A1

Bell 407

Cessna 210

Beech V-35 Bonanza

North American T-6 Texan

Robinson R-44

Bell Long Ranger L3

McDonnell Douglas DC-9

38851394R00155

Printed in Great Britain
by Amazon